Stanley Morgan, author of the sensationally successful saga of Tobin, stud of the seventies, is also familiar to the public through his film-acting career and voice-over recordings for many well-known television commercials. His sales in the Tobin series have been phenomenal and his status is now assured as one of today's most popular paperback writers in Britain and on the Continent.

By the same author
in Mayflower Books

THE SEWING MACHINE MAN
THE DEBT COLLECTOR
THE COURIER
COME AGAIN COURIER
TOBIN ON SAFARI
TOBIN IN PARADISE
TOBIN IN TROUBLE
TOBIN FOR HIRE
TOBIN IN LAS VEGAS

and

OCTOPUS HILL
MISSION TO KATUMA

Tobin Takes Off

Stanley Morgan

Mayflower

Granada Publishing Limited
Published in 1973 by Mayflower Books Ltd
Frogmore, St Albans, Herts AL2 2NF
Reprinted 1973 (4 times), 1974, 1975

A Mayflower Original

Made and printed in Great Britain by
Richard Clay (The Chaucer Press) Ltd
Bungay, Suffolk
Set in Linotype Plantin

THE STORY SO FAR: Devilishly handsome Russ Tobin, ex-sewing machine man, ex-debt collector, ex-T.V. commercial actor and all-round first class chap has just completed his first season as courier for Ardmont Holidays in Majorca and I, I mean *he* is now faced with something of a dilemma, namely: where does he go from here?

Fortunate man that he is, he has a world of choice before him. The series of White Marvel detergent commercials (in which he *stars*) that are currently annoying the British nation on T.V. five times a night and ten times on Sundays have provided him with financial independence for a whole year. Freedom is his. But the decision regarding his next destination is a matter of pressing concern. Where to now—Tokyo? Rome? Wagga Wagga?

We discover Russ and his close friend and fellow-lecher, Patrick Holmes (Ardmount courier, Irish charmer and professional bird-fancier) in the Bar Figero in downtown Palma. It is Friday, the fourth day of November and the very last day of the Ardmont season. Gone now are the summer days of hot blue skies and even hotter brown women. The evening is cool and rain is imminent. The season is about to die.

On this, the eve of their departure from Majorca to London, seated at the bar before comfortingly large scotches and soda, the two men confer about their future plans. Patrick opens his mouth to speak, changes his mind and first drains his glass, then continues, uttering a sentiment that so typically illustrates his unbounded Irish generosity, the breath-taking enormity of his Gaelic heart. NOW READ ON!

'Russell, I will ... but only to please you ... and thank you for askin'.'

'Mm?' I wiped the drip off my chin and looked at him. 'Patrick,' I sighed, 'during these past nine months of our close and immensely compatible association ... these weeks of fraternal fun and friendship ... these countless golden hours of comradely bonhomie, there has been and, alas, still is but one small blot to mar an otherwise perfect relationship ...'

He turned to me, appalled. 'Russell ... can it *be*? Whatever is it?'

'Simply that most of the time I haven't the slightest idea what the hell you're talking about. "You will but only to please me and you thank me for asking you" *what*?'

His green eyes widened innocently. 'Why—have another scotch, Russell! Jaze, is me hearin' failin' me? I could've *sworn* yuh said "Patrick, for old times sake and in memory of a fabulous faded summer, will yuh not have the other half?'

'Yes and no, Patrick.'

'Mm? Ah, now you're bein' just a touch mystifying yourself.'

'Yes—your hearing *is* failing you ... and no, I did not say have the other half.' He slumped, dramatically crestfallen. 'But,' I went on, circumventing tears, 'in memory of a fabulous faded summer, Patrick, *will* you have the other half?'

'Begob,' he smiled, 'that's decent of yuh—to say nuthin' of totally unexpected.'

I signalled the tubby barman, Frederico, he of the bulbous, cratered nose and slicked-down hair the colour of wet liquorice. He came up swiftly, delighted to be of service if only to pass the time. The bar was deserted.

'Gentlemen?' He wreathed a genuine smile as though pleased to have the time to do it. Even a month ago there would have been eight million tourists in here working him to a froth.

'Two more biggies, Fred,' I said, 'to keep the winter out. And have something yourself.'

'Take the offer,' advised Patrick. 'It's his last night.'

'You leave tomorrow?' asked Frederico.

We both nodded solemnly.

'But you will be back next year?'

I shook my head. 'I don't think *I* will. Patrick is destined to plague you for at least one more season but not I. But try not to pine, Fred, there'll be others.'

He made sounds of commiseration while pouring himself a large slug of something out of a bottle with a twig in it. 'If you won't be here, Russ,' he said, corking up, 'where *will* you be?'

I shrugged.

Patrick said to him, 'Russell is now a man of not inconsiderable fortune, Fred. He can go anywhere he likes, do virtually what he wants without the immediate need to earn a crust. We are discussing the problem of his eventual destination at this very moment but up to now we haven't got further than Palma airport. What do you suggest?'

'Copenhagen,' replied Fred, without needing to think. 'City of free love and legal filth. There a man could die happy.'

'And scratching,' I said. 'No, not my scene, Fred. Try something less obvious.'

'Poaki?' he suggested.

I glanced at Patrick, he at me. 'Where?'

'Poaki,' said Fred. 'In China. There is a rumour there are sixteen women to one man there.'

'Mm,' I said thoughfully. 'Highly appropriate name. I wonder who the one man is—and how much is the fare.'

Patrick groaned. 'Aw, Russell ... how *can* yuh think of it—after the summer we've just had?' He turned to Fred. 'Fred, you are lookin' at two extremely exhausted libidos. I personally am heading straight for Dublin to sleep the winter through. And *please* .... don't even mention that word to be before next March.'

'What word?' I asked.

'Crumpet.' He winced and shut his eyes. 'There—yuh made *me* mention it. Look! See what it does to me, me hands are shakin' uncontrollably ...'

'Don't pick up that scotch, for Godsake ...!'

'I won't ... I won't. I'll sip it from the bar.' He lowered his lips to the glass and sucked off the top half inch. 'Ah, that's better. But don't ever mention that word again.'

'Good season, then?' asked Fred, with an appropriate leer.

'Better than ever,' grinned Patrick. 'You know, I do believe the seasons get better each year.'

'Undoubtedly due to your ever-pullulating power over women,' I said with deep insincerity. 'To say nothing of your excitingly maturing good looks, your bourgeoning finesse, your Emerald-isle charm and your general *je ne sais quoi.*'

He regarded me with unabashed delight. 'Russell ... but *how* you've come on with the words and the wisdom! Sure, it could almost have been an Irishman that said that. And yuh not only have the poetry but the perspicacity to go with it. Right on the button—every pearly word of it.'

But kidding aside it had been a good season. A fabulous season. As I gazed into my scotch, fleeting memories of the golden days passed before my mind's eye. There, in the bubbling amber, lying naked in the sun on the balcony of my flat—the lovely Donna. As I enter the room she turns her head, smiles devilishly, refreshed and recharged by sleep, and rises, ready for the attack. 'Kom here, man . . .' I smile to myself, remembering the ludicrous incident of the vicar and the soda syphon and of Donna's laughter ringing through the apartment. The picture fades. I see Lila next . . . then Claudia . . . beautiful girls . . . tanned, handsome girls . . . and here was the lovely Japanese doll, Sin Wen, standing before me waist-deep in soap suds in Count Buenano's unbelievable bathroom . . .

How long ago they all now seemed. Perhaps I was an idiot to even contemplate not coming back for another season. But no . . . life had to go on. Out there, somewhere in the world, there could be an even better season—certainly a different one. Tobin had to move on.

'Africa,' I said suddenly, surprising myself almost as much as I surprised Patrick.

'Mm?' he said, frowning at me. Then, with comprehension, 'Ah, I wondered whether that had been running through your mind.'

'It's been running through it ever since the party, Patrick. I'm rather tempted.'

To explain: last June, at Harry Onion's party, I met a man named Frank Chappell. Harry Onions, a Cockney scrap-metal millionaire, had taken over Count Buenano's château for a month and had started off his summer season with a festive bang of impressive proportions. Patrick and I, together with another pal of ours, Tony Dane, had been invited to the party and during the evening Harry had introduced me to Frank Chappell.

It transpired that one of Harry's many sidelines was a partnership with Frank in a tour-operating business involving photographic safari tours from London to Central and East Africa. Knowing that I was a courier with Ardmont and that my season would be finishing in November, Chappell asked me if I was interested in doing a season with them in Africa. I replied that I hadn't yet made up my mind what to do but I felt I wanted to work on some independent travelling with the money I'd earned from White Marvel. Chappell then suggested it might be more profitable for me to do a season with them (all travelling expenses paid, of course) and then if I wanted to see more of Africa, to go my own way after the season had finished. It made good sense and the idea had been at the back of my mind all summer.

Patrick was saying, 'I must admit, Russell, that at first I couldn't see why you should work your pollies off on safari while you've got all that luvly money in London, but Frank's suggestion has it's merits. You now know couriering backwards—and provided you pull yuh socks up and learn it forwards the way it's supposed to be done, there's no reason why the job out there should be any more difficult than it's been here. Quite possibly it'll be more exciting. You'll undoubtedly be dealin' with a wealthier set of clients altogether *and* gettin' yourself into a higher-class mess of trouble as a result. And, as you well know, association with the wealthy has its own perculiar rewards . . .'

I grinned at him, knowing he was referring to the wealthy and beautiful Caroline Courtney off the good ship *Kandy King* with whom I had briefly and almost (for me) disastrously associated in June. 'High-class mess of trouble' described Caroline to a T. I wasn't sure I was in a hurry to repeat the experience and told Patrick so.

'Aah, way with yuh,' he scoffed. 'You enjoyed every terrifyin' minute of it. It's not every day a man gets kidnapped aboard a millionaire's yacht and almost bum-rushed to mysterious Algiers . . .'

I winced. 'Patrick, don't *use* that expression, it's too damned accurate for comfort. Anyway, forget that. This African thing does appeal to me. Six months of dashing around in a Land-Rover with beautiful rich people can't be all misery . . . and it would save me a lot of money . . .'

'Then why don't you call Frank Chappell next week and find out if the job's still open?'

'I will, I will. That's what I'm going to do.'

'Well, then . . .'

'Well, then—what?'

'Well, then, the problem's solved, isn't it?'

I looked at him, then grinned. 'Yes . . . yes, it is. That's where I'm going—Africa.'

'Thank God for that,' he sighed. 'Now I can hibernate in peace. Frederico! . . . two more of the same, please. Be Jaze, I'll pay—out of sheer relief.'

Fred came up, polishing a glass he'd already polished four times.

'He's decided,' said Patrick. 'He's goin' to Africa.'

'Africa!' said Fred, slopping the scotch into our glasses. 'Now there's one place you'd never get me.'

'Oh,' I said. 'Why not?'

'You keeding . . .? With all that malaria . . . and dysentery . . . and bilharzia . . . and poisonous snakes . . . and maneaters . . . and spiders . . . and . . .'

'Fred! Cut it out!' cried Patrick. 'God, man, you don't know what you're doin' to me . . .!'

'Had an uncle who went to Africa,' Fred said solemnly, shaking his head. 'Died the most terrible death . . .'

'Fred,' Patrick pleaded, in anguish.

'He was plucked from his tent in the dead of night by an elephant . . .'

'Fred, will you stop it! Russell, don't listen to him . . .'

'They found his right arm first,' Fred went on, 'then his left leg—a lion was eating that . . .'

'Fred, so help me . . .' groaned Patrick.

'Next they found his left arm and his right leg. The hyenas had those . . .'

'If you destroy his nerve I shall never drink in here again!' howled Patrick.

'They never did find the torso,' said Fred sorrowfully. 'But they found the head. A bunch of monkeys were playing football with it. And d'you know—the head was singing!'

Patrick stopped, mouth open. 'Singing?'

'Yes, singing. He had a very good voice, my uncle. As a boy he was head chorister in the Madrid choir . . .'

'Singing what!' exclaimed Patrick.

'I . . . ain't got no . . . bo . . . dy . . .!' sang Frederico, and went back up the bar, roaring with laughter.

'You're too bloody smart for a Spaniard!' Patrick shouted, and Fred laughed all the harder. 'He's gettin' punchy,' Patrick said to me. 'He's got the end-of-season twitch.'

'Can't blame him,' I said. 'It must be deadly dull after the summer trade. Patrick, let's *do* something, for Pete's sake. We can't spend our last night like this. It'll be a poor do if we get on that plane sober tomorrow morning. I personally don't intend to go to bed.'

'Agreed!' Patrick agreed, with the intensity of enthusiasm he reserves only for booze-ups and women, though not necessarily in that order of priority. 'Let us stroll across to Dirty Dick's and have one there, then on to El Jarrito and say *adios* to Juanita. The little darlin' would never forgive us if we slipped off the island without sayin' goodbye.'

We bade Frederico goodnight and goodbye and he shook our hands with genuine regret that we were leaving, probably because there was no one else in the bar to talk to.

'Send me a postcard from Poaki, now!' he called as we reached the door.

'I will,' I called back. 'Provided I've got enough lead left in me pencil!'

We pushed through the door into the narrow street that leads down to the beautiful Plaza Gomilla Terrano, and as we left the protection of the high buildings and entered the open square the sweeping cold wet sea wind cut through our thin summer jackets making us gasp and groan. By English winter standards the wind was possibly not all that cold, but by Majorcan standards, and after the long hot summer, it was bloody freezing.

Patrick moaned, 'Aah, this is when I'm glad to be leavin' the island. It's paradise in summer but as dreary an' dead as Bournemouth on Boxing Day in the winter—and somehow twice as depressing. It's just not right that winter should come to a place like this.'

I agreed. The lovely tree-lined square which only a month ago had been bustling with life, filled with sun-tanned tourists strolling in the evening cool or sitting at the pavement cafes, was now desolate, windswept and cheerless as a cemetery. There were fewer than ten other people in the entire square and they, like ourselves, were huddled into their coats and appeared to be heading quickly for one or other of the warm, enticing bars.

Then, half-way across the square, the rain caught us. We broke into a run, pelted across the square, ran down a narrow street and fell breathless and well rain-spotted into Dirty Dick's. Compared to the temperature outside, the bar was like a furnace. It was also unbelievably smoky, reeking of Continental cigarettes, most of which were being smoked by Dirty Dick himself, simultaneously.

Dick is one of life's *real* people. He's a real eater, a real drinker, a real smoker and a very real fornicator. Dick *must* have a lighted cigarette always within reach and, since it is a very long bar, he stations as many as seven lighted fags in ashtrays down its length.

One of the other very real things about Dick is his weight problem. He carries two hundred and eighty pounds around on his six-feet frame and most of it on his belly. Dick's corporation is the subject of a great deal of thoughtful speculation among his regular male customers, because they cannot visualise how he manages to do all the fornicating he's reputed to do with a protuberance of that grandeur. Still, where there's a will . . .

Dick, whose full and proper name is Reginald Schick, is a forty-something-year-old American Armenian who settled in Majorca five years ago after serving ten years in the American navy. He has been everywhere, done everything and you know it just by looking at him. He is big, tough, crude and rude and just the sort of fellow to have on your side in a bar brawl, though nothing of the kind ever happens in his bar. One glare from those coal-black eyes, set in a forest of jet black beard and straggly black hair, is normally sufficient to quell the most promising disturbance.

Around the end of September Patrick and I saw him clear the bar counter with unbelievable agility, grab two big troublesome Norwegians by the scruff of their necks and propel them through the door as though they'd been a couple of naughty children. All good entertaining stuff. And testimony to the attractiveness of his flamboyant character is the fact that, unlike the El Figero bar, and probably most other bars in Palma right now, Dick's place was three-quarters full, mostly local people and all men.

We fought our way through the thick blue fug and approached the bar. Dick, down at the far end and almost totally obscured by the Disque Bleu mist, finished serving a customer, took a drag from the fag in number seven ashtray and rolled towards us, taking a coin from his pocket as he came.

'Christ, I mighta known. Now the day's bin completely lousy. Whatdya cry?'

'Heads,' I said.

'Tails,' insisted Patrick.

'Make yuh goddam minds up, will ya?'

Patrick bowed deferentially to me.

'Heads,' I said again.

Dick flipped the coin and pulled a disgusted face. 'Mighta known that, too. O.K., what d'you bums want?'

'We won!' Patrick cried with astonishment. 'We actually won!'

'About time,' I said.

Patrick rubbed his hands with glee. 'Dick ... I've been waiting all summer for this moment. I, personally, and speaking for myself, will have a small quadruple brandy—and not the local pig swill, the Napolean stuff yuh keep under the bar.'

'Yeh, me too, Dick,' I said. 'And thank you kindly.'

Dick gave us a one hundred proof Bogart sneer and reached for a bottle under the counter. 'Goddam courier bums,' he scowled, slopping enormous shots of the very good brandy into two balloon glasses.

'And served with such spontaneous generosity of heart,' Patrick observed, smiling at me with supercilious exaggeration.

'Oh, Dick's all heart,' I agreed.

Dick threw us a glare designed to frighten Mafia bosses into giving State's evidence.

This flipping a coin business was, by the way, one of the unique features of Dirty Dick's bar. The first drink of the evening, if the customer so wished, was tossed for. If he won he could order anything he liked; if he lost he paid double for the drink he ordered and the extra money went to a children's orphanage up in the hills.

Whether it was pure luck or fiendish skill I wouldn't know, but the orphanage won ninety per cent of the time and nobody minded. I had a feeling Dick had only let us win this time because he knew it was our last night in town.

He plonked the glasses ungraciously before us and pulled a big drag on fag number two. 'Hope it chokes ya,' he growled.

'And our best wishes to you, Richard,' said Patrick, raising the glass and sipping the brandy appreciatively. 'Only sorry I won't be around to enjoy the welter of hospitality that emanates from that side of the bar until next March. Gob, I'm going to miss your cheery face and merry banter this long Irish winter. Russell, I'm afraid, will not be returning next year and will no doubt be the poorer man for that.'

'Oh, yeh? So where will you be bummin' around next year, Tobin?'

'Africa,' I said archly. 'King Billie of Upyatuckus has invited me for a season of shaws shooting. I leave next week.'

'Shaws shootin'?' he said suspiciously. 'What's shaws?'

'Well, that's very kind of you, Dick, I'll have another brandy.'

Patrick collapsed with laughter. 'Got the bugger! It took us all season but we finally nailed him. Now I can retire a happy man.'

'Very comical, I'm sure,' sneered Dick. 'You Limeys have got the goddamed wierdest sense of humour I ever heard—an' I've lived with Eskimos! Jeezus, I thought they were yacall—but you guys have got 'em beat ta hell.'

'Yacall?' I said. 'What's yacall?'

'Well, now, that's mighty nice of you, Tobin, I'll have a fifth of scotch!'

He roared with laughter and disappeared down the bar, picking up a lungful from fag number four on the way.

'Curses!' I cried. 'Foiled by a bloody Yank!'

Patrick was shaking his head ruefully. 'I think it's time we were on the plane, the season's beginning to tell. First Fred the Majorcan and now Dick the Yank. Fancy being caught twice in one evening—and by two foreigners! We badly need a rest, Russell.' He sipped his brandy and grinned, shaking his head. 'What's yacall ...?' he muttered to himself. 'Fancy fallin' for that ...'

'All right, Smartarse, admit you were just about to ask him yourself.'

Patrick looked up, grinning, and was about to answer but stopped, his eyes widening in a way that indicated only one thing—women!

I heard the door open behind me and felt the swirl of cool air around my neck. A party had entered, four, five, six people, talking and laughing. I raised an enquiring brow at Patrick.

'Aircrew!' he breathed excitedly. 'Two men and *four* birds . . .!'

'Whadtheylike . . . whadtheylike . . .?'

'The men or the women?'

I tutted and lisped, 'The chaps, silly . . .'

'Hang on, they're coming over, you can see for yourself.'

The group passed us and spread themselves along the bar. They were all in uniform but hatless. Both men were in their late thirties; the girls much younger. One guy was big—broad-shouldered, going to paunch and sported a dark, flamboyant moustache. Clinging to him like a shadow was a pretty brunette with a cracking figure, a cuddly little handful.

The other man, a bit younger, was slim and conventionally airline handsome, brown, wavy hair and sharp features. His bird was a blonde, not a bad figure but her bottom was a touch too big for the rest of her.

Of the remaining two girls, one was a red-head, the other blonde. The red-head was very striking. She had everything, face, figure, style; instantly appealing and very sexy.

The little blonde was obviously the character of the group. She was small, vivacious and walked with a cheeky swagger, and as she reached the bar, she exclaimed, 'God! Smells like a Marseilles brothel in here!'

'Often wondered what you did before you took up flying, darling,' said the bottomey blonde with Wavy Hair.

'Ho ho—fun-nee,' said Cheeky. She sneered a smile at Red Head standing at her side. 'Well, at least that's over for another year. It gets to be a bit of a strain waiting for Janice's annual wit.'

The red-head laughed but only with her mouth; her eyes were sweeping the room through the big mirrors, checking it out for the talent. They caught sight of Patrick, held him for an instant, switched to me, tripped my switch with their lazy directness, flicked back to Patrick for another look and then returned to Cheeky. But the damage had been done. She was interested in the two fellas along the bar, interest quite possibly born out of boredom but fulsome nonetheless. I knew she'd look again, in her own sweet feminine time, if for no other reason than there was nothing else worth looking at in the room. I didn't think she'd go for any of the Majorcans there.

She took about a minute to get around to it, then, on pretext of addressing Wavy Hair, she had another look, this time a longer one, but, dammit, it was nearly all at Patrick! Curses! Mind you, you couldn't really blame her, he's a very good-looking lad . . . in his own Irish way, you understand. His nose some may think just a *leetle* bit too straight and his hair just a *touch* too luxuriant and curly but there's no doubt one or two women have found him attractive in the past . . .

'Did yuh see that!' he whispered, side-mouthed, swallowing hard. 'Did yuh see the look I got from the *gorgeous* creature with the copper hair?'

'Mm? . . . no, can't say I did . . .'

'A real *scorcher*, Russell . . .'

'Yeh?'

'Hey, now, we've just got to *do* something about this.'

'Such as what?'

'I dunno—but somethin'. I reckon they're all on the town for the night. They can't be flying if they're drinking.'

'Since when?'

'Well, they're not *supposed* to be drinking if they're flying. Y'know, this could be the makings of a fair old final night.'

'Oh, sure—you with the red-head and me with the female Bob Hope . . .'

'Ah ha! so you fancy the red-head yourself. Too bad, too bad . . . still, that's life.'

'Like hell. I'm not giving up that easily. It'll be a fight to the death, Patrick.'

He grinned at me. 'Yes?'

'Too right.'

He put his hand out to shake mine. 'You're on—and may the best man win.'

'In that case why don't you retire now and save yourself a pile of disappointment later.'

'Ha!' he laughed, and half the bar turned to look at him.

Dirty Dick finished serving at the far end of the bar and came to serve them, demolishing fag number three and lighting a fresh one as he came.

'Yeh, what'll it be?' he asked the group, blowing smoke at them.

'Are you Dirty Dick?' asked Cheeky.

'Sure, don't I look it?'

'Well, I'll have one of your vile vodkas and a touch of tetanus tonic.'

'Ya want any lousy lemon in it?'

'No, just as bad as it comes.'

This banter got the group going. Each of them, ordering in turn, used the 'dirt' theme—a germ-ridden gin and ginger ... and unwashed whiskey and water ... and Moustache, who I guessed was the aircraft Captain, capped the lot by ordering a gangrenous Gordons and grapefruit.

Dick gave one of his rare smiles. 'Say, I reckon you folks have given me an idea. I'll get a new drink list made up usin' that theme.'

All the while this was going on, the red-head kept flashing a look at us now and again. Cheeky also had a peek or two but not with the same kind of interest, though one time she did pass a remark to the red-head who smiled and nodded and it was obvious the remark had been about us.

At an appropriate moment Patrick caught Dick's eye and motioned him over.

'Jeez, don't tell me you pikers are orderin' a second drink already. You've only bin here four hours.'

'No, we're not,' said Patrick, *sotto voce*. 'Lissen, Dick, do your stuff for two of your best customers and get us into that group.'

'Don't confuse me—is it for you or for two of my best customers?'

'What d'you reckon on this bunch, Dick?' I asked. 'They're not flying, hm?'

He shook his wise old hairy head. 'Hell, no, they're not properly dressed. They got no hats. I reckon it's an emergency stop-over—otherwise they'd be in civvies.'

'How come you know so much, Dick?'

'Because I'm a smart bastard, that's why.'

'O.K.,' said Patrick, 'then show us just how smart and get us in there.'

Dick looked at him, nodding sagely. 'You got hot pants for

the copper job, huh, yuh randy Mick?'

'It won't do him any good,' I said. 'I saw her first.'

'You, too, huh, Tobin? Well, that figures. I always thought you were a coupla schmucks when it came to sizin' up broads.'

We stared at him. 'What d'you mean?'

'Hell, I reckon the little blonde any time before the red.'

'You do?' I said.

'Sure ... the red's too obvious. She's a teaser. The smartass blonde don't have so much goin' for her—except her humour—but instinct tells me ya'd die of exhaustion rather than laughin' if she got ya bedded.'

Food for thought. He shuffled off, blowing smoke like an old 2–4–2 steaming out Waterloo, leaving Patrick and me pondering his wisdom.

I sneaked another and more careful look at the little blonde, aware that Patrick was doing the same. Yes ... Dick *could* be right ... and yet ... nah ... *could* he? My money was still on the red-head.

We watched Dick approach the group, lean over towards the spare girls and talk earnestly to them, flicking his head a couple of times in our direction. The girls gave us yet another, somewhat hasty glance in the mirror, grinned at each other, then nodded to Dick.

'He's done it!' breathed Patrick. 'By Gob, he's done it!'

Dick came strolling back, pausing to quench a small fire roaring away in ashtray number five.

''Kay, you slobs, they're all yours. Go down an' buy 'em a drink.'

'Dick, you are altogether too much,' exclaimed Patrick. 'Next season, so help me, I'll bring in twice as many clients to drink your wholesome liquor.'

'Huh—those bums! The last bunch you brought in ordered twenty-seven coffees and a coke.'

'*I* didn't know they were all bloody Baptists!' Patrick protested. 'They were doing a tour of Palma and ...'

'Are yuh goin' to sit there all night playin' with yaselves or are yuh goin' to chat the broads?'

'Sure, sure, we're going. Er, Dick, what did you tell them about us?'

He gave an evil grin. 'I told them you were a coupla queer

writers doin' a story on Palma airport an' yuh wanted some background material on stranded aircrew.'

'Beautiful!' exclaimed Patrick. 'Dick, you're a genius.'

'So—I'm a genius. You'll be orderin' champagne, no doubt . . .'

'Get stuffed.'

Patrick swivelled off the stool and headed for the group, me close beside him, ready to circumvent any tricky move. For a good-hearted, charming-natured bloke he can be very sneaky when it comes to birds.

We approached the girls. They were pretending to be talking about something else but the blonde was giving her pal a running commentary on our progress.

Patrick edged in at the last moment with a diabolical side-step that had me falling over a stool. 'Oops! Sorry . . .' I said, catching the blonde's elbow and spilling her drink. I glared at Patrick who wasn't looking. He was basking in the red-head's amused smile and winding up his entire stock of Irish bull, ready for the off.

'Ladies,' he began, 'it's more than kind of yuh to give us your precious time. My name is Patrick Holmes . . . and this is my alcoholic co-writer, Russell Tobin.'

The introductions were made. The red-head was Annabel Muir; Cheeky was Jane McElroy; the blonde with Wavy Hair—Sarah Langton; the Captain's bird—Jane Preston; Wavy Hair—who I gathered was co-pilot/navigator—Dewi Davies; and the Captain's name was Tiny Timm. True. His real Christian name was Hereward (true again!) but he was nick-named Tiny (what else?).

'Dirty Dick told us you were writers,' said Cheeky Jane. 'What do you write?'

PATRICK: Books.

ME: Plays.

'Er . . .' I said, looking at Patrick.

PATRICK: Plays.

ME: Books.

'Well,' said Patrick, scratching his eye, 'sort of bookish plays, actually.'

'Or, indeed, you might call them playful books,' I said.

'Indeed you might,' said Patrick sagely. 'Yes, playful books it is . . . and we're both lying through our teeth because we're not writers at all—unless you count the odd postcard home. We're a couple of couriers with Ardmont Holidays retired for the season. There, it's out and I feel a whole lot better.'

The girls laughed and Jane said, 'Honest . . . at least they're honest.'

'Sorry about the temporary deception,' I said. 'It was Dick's idea, not ours. Shall we crawl back to our part of the bar now or wait till later?'

Jane shrugged at Annabel. 'I suppose they might as well stay.'

'We'll be leaving soon anyway,' said Annabel.

'Flying?' I enquired.

'Depends on how many we have here,' said Jane. 'No, not tonight. Tonight we are gloriously grounded—for the first time all summer, would you believe.'

'Oh, you come to Palma often?' I asked.

'About forty times a week,' Annabel said dolefully. 'You begin to feel you're attached to London by a piece of elastic. No sooner do we hit the Palma runway than whooosshh! back we go again.'

I frowned. 'You mean you don't ever get out of the airport?'

They both laughed cynically. Jane said, 'We're lucky to get out of the plane. We're down and up again in an hour and a bit. A cup of coffee, a quick trip to the loo and it's hey ho for Heathrow.'

'Sounds a bit busy,' Patrick remarked.

Annabel said, 'I must have been to Palma two hundred times and I don't even know where the main street is. And we had to get engine trouble in winter! Jane and I were going to do the town tonight—look at the shops and the squares—and look at the weather! So we're sight-seeing some of the bars instead—getting wet inside rather than out.'

Dick, I thought, you're wrong—this is a very sexy lady. No woman with such a big, soft mouth and naughty blue eyes could be anything but. Well, there was only one thing for it—Patrick had to die. I would do it quickly. But how? I could ply him with drink and lay him out for the night . . . no, that was no good. His capacity for liquor was second only to his capacity for the other which was awe-inspiringly prodigious. It would cost me a fortune and get me nowhere. I could run him over—

gently! No, that was out. I no longer had the car. The Mercedes I'd rented all summer had gone back that morning and we were taxiing all over the place.

Ah! I could lure him to the gents' loo and lock him in! Mm, possibility ... though he'd probably start singing and bring the cops running thinking someone was being garrotted. No, nothing would come immediately to mind. I'd let it stew, but in the meantime I would get back in there and thwart the sod because he was making far too much headway with Annabel, waxing lyrical about the wonders of Ireland, the lakes, the mountains and all that rubbish. Jane was very attentive, too. She'd stopped being funny and was listening with rapt attention to his lilting Irish tones. Hell, he was going to finish up with both of them!

'... sure, there's no cleaner, softer air in the whole world than you'd find in the Connemara Mountains. I remember as a lad goin' on a three-day hike with me dad. We spent a whole day fishin' in Lake Corrib, then struck out on foot ...'

'Er, anyone for a drink?' I asked brightly.

No one took a blind bit of notice. The Captain was deeply engrossed in whispered somethings with Janice Preston who was surreptitiously stroking his thigh beneath her handbag; and Wavy Hair was gazing into Sarah Langton's dreamy eyes as though they were having it off by thought transference.

I was doing a solo.

Patrick was really getting into his stride. '... we camped the first night on a gentle slope close to a little tumbling brook and I awoke next mornin' to the tinklin' sound of the pure crystal water trippin' over the moss-covered rocks. Sure, if yuh haven't woken to that sound, yuh can hardly say yuh've lived ...'

I tried again. 'Annabel, would you like a drink? Jane, how about you? Sorry to interrupt, Patrick ...'

'Not at all,' he said generously, grinning secretly. 'It was remiss of me, girls, goin' on like that and not noticin' you were empty.'

'It was fascinating,' said Annabel. 'Ireland's one place I've never been to. I must see it.'

'Well, then,' said Patrick, 'let Russell buy us a drink and I'll tell you what you ought to see when you go.'

'Thanks, buddy,' I said cheerily. 'That's big-big. What would you like, ladies?'

After I'd given Dick the order, I got in quickly. 'Er, either of you know anything about Africa?'

'No,' they chorused.

Annabel said, 'Go on, Patrick . . .'

'Aah, I don't think I ought to be hoggin' the conversation,' said the lying swine. 'I'm sure you girls have been to far more interestin' places.'

'Oh, sure,' said Jane. 'You want a vivid description of Zurich airport, or Orly, or the John F. Kennedy . . .? Tell you what, we'll swap you a prose-poem on Tipperary for a loo-by-loo commentary on the ladies' rest-room at Gatwick.'

'Done!' laughed Patrick. 'I've always been intrigued by the ladies' rest-room at Gatwick.'

'*Kinky*!' I murmured.

At that moment Captain Tiny Timm got off his stool and moved over to talk to all the girls. 'It's nearly eight thirty, I think we'd better move.'

My heart sank. Patrick looked mortified. 'Sure, you're not off already?'

Annabel explained, 'Tiny's the only one of us who knows anybody in Palma. When we heard at five o'clock tonight that we would be grounded until tomorrow noon, he did some phoning and came up with a party. We've no idea where it is or whose it is, except it's an airline party, and frankly we didn't care. It's better than sitting in a hotel room.'

I noticed she'd said 'didn't care' and not 'don't care'. It implied she was sorry to leave. The feeling was mutual.

'Ah, that's too bad . . .' said Patrick, with a suitably wan smile.

'Are you two completely at a loose end?' Jane asked.

'Double loose,' I said. 'We fly out at nine tomorrow morning and we are determined not to fly sober.'

'So who flies sober?' she quipped. 'Hang on a minute.'

She left us and went and whispered something to Timm. He shrugged non-committally and thought for a moment. Finally he spoke to her and she came back.

'He'll give his friends a call, see if it's all right for you to tag along.'

'That's very good of him,' I said, 'but we don't want to trouble him.'

She smiled. 'If the Spanish airline parties are anything like the British, French, American and you-name-it airline parties, this one is open house. I've never known a fly party yet that didn't attract some gate-crashers before throwing out time.'

Tiny crossed the room and disappeared down the corridor that led to the toilets and the telephones. In a few minutes he was back and came over. 'Yes, fine, we'll take taxis. You four take one, we'll take another.'

Patrick and I thanked him and he smiled, nodding at the girls. 'Got to keep my crew happy. These two would sabotage the ship if they got the hell in. Can you imagine a full load of passengers at thirty thousand feet and the doors to both toilets nailed up?'

'We would, we would!' said Jane. 'But not on a milk-run to Palma, Tiny. We'd wait for a seven-hour flight to New York.'

He winced and walked away with his legs clamped tight, in agony.

The group began to move.

'G'bye, Dick!' I called. 'Wherever you are!'

Dick came out of the fog. 'G'bye, you bums. Keep it clean, now.' He hung out his huge hand and shook ours. 'See yuh next year, Holmes, if ya don't disintergrate in the meantime. Jeez, you look awful.'

'Thanks a lot, Dick—and stay as sweet as you are, don't let a soul ever change you.'

'Up yours, Holmes. G'bye Russ, watch out for the dreaded yapoison in Africa, now.'

'What's yapoison?'

'Another fifth of scotch!' he roard. 'Jeez, are you guys dumb!'

We left him choking on a butt and followed the girls outside.

'Phew!' went Jane, breathing air. 'How can he live in there?'

'Who's living?' I said. 'Dick's been dead for years, it's the smoke holding him up.'

We collected two cabs from a rank near the square. The drivers were profusely polite, delighted to be working. Holmes pulled another fast one here, taking gross advantage of my genteel nature. I held a rear door open for Jane, expecting Annabel to get in next, then I was going to nip in quick before Holmes had a chance, leaving him the front seat with the driver. But the crafty sod nipped in after Jane, saying, 'I'll sit between you girls. Russ likes to ride in front. It's a throwback to his childhood, he gets sick in the back. Got enough room, Annabel?'

Annabel squeezed in, tight up against him, and stopped my heart with a flash of slender thigh as she raised her legs over the sill. I sneered at Patrick and got in front with the driver.

'Follow that cab!' I said in Spanish, seeing the other one tear away.

He turned to me, deaf as a post, and breathed in my face, 'Señor?'

Phew! Garlic and cheese, right up the hooter. I took out my hanky and pretended to blow my nose. 'Follow dat cab in frond,' I repeated.

And now my mind began working in deadly earnest about killing Holmes—and to hell with gentility. Listen to him, laughing with them, his thigh pressed with indecent familiarity against hers. Curses—for the fourth time!

'Will you be on the Palma run next season?' he asked her.

'Yes, probably.'

'Then you must arrange some more groundings—between March and November.'

The girls agreed. Patrick went on, 'Unfortunately, my buddy won't be here. He'll be in darkest Africa.'

Jane said, 'Sounds exciting. What will you be doing, Russ?'

'If I get the job, it'll be working as courier on photographic safari tours.'

'Wonderful. I wouldn't mind getting a job on the Africa run. At least you get breathing time at the other end. A friend of mine flies with B.O.A.C. She stops off at Karachi, Entebbe, Nairobi and trolls into London in mid-January with the most hateful tan. I must think about it.'

'You girls all right?' Patrick enquired diligently. 'Not too crushed?'

'Perfect,' said Annabel. 'I'm so comfortable I could go to sleep.'

'Go ahead,' said Patrick. 'Put your head on my shoulder. I'll give you a nudge when we get there.'

I'll bet you will—and I know where she'd get the nudge, son.

Fortunately the journey was fairly short-lived. About three

miles out of Palma we entered a residential section I'd never seen before. The houses were enormous, set way back from the road in acres of gardens, and very opulent. The girls were behaving like girls, 'oo-ing' and 'aah-ing' as they caught sight of the houses through wrought-iron gates, sighing at the illuminated landscaped gardens, gasping at a particular piece of grand architecture.

'Oh, what it is to have money,' sighed Jane. 'I'd love to see inside some of those villas. Huh, I bet the one we're going to is the poor relation of the street—the rabbit hut amidst the mansions, it always happens.'

But this time she was wrong.

Suddenly we turned through open gates in a high stone wall and jerked forward in our seats. The place was fantastic. There must have been two or three acres of garden—sweeping lawns and hundreds of flower beds—in front of the house. Tropical colour blazed in artificial lighting—roses, geraniums, poinsettia, a thousand others ... and spiky thrusts of cactus grew in controlled profusion among the rockery strewn with masterly abandon in a series of ascending terraces between the lawns and the house.

We followed a gravel path to the side of the house which was immense—long and low and very beautiful, a mixture of traditional Spanish and ultra-modern Hollywood. In front of the house was a wide patio, landscaped with shading trees and exotic tropical plants set in beds and pots and troughs. Over to one side there was a rose-arbour which surrounded a stone fountain and fish pond, undoubtedly a cool, delightful place to sit on a hot summer afternoon—the arbour, I mean, not the fish pond. Though, I don't know ...

'What a place!' exclaimed Jane, as we crossed the patio. 'Whose place can it be, Tiny?'

Tiny shrugged. 'Damned if I know. I just phoned a friend of mine in Palma Traffic Control and he told me to bring you here. I must say it's a fraction bigger party than I reckoned on. Just look at the cars over there—there must be five hundred people here!'

He led the way to the front door which was ajar and with a perfunctory ding on the bell he went in.

There was no hallway; we walked straight into the incredible lounge, as big as a soccer field and as modern as the day after tomorrow, the sort of room that results from giving a young, very with-it architect an enormous cheque and then defying him to spend it. The walls, built of glass or stone or timber, supported scores of modern art pieces—cubist and abstract paintings, seascapes, three-dimensional projects, works in metal—seizing the eye with interest and warming the room with colour. The furniture was a pot-pourri of modern inventiveness—deep armchairs in burnished hides, chrome and leather pieces and squashy leather sacks that moulded themselves to the contours of the body using them.

The focal point of the room was a circular fire pit set on a raised section of the floor, above which hung a huge beaten-copper canopy-chimney. The polished copper, reflecting the glow of the fire within the pit, endowed that part of the room with a rich warmth, and it wasn't surprising on this cold wet night that a great many guests were clustered around it, either standing or sitting on the carpeted floor or on the steps leading to the raised section.

There must have been a hundred people there, of all ages, dressed, for the most part, informally. They were making the usual happy party noises, drowning the background of stereo music that seeped in from hidden places all round the room.

The girls' eyes were wide. Jane said, 'Tiny, I believe you've made my night.'

'Quite something, hm? You all go over to the bar, there, and I'll try to find my pal, Tony, and let him know we're here.'

Over on the far side of the room, beyond the fire pit and on the same raised section, was a crescent-shaped bar built of white stone and what looked like ebony wood, a clever contrast of black and white. Some thirty people were crowded round it. As we crossed the floor to join them, feeling a bit self-conscious at walking in on an obvious 'in-group' thing, I noticed several men nudge each other and stare at the girls—particularly at Annabel. It wasn't surprising; she stood out easily as the best-looking bird in the room.

We approached the bar and squeezed in. There were two barmen on duty, young, dark-haired fellows in white jackets. One nodded to us then glued his eyes on Annabel. I had a feeling then we were going to have trouble with this bird.

'Señorita . . .?' he enquired, ignoring the rest of us. Annabel ordered and we eventually got some sense and a drink out of him.

Annabel detached herself a little way from the group and stood near the fire, gazing out at the room, trying to make out she didn't know the attention she was getting from half the males there. Patrick, I thought, you've got your hands full, son. This one's a flirt. Dick, I think, was right.

Suddenly she turned and walked up to me, flashing me a loving smile. 'Got a cigarette, Russ?'

'Sure.' I almost dropped my drink in anxiety to get the packet out of my pocket.

She accepted the light with an upward sweep of her eyes that bowled me over like a bowling ball. 'Thank you. Where, er, where do you come from?'

'Where was I born?' I asked, wondering what game she was playing now. 'Er, Cheshire—a little village in Cheshire—in a house remarkably similar to this one, except the lounge was no bigger than that fire pit and the backyard was a touch smaller. This is quite a place, huh?'

She gazed around the room, posing beautifully for the fellas. I caught Patrick in the corner of my eye. He was gnashing his teeth silently and pretending he didn't mind her talking to me.

'Oh, here comes Tiny,' she said. 'Is that our host, I wonder?'

Captain Timm was walking towards us accompanied by a thin, saturnine man, middle-aged, dark olive skin. They stopped in the centre of the room, talked for a moment, then Tiny came on alone, the other man walking back the way they'd come.

Tiny came up with a secret amused smile in his eyes, and called the girls together.

'Is that man our host?' Annabel asked him.

He shook his head, smiling more deeply. 'No, that was Tony Calvi, my buddy from Traffic Control. Well, girls, it looks as though we picked the right night of the year to be grounded. Our host is none other than . . . Calvario Bastar.'

Annabel gasped. Jane gaped. Janice and Sarah let out squeals of delight. Dewi raised an impressed brow. Patrick and I looked at each other and sighed. If there was one guy in the world whose party you *don't* bring a good-looking bird to—it was Calvario Bastar.

Tiny Timm was saying, 'The party is an annual wing-ding that Bastar throws for the people who have helped him to another ten million during the year. It's *really* open-house—do as you damn-well pleasey. There's a mountain of barbecued food at the back of the house—around the indoor pool. Girls, you've got to see that pool! You can't miss it—it's just before you get to the zoo . . .'

'Zoo!' gasped Jane. 'You're joking.'

Tiny grinned. 'I'm not. There are lions, tigers, gorillas—the works.' He swept his hand towards the lounge. 'You think *this* is impressive—wait till you see out back. Well, help yourselves, it's all yours. I'm for a drink.'

Jane grabbed his arm. 'Come on, Tiny, you're holding out. Where *is* he? Is he *here*?'

'Sure—he's around the pool, doing his thing off the top board for the ladies. You know Bastar.'

'Not intimately enough by half,' growled Jane.

Tiny shrugged. 'He's all right if you like the type.'

'I like, I like!' said Jane breathlessly. 'Oh, I've *got* to see this one in the flesh. How do I get there?'

Tiny pointed across the room. 'Through the glass panels beyond the staircase and across the rear patio. Just follow the sound of adoring female sighs—Bastar will be smack in the centre of it.'

I could understand Tiny's attitude towards Calvario Bastar, even though I'd never met the man. Bastar was one of those fellows who are just too much of and too good at everything to be popular with men. To begin with, at thirty-four he was filthy rich. Grandad had started the Bastar ball rolling with a lifetime dedication to breeding the finest fighting bulls in Spain. His son, Bastar's father, had inherited this lot and had expanded into hotels, the car industry and clothing. Then came Calvario, inheriting not only daddy's vast fortune but his god-like handsomeness as well, the dark-eyed, dark curly-haired good looks that demolished women at a thousand yards and brought him as much fan-mail as a leading film star.

Bastar was always in the news, always creating a stir somewhere in the world. He was an expert skier, racing driver, swimmer and diver, bob-sleigher and polo player. He was a financial wizz-kid who had increased his inherited fortune a couple of times over, expanding into, among many other things, airline catering—hence, I supposed, this party for airport personnel.

But of the many accomplishments for which Bastar was famous, one in particular brought him more publicity than all the others combined. Bastar was a bugger for and with the women. In every photograph I'd ever seen of Bastar—in magazines, journals, colour supplements—he'd always had a superb-looking woman on or in his arms and never the same woman twice. He was for ever being snapped in St. Tropez, St. Moritz, Rome, Paris, Le Mans. He'd be seen gambling in Monte, sailing in the Caribbean, bull-fighting in Seville—and always surrounded by a cluster of beautiful, adoring birds.

I had read that among certain men he had earned the nickname, probably well-justified, El Ladron—The Thief, because of his propensity for stealing their women. And it was rumoured, again with probable justification, that Bastar had been challenged more than once to a duel, though I don't know whether he ever fought one.

It was also common knowledge that besides El Ladron he was also known, by both men *and* women, as El Bastardo (which hardly needs translating), an epithet earned not only for his swaggering, insufferably high-handed attitude towards people but also for his broad streak of olde worlde Latin cruelty when dealing with animals.

However, this latter testimony to his character was, I admit, mostly gossip gleaned from such places as the barber's shop and the Bar Boom Boom where reputations are enhanced and destroyed daily by men whose opinions probably don't matter a damn anyway, and yet if only a quarter of what was heard and half of what was read was true, Calvario 'El Ladron' 'El Bastardo' Bastar was still one hell of a fella and out of sheer curiosity I had to take a peek at him.

Well, we got a peek all right—and a damned sight more beside. And if Patrick and I had had any sense we'd have hotfooted it out of that house after the first brush with Bastar and spent the evening getting pleasantly and uncomplicatedly shickered at Dirty Dick's place.

But we didn't.

Will I never learn . . .?

TWO

Jane and Annabel were off like a shot, saying to Patrick and me, almost as an afterthought, 'You two coming?' We followed them across the room, past a splendid open-tread staircase and out of an open glass panel to a covered patio. Here the girls stopped abruptly and we caught up with them.

'My God, would you *believe* it?' Jane gasped.

'Yes,' I said. 'But only because I'm looking at it.'

The wing of the house, running back at right angles from it, was made entirely of glass, huge panes in a slender frame, so slender the struts were hardly noticeable. And inside was the pool ... well, not just any old swimming pool but a landscaped complex of lawns and flowers and shrubs and palm-trees and sun-chairs and lounging couches and a bar and the barbecues ... and people ... and more people ...

'It's too *much*!' Jane squealed, holding her face. 'All this *and* Calvario Bastar ...! Oh, let's go in!'

We entered through a glass door in the panelling. It was like walking into summer, warm and moist and noisy. There must have been a couple of hundred people in there, some of them swimming or messing about in the water, but most of them at the bar or sitting around the pool.

The pool itself was immense and very deep beneath the diving tower which must have been twenty feet high, having three boards at different heights. But as far as the girls were concerned it might have been a tennis court. They had minds for only one thing and finally they spotted him, ringed by a dozen women at the far end of the pool, towering above them, a six feet four, bronzed, bare-chested, curly-haired Adonis in gold bathing trunks, a towel round his muscular shoulders.

Jane drew in a breath. 'There he is! Oh ... isn't he *gorgeous*?'

'Gorgeous,' replied Patrick, affecting a yawn, winking at me.

Annabel said excitedly, 'Come on you two, take us over. We've got to get a closer look.'

'Oh, we do have our uses, then,' cracked Patrick.

'Take the short-cut across the water, girls,' I said. 'You're treading so much air you'd never sink.'

The humour was lost on them; they were gone. We started off, casually strolling the length of the pool, making out we were interested in the plant life. To be fair, the closer I got to Bastar the more I had to admit what a fantastic looking fellow he was. He was built as a super-sportsman should be—wide of shoulder, narrow of waist, with a subtle corrugation of stomach muscles that reminded him of Lonnie Donnegan's skiffle board. And he *was* extremely handsome with a straight, proud patrician nose and strong jawline, and his dark curly hair worn long on the neck. As a kid I imagined he'd been good-looking enough to be called pretty, but maturity had knocked the corners off and had given him a few bags and crags that women went bonkers over and a trace of grey around the ears that would really finish them off. Was there *nothing* this guy didn't have?

One thing he certainly did have was the complete attention of every woman in his group. He was talking to them, in Spanish, effortlessly charming them, making them laugh, very much the noble lord surrounded by serfs and sycophants. As we got quite close I noticed the men on the fringe of the group. There were two of them, as tall as Bastar and if anything bigger built, real bulls, hard-eyed, unsmiling, taking no part in the conversation, just keeping a general eye on things. I didn't need two guesses. They were bodyguards. Maybe the rumours of Bastar's duels were true.

Now we were quite close to the group. Bastar up to this point had not been facing us direct so had not seen us approach, but now he turned to address a couple of women on his left and in doing so looked up. He paused fractionally in mid-sentence, then went on talking but kept his eyes on us, sweeping across the four of us until he spotted Annabel. They didn't move again for a long moment.

When they did it was to come back for a more searching inspection and as they locked on to me I felt suddenly nervous, even frightened. He had the eyes of a lynx. They were dark and unblinking and behind this gaze I could feel him analysing my worth, wealth, position, degree of challenge in business, women, sport . . . then, finally, having computed negative right across the board he dismissed me and swung over to Patrick. When he'd done with the three of us, his eyes went again to Annabel and the severity of his expression softened into the lop-sided, boyish grin that as much as anything else about him earned him the nickname The Thief.

I glanced at Annabel. She was flushed, bright-eyed and breathless. She returned Bastar's smile but didn't quite make it and the smile ended more as a nervous quiver of the mouth. I transferred my glance to Patrick. He knew he'd lost her. His expression was doleful and resigned, as though for him the fun had suddenly gone out of the evening.

Bastar made his excuses to the group and moved through it towards us, concentrating on Annabel, smiling charmingly, extending his hand.

'Well, now, who are you? You've obviously just arrived since I would have noticed you ...' a quick shift of the eyes to embrace the three of us '... all ... before.'

'Yes, we have just arrived,' said Annabel, fighting nervousness, endeavouring to stay cool. 'We ... that is Jane and I ... we ...'

Bastar transferred his eyes to Jane, demolishing her with his grin. 'Hello, Jane.'

'... Jane and I are part of Captain Timm's grounded crew ...'

'Captain Timm?'

'Er, yes ... I believe we were invited through a friend of Captain Timm's—Tony Calvi ... of Palma Airport ... he's head of Traffic Control ...'

Bastar either didn't know what she was talking about or just plain wasn't listening. 'It's of no matter,' he said easily, his eyes steadily on the movement of her mouth. 'You're very welcome. Have you no drink? Here, you must have mine.' He handed her a tall glass of green stuff with a couple of cherries in it and said to Patrick and me, 'Gentlemen, the bar is at your disposal ... at the far end of the room. Perhaps you'd care to avail yourselves of a drink and bring one for Jane?'

And with that he turned back to the group taking Annabel and, without much interest, Jane with him.

Patrick and I stood rooted, staring after him, aware that we were being watched by the two bodyguards on the far side of the group.

'Son,' I said, '... we've been dismissed.'

He nodded, benumbed. 'Hm hm.' He drew a deep breath and

let it out slowly.

'How d'you think we ought to do it?' I asked.

'Mm?'

'Kill him. How d'you think we ought to kill him?'

'Just what I was thinkin'. I think I'd like to nail him by the scrotum to the top diving board and push the rest over the edge.'

I winced. 'Ouch! You're that mad, huh?'

'He's a bastard all right.'

'A pig.'

'Mm,' he went, thoughtfully. 'Well, I'll tell yuh, one thing he's not goin' to do is spoil my last night on the island . . .'

'Hear hear.'

'Let's hope Dick was right and she spoils *his* evenin'. Anyway, what's it to me, I only met her an hour ago.'

'Quite.'

'And if there's no other way to get back at the bastard, I can at least ruin him with liquor bills. Come on, let's get a drink and see what else is floating around.'

'Spoken with wisdom rare in one so young.'

All of which was bravado to cover up the hurt we both felt at Bastar's dismissal. I knew, of course, that Patrick had felt it more keenly than I because I knew he was really quite bowled over by Annabel. What I didn't know was *how* keenly and how determined he was to get back at Bastar. If I had I'd have taken him home there and then.

We approached the bar, ordered two enormous scotches and stood with our backs to the bar, surveying the room. I lifted my glass. 'Well, here's to women.'

He grinned, returning to his normal cheerfulness. 'What I say is—screw 'em . . .' he sighed dramatically. 'And ain't that the root cause of all our trouble. See anything nice lying around?'

I nodded. 'Mm mm, one or two. All is not lost, Patrick, the night is still young.'

'Indeed it is. Let us stroll around and see what mischief befalls us.'

'Fancy a swim?'

'Ah, not yet awhile. I'm just beginning to feel a nice alcoholic edge and no desire to spoil it. Later, perhaps.'

We did a circuit of the pool, giving Bastar's group a wide

berth, mainly because we had no desire now to reunite with the girls but also because we did not like the way the two bodyguards were watching us.

'Not the most affable of gentlemen,' Patrick remarked, sidemouthed.

'Distinctly unjovial. Let's get back to the bar.'

By half past ten we were both very squiffed.

'Lissen ...' said Patrick, trying to get me in focus. 'What d'yuh say we quit this over-sized birdbath and have a look at that zoo Tiny talked about? I've an idea the animals will prove better mannered than some of the humans we've met so far—partic'ly if we can locate the pigs.'

'Ooh,' I winced, 'that was straight from the armpit. I'm glad I'm on your side, son.'

'Ah, Bastar kinda got me Irish up, the silly man. I don't easily lose me temper but he did it for me tonight. Come on, let's go huntin'.'

Out through the glass door we went, shutting the echoey noise and steam heat behind us. The night was cool but there was no rain and a sprinkle of stars were showing through a gap in the heavy cloud. There was a bit of moon now and again but it was a poor, watery, half-hearted thing. We stood on the patio and breathed the fresh air.

'Wow!' laughed Patrick, shaking his head. 'Boy, I do believe I'm the tiniest bit fractured.'

'Have no fear, Tobin's here. I shall guide you through the valley of the shadow of zooland ... wher*ever* it is.'

'Hey, Russell, it's dark. Which way d'we go?'

'This way,' I said, taking his arm.

'Ha!' he laughed. 'Talk about the blind leadin' the paralytic!'

'There!' I said, pointing. 'I distinc'ly saw some lights through the trees. It's that way.'

We started off across the patio, descended several stone steps, and as my eyes adjusted to the dark I spotted a gravel path leading into the tangle of trees. We took it. We hadn't gone more than twenty yards along it before the darkness closed in around us, total, impenetrable. Then I lost Patrick and was about to call when I heard a splash and an Irish curse.

'Patrick ...? Where are you? What have you done?'

'I've stuck me foot in a hole! Me best brogue is full of

water!'

'Keep talking, I can't see you. Have you got a match?'

'No.'

'Keep making a noise. Sing something.'

'Anything special? How about the "Rose of Tralee"?'

' "Who put the lights out" would be more appropriate. What a daft way to run a zoo. Where are you?'

'Right here. Just follow the sound of the dripping sock.'

I struck a match and revealed the luckless Patrick standing on one foot beside a rain puddle, wringing out his woolly.

'Hardly your night, cock, is it?' I said consolingly.

'Why don't they put some flamin' lights down here?'

'Maybe it's Bastar's way of giving the ladies an extra thrill when he brings them down to see the other animals. Come on, get your sock on, there's a glimmer of light through the trees.'

I dropped the spent match into the puddle, plunging us once again into darkness. Patrick got his sock on and we set off again, following the tiny distant speck of light, creeping cautiously along the narrow path.

'It's bleedin' spooky in here, mate,' I said.

'Want to hold my hand, Russell,' he lisped.

'Sure, sweetie. I wouldn't like to spend the night in here, all the same.'

'No,' he said, then chuckled. 'I'd surely rather spend the night in Gladys than in here.'

'Gladys? Who's Gladys?'

I heard him sigh. 'It's a saying, Russell . . . a saying.'

'Oh, I thought you were on to something good for a minute . . . hey! It's getting lighter . . . there—at the end.'

We came unexpectedly on a sharp bend in the path and when we reached it we saw the zoo. It was a huge tarmac-ed clearing with lines of cages and grassed compounds with stone-built animal houses in them. The lights we'd seen through the trees were three or four working lights on top of some of the cages, obviously not the complete lighting for the zoo because the place was dim, gloomy, miserable.

We stood at the entrance in silence, listening, hearing nothing, not a thing.

Patrick looked at me, weaving a bit. 'What d'you think?' he whispered.

'I think it's a zoo,' I whispered back.

He curled his lip at me. 'Should we go in?'

'Why not? Come on.'

Slowly, stealthily, we ventured in, surrounded by silence. There was no sign of life. It was eerie, standing there among the dead, deserted cages, the dim, shadowy recesses of the buildings. I turned round slowly, believing that someone—or something—was watching us, beginning to regret coming in. Then:

'Listen!' hissed Patrick.

I leapt a foot in the air. 'What is it?' I whispered, heart thundering, peering frantically into the shadows, prepared to run like hell.

'Nothing,' he said. 'Funny, isn't it?'

'You great narna!' I gasped. 'You frightened the wits out of me.'

'Well, it *is* strange! You'd expect roars and chatterin' and stuff.'

'*I* can hear chattering, mate—it's coming from my bleeding teeth!'

'Aah, there's nuthin' here to hurt yuh, the poor dumb creatures are fast asleep. Come on, let's go on through, see what's here.'

Despite his alcoholic courage, Patrick still peered about him as we went on slowly through. I didn't like it at all. The persistent premonition that we were being watched was trickling icy fingers through the hairs on my neck. I wanted to turn tail and run, back to the house and the comforting company of several hundred jovial souls. But, dammit, as long as Holmes advanced, so would I, and advance he did, right through the clearing and out the other side—and into view of a shoulder-high wooden barrier that swept around in a wide crescent.

'Now what d'you suppose that is?' he whispered.

'A tank trap?' I suggested.

We approached the barrier and looked over.

'A bullring,' said Patrick. 'A practice bullring. I wonder where he keeps his bulls?'

'Probably in his trousers, same as all the other fellas.'

'See, the lights up there on the poles. D'you suppose he fights here at night? Come on, let's hop over.'

'What for?'

'I've never been in a bullring. I want to savour the atmosphere, the thrill . . . the danger.'

'What—without bulls?'

'Of course. D'you think I'm mad?'

He cocked a leg over the barrier and dropped into the sand. Ah, well. . .

I dropped down beside him.

'Feel it!' he whispered dramatically. 'It's different in here, isn't it?'

'Of course it's different. We're in it. It's different from being outside it.'

'Think of the crowds . . . banked to the sky on a broiling Sunday evening. The matador enters . . . proud, erect, totally unafraid . . .' He began to strut the ring, stiff-legged, chin high, arm bent to the cape. 'The parade is over . . . the crowd starts . . . the first gigantic bull thunders into the ring . . . *olé* . . . *olé* . . .' Patrick made a couple of passes with an imaginary cape, getting his legs so twisted up he almost fell.

'Patrick!' I yelled. 'Look out—behind you!' and started running for the barrier. He didn't bother to look round; he just lit out for the fence and cleared it in one, landing in a heap on the outside. I sat up there, straddling the fence, laughing meself sore. 'The matodor exits . . . proud . . . erect . . . totally unfraid . . . !' I laughed and blew an enormous raspberry.

'Very funny,' he said, dusting himself off.

'Some bloody matador. Come on, cock, let's go back. I need another drink.'

'Ah,' he said, his eyes lighting up. 'A perspicacious thought, Russell.'

'Jeez, you need one if you can say perspicacious.'

We started back, venturing once more between the lines of cages, at once feeling the tingling silence, the disquieting gloom, glancing about us and behind us as we went. We had cleared the first two or three cages and were passing close to another when it happened. A gigantic black shadow suddenly shot out of the animal house and with a terrifying roar flung itself at the bars inches to my left. With a yell I leapt sideways and slammed into Patrick who staggered backwards, arms whirling, teetered four yards on his heels and finally fell on his arse, me on top of him.

'Jeezus Christ!' he cried. 'Get up ... get up!'

'What the hell is it!'

'Don't care ... let me get up!'

The monster was still roaring away, pounding the bars and roaring for all it was worth, shattering the silence of the zoo. I staggered to my feet, pulled Patrick up and stared at it.

'Holy mother, the size of it!' gasped Patrick, edging back automatically. We were staring into the savage black mask of the biggest, ugliest, most ferocious gorilla imaginable. It's little piggy eyes were furious black fires of unadulterated evil, and its mouth, wide open and screaming, was a nightmare hole of murderous yellow fangs. Even behind heavy bars it was a terrifying sight because it looked powerful enough to bend them open without effort and leap through.

We backed away from it until we reached the cage behind and leaned against the bars, hypnotised by the gorilla, watching it going berserk, leaping up and down and screaming at us, then, hell, from right behind us came another terrific roar. We shot round, and came face to face with a bloody great tiger, an enormous sod, eighty feet long with a head the size of a sea mine.

That was enough for us. We shot—straight down the path between the cages and round the bend into the woods. Almost! We didn't make the woods. Standing there in the middle of the path was a giant of a bloke, six feet six if an inch, and built like the gorilla, except he wasn't so hairy. In fact his bullet-head was shaved. He stood feet astride, dressed in riding breeches and boots, a rock, immovable, fiercesome, though not half as fiercesome as the two dogs at his sides. Dobermans! Two evil-looking buggers, held on short chains by Goliath, straining to get at us, growling and rumbling, instant quivering death waiting for the command 'KILL!'

'Vat are you two doink here!' Von Shitehork demanded, his voice booming through the zoo.

His tone set the dogs off. Rumbling thunder sounded in their throats, fangs glistened in the light, saliva dripped to the road. The German choked off the noise with a ringing command in Kraut and a murderous jerk on the chains, but although the noise stopped, the dogs maintained every vestige of their quivering vigil.

'Vy are you disturbink my enimals! ?' he demanded.

Patrick coughed. 'Well . . . I . . . we . . . that is, we, er . . .'

'That's the stuff, Patrick, you tell him.'

I thought I'd have a go. 'Well, you see . . . I . . . we . . .' For some reason I felt compelled to turn and point towards the gorilla who was nowhere to be seen. 'You see . . .'

'Are you guests of Señor Bastar! ?' he growled, getting full Germanic mileage out of 'Bas . . . taaar!'

'Well, of course .. yes, we certainly *are*,' said Patrick, settling down a bit.

I caught the valiant defiance of his tone, and went on, 'We didn't disturb the animals . . . they disturbed us! That bloody gorilla scared the daylights out of us. Its mad! Crazy! An unprovoked attack as we walked past the cage . . .!'

The German's face set even harder as he drew himself up indignantly. 'That gorilla, my friend, is a vild enimal and a very beautiful vild enimal, captured by Señor Bastar himself! Of course he will re-ect violently if you disturb him.'

'We didn't disturb him!' I protested, keeping an eye on the dogs who appeared to be gaining ground. 'We were *creeping* past his cage!'

'Ho! So! Vy vere you kreepink! ?'

'So as not to wake the bloody thing up!'

'You are not supposed to *be* down here!' said Fritz. 'Zer are signs saying you must not kom down here unless accompanied by Señor Bastar or one of his staff . . .'

'Well, we didn't see any signs. Where are they?' asked Patrick.

'Back zer—et ze beginning of ze path.'

'It was so dark back there we could hardly see the path, never mind the signs.'

'Quite!' barked Fritz. 'Ze lights are kept off purposely to discourage guests from vandering down by themselves. Normally the darkness is sufficient deterrent. It is very dangerous down here. It is fortunate for you the dogs vere not loose! I suggest you now return to the house and kom down later with Señor Bastar. You vill hef plenty of opportunity to see the enimals then.'

He moved to one side and beckoned us to pass. As we reached him and the bitterly disappointed dogs, he said in taunting tone,

'You are obviously two very brave fellows. Perhaps you vould like to demonstrate your bravery for us later in ze bullring, hey?'

We gawped at him.

'Oh, don't vorry,' he said snidely, 'zey are only leetle bulls. Señor Bastar vould not dream of exposing his guests to any *real* danger.'

With that he turned and marched off towards the zoo. We moved into the darkness of the trees, then, at the bend, turned and looked back. He was standing there watching us—he and the dogs.

'As the man said,' said Patrick, as we groped our way back to the house, ' "What steps would you take if suddenly confronted by that gorilla in the dark?" And the snappy catch answer is: "Bloody big ones." Russell, I did not like the looks of German George one bit. Come to think of it, from the point of view of congeniality there wasn't a haputh of difference between him and those heathen dogs. Surely he didn't mean those devils run around here loose?'

I shrugged. 'I don't know. It's private property and there are a lot of valuable animals down there.'

'Meanin' what!? Who in his right mind is going to try and nick that bloody gorilla—or the tiger! Those Dobermans are killers, y'know. If they'd been loose tonight I'd have taken me chances and nipped in with the gorilla rather than face them. Gob, I could use a drink.'

'Well, you did say you wanted a bit of excitement on your last night.'

'Ha! excitement—yes. A seizure—no. The festivities can stay this side of heart-failure and still please me enormously.'

I was glad of one thing—all the excitement had taken Annabel out of his mind—or so I thought. He now appeared his own jovial self, prepared to make use of Bastar's facilities and have a marvellous time. Well, we did make use of his facilities and that's how, eventually, we got separated—and how Patrick got *us* into all the trouble. Y'know, the fella's just not to be trusted on his own.

THREE

Well, believe it or not we actually got back in the pool room without further incident, which, the way things had been going, was little short of miraculous. We ordered two very big drinks at the bar and once again stood casing the joint.

'Aha!' said Patrick. 'Over there.'

I followed his gaze. There were two little swingers sitting on the side of the pool, dangling their feet in the water, sipping drinks through straws. They were quite pretty, had good figures and looked happy, uncomplicated souls, good for what we both needed right then—a giggle. One had long brown hair loose about her shoulders; the other had blondish hair caught in a pony tail. They were both about twenty years old.

'Mm,' I said. 'Fancy a stroll, Holmes?'

'After you, Watson.'

There was little point in subtle, time-wasting tactics. Patrick said boldly, 'Ladies, there are several ways in which we can approach and pester you and we'd like to know if you have any preference—or shall I just suggest—"I'm Patrick ... he's Russell ... and would you like a drink with us?" '

They laughed and I knew we were in. 'Thank you,' said the dark one, a nice little thing with big black eyes and a promising moustache, but very nice teeth and a fair bosom nearly in her swimsuit. 'My name is Victoria. This is Consuela.'

'Lovely names, both,' said Patrick, looking down Consuela's cozzy. 'What would you like to drink? Russell will gladly get you one.'

We all sat around a little white table and chatted. The girls, it transpired, worked as receptionists in one of the Bastar hotels on the island. We kidded them a lot and when things got too much for them they plunged in the pool for a quick swim.

After half an hour or so I could see Patrick was getting nicely smashed again, not surprising since he intended to and was drinking nothing smaller than quadruplets. I can always tell when it happens, apart from seeing him fall down, because he gets gradually more Irish than Gilhoolie's pig and begins 'bejazeing' and 'begorra-ing' all over the place.

The girls, emerging from their third plunge and standing

before us dabbing themselves dry, obviously noted that we were both beginning to feel the effects of the Highland sauce and Victoria suggested gaily, 'Come on, why don't you come in for a swim, it's really beautiful.'

'Bejaze,' said Patrick, 'and wasn't I thinkin' the same thing meself. Russell, d'you feel like a plunge?'

'What about swimsuits?'

Consuela said, 'Oh, they're in the dressing rooms. Just help yourself. It's through that door, there.'

'Come on, son,' I said. 'You'll need help to get your shoes off. See you girls in a few minutes. Don't run away.'

Patrick climbed unsteadily out of the chair and we went through the door and along a corridor that had a sign saying 'SEÑORS' on one side and another saying 'SEÑORAS Y SEÑHORITAS' on the other.

'That's the one for me,' said Patrick, weaving towards the S-y-S sign. I caught him by the arm and turned him in the men's place.

'Patrick, you're squiffed. You'll have to cut down on those quadruplets or you'll never make the plane.'

'Ah, forgot to tell yuh—I'm not flyin' home tomorrow. I've decided to take the job after all.'

'Job? What job?'

'Gorilla's companion. Good wages, I hear. Six boxes of Band-aids a week and all the bananas I can eat. And with a bit of luck I may even get to walk the Dobermans.'

'You *are* squiffed.'

'Squiffed but happy. Now, where're the cozzies?'

The room was lined with wall-lockers. In each open locker hung a pair of swim trunks made of an elastic-type material that would fit any size. I slung a pair at Patrick and we were changed in a couple of minutes; we would have been even quicker if he hadn't fallen off the bench while trying to undo his shoes.

'Whatya doing down there?' I laughed.

'Gettin' up,' he said, rubbing his elbow.

'Come on, the birds will have flown.'

We finally made it. Patrick entered the pool doing one of his ridiculous walks, shoulders spread, bottom stuck out, then paused on the edge of the pool, flexing his muscles and posing like Mr. Universe, making the girls laugh. I walked up behind him and gave him a tiny push with my forefinger. With a cry of mock dismay he keeled over, then leapt into the air and came down in a daft dive, a Goofy dive, legs bowed and his hands held close to his chest. He hit the water with a heck of a belly flop and half-drowned ten people sitting close by. I dived in after him and the girls followed and for ten minutes we sky-larked around, ducking each other, Patrick standing on my shoulders and doing ridiculous dives. Then we got out and had another drink.

At this moment a mild roar of approval sounded in the region of the diving boards and Bastar broke from his substantial group, slung his towel at one of the bodyguards and began to climb the steps of the tower to the twenty feet board.

'Oh, here we go,' Consuela murmured.

I looked at her, surprised by her tone. 'Don't you like Bastar? I thought all you girls were potty about him.'

'Here are two that aren't,' said Victoria. 'He's terribly rude. He stays at the hotel occasionally. The girls hate him.'

Bastar had now reached the top of the tower. He paused, summoning concentration, then advanced along the board with a slow, affected deliberation that was pure melodrama. He reached the end of the board and paused again, toes curled over the edge, head erect, his gaze fixed unblinkingly on the opposite wall, arms out straight ... and then he paused ... and paused ...

The crowd was hushed, the huge room breathless; even the water seemed to have calmed. Finally, when all was absolutely quiet, when he had the undivided attention of every serf in the room, he rose slowly on his toes, inclined slowly forward, rigid as a board and took off, executing the most perfect swallow dive and entering the water like a knife blade, barely disturbing the surface.

The crowd erupted in thunderous applause. Bastar surfaced, threw the water from his head with a practiced flick and smiled boyishly, then cut for the side in a powerful crawl.

Patrick was applauding with the rest of them, a little *too* heartily, I thought. 'Excellent ... excellent. Give the man nine out of ten for that one.'

'Nine?' I said. 'Why only nine, Patrick?'

'Because it wasn't perfect, that's why.'

'What the heck do you know about it?'

'What do *I* know about it! Jaze, wasn't I the champion of Ballybigsplash three years runnin' and only *just* failed to reach the finals in Dublin.'

'Why?'

'Sure, I missed the bus. Man, a fella wouldn't have to be all that terrific to beat Bastar. I'd do it meself but it's considered bad manners to show up your host.'

'Oh, go on, Patrick,' I chided, 'force yourself.'

'Yuh mean it?'

'Of course,' I said, winking at the girls.

'Right then, I will.'

He started to get up and we laughed, knowing he'd sit right down again or do a somersault into the pool or something. But he didn't ... and the next thing we knew he was doing his funny walk along the poolside, heading for the diving tower.

'He's going to do it!' gasped Victoria.

I shook my head. 'No, he won't. He'll jump off the low board or something. I don't think he's ever dived from twenty feet in his life. He'll probably turn round and come back in a minute ...'

But Patrick wasn't turning round. By now he was approaching the crowd of admirers surrounding Bastar who was drying himself and accepting the plaudits for the dive. Still doing his funny walk he passed the group, nose held mockingly in the air, reached the steps of the tower and began to climb.

'Oh, my God ...' I whispered. The girls just stared, open-mouthed.

Slowly, as he ascended, the room became aware of him. Talk began, then laughter, then a roar of laughter as he purposely missed a step and tripped. I glanced at Bastar. He and his crowd were gazing heavenwards. Bastar's face was set, puzzled, grim. I could see a muscle working in his cheek as he clenched his teeth.

'Oh, hell ...' I said. I saw it all now. Patrick would dive; it was his way of getting back at Bastar. He was going to make a fool of him. I didn't know whether to watch or head for the dressing room and run. I had the terrible feeling there was going to be trouble.

Patrick had now reached the very top and, emulating Bastar, he paused and shuffled his feet, drawing a ripple of laughter from the crowd. I glanced again at Bastar. Now he was glaring up at Patrick, dark with rage. His bodyguards were now beside him, looking perplexed, helpless. Oh, Patrick, you idiot, what have you done.

Patrick was now advancing along the board with a jerky walk, bottom out, elbows out, like a ruptured duck, nose held arrogantly high, legs all stiff and peculiar. The crowd were loving it. It sounded to me as though many of them had waited a long time for something like this to happen. All around me I could hear subdued cries of 'Bravo . . . bravo' and 'Who is it?'

Patrick was at the end of the board, toes curled over the edge, head erect, arms out straight, eyes fixed on the opposite wall . . . then he paused . . . and paused . . . and paused. Don't over-do it, you twit, I prayed. Go on, dive . . . dive . . .

A shout went up from someone in the crowd. 'How much longer!?' and Patrick bent his arm and looked at an imaginary watch. A terrific roar of laughter rang from the crowd. Bastar was beside himself. He was talking rapidly to his bodyguards who didn't know what the hell to do. What *could* they do?

Suddenly Patrick rose on his toes, bent his knees double and launched himself off in his crazy Goofy dive. Down he came, legs bowed, hands together against his chest, sickeningly parallel to the water. The crowd roared again and was on its feet, shocked that Patrick was going to belly flop from twenty feet. But he didn't. At the very last moment he straightened out, ducked his head, shot out his arms and entered the water with hardly any more splash than Bastar had made.

The crowd went wild. Patrick broke surface to thunderous applause and shouts. Emulating even Bastar's flick of the head he struck out for the side in an exaggeratedly stylish crawl, acknowledging the applause with a wave of his hands as each came out of the water.

Bastar had gone. The bodyguards had gone. And the group of sycophants was milling around like a leaderless herd of sheep.

Patrick hauled himself out of the water and flopped into his chair, gasping for breath, and swallowed the remains of his scotch. '*Now* d'you believe I was champion of Ballybigsplash?' he grinned.

'Patrick, you blithering idiot ... Bastar's livid with you! You're in trouble, you big dope.'

'Serves him right. Now we're quits.'

'Well, let's hope *he* thinks so. You didn't see the way he and his gorillas were looking at you up there.'

He shrugged with alcoholic indifference. 'Ta heck with him ...'

At that moment an announcement, in Spanish, came over the tannoy system that had, up to now, been providing quiet background music. 'Ladies and gentlemen ... Señor Bastar wishes to announce that the zoo is now open for your enjoyment ... and hopes that you will all attend the Fiesta of the Little Bulls in the plaza beyond the zoo. This is a golden opportunity for all you brave would-be matadors to show your skill and valour against these highly-dangerous killers!' (Jeers of derision from the crowd.)

'Oh, I want to see the zoo,' said Victoria. 'Will you take us down?'

'Of course,' I said. 'Come on, Holmes, let's get dressed. We'll be about ten minutes, girls.'

'We'll be fifteen, we have to dry our hair,' said Victoria.

We left them in the corridor and went into the dressing room, which was crowded. As soon as we entered, the congratulations began to rain on Patrick's head.

'Amazing dive, my friend ... far more entertaining than any other I've seen this evening.'

'Bravo ... a lesson may have been learned tonight.'

And so on. All good suicidal stuff. Patrick, I'm sure, was still not fully aware of the flap he'd caused because he was far more interested in drying his feet than in the plaudits. He was just smiling benignly and nodding and taking his time with each toe, so much time, in fact, that I was ready long before him.

'Look,' I said, checking my watch, 'the girls will be ready. I'm going for a slash down the corridor and I'll see you back at the table, huh?'

'Slash away, old cock,' he said generously, waving his hand. 'Enjoy life to the full.'

'Well, hurry up, eh, we'll be waiting for you.'

It took me two or three minutes to find an empty stall in the gents and another five before I joined the girls who were fixing their faces at the table.

'Patrick won't be long. He's having a little trouble with his feet.'

'Oh, what's wrong with them?' asked Consuela.

'They're on the end of his legs. In his condition that's a long way down. Hey, would you girls like some coffee while we're waiting?'

They said they'd love some so I went to the bar and brought four back. There was still no sign of Patrick. And when we'd finished the coffee there was still no sign of him.

'He's probably fallen asleep in a locker,' I said. 'I'll go an' chivvy him up.'

I went down the corridor and into the dressing room. There was nobody in there. Aha! I thought. Nature will have it's little way. He's gone for a slash. But he wasn't in the gents either. Aha! I thought. While I was in the dressing room he came out of the gents and went back to the pool room. Back *I* went to the pool room.

'Where is he?' asked Consuela.

'Hasn't he shown up?'

'No.'

'That's odd. Where the devil could he have gone to?'

The daft sod probably turned left instead of right out of the changing room, I thought, and won't realise it until he reaches Palma . . . or North Africa.

Five minutes later he still hadn't showed and the girls were getting impatient. I didn't blame them, there was nobody but waiters left in the pool room.

'Oh, come on, girls,' I said. 'I'll take you down. Patrick will have to find us.'

We went out of the glass door and across the patio. Ah, what a different scene now. All was floodlit—the paths, the trees—even the signs which said: 'IT IS DANGEROUS TO PASS BEYOND THIS POINT WITHOUT PERMISSION AND ACCOMPANIED BY STAFF. DO NOT ENTER! BEWARE OF THE DOGS!'

How different now the stroll between the trees. We joined the throng of people and walked towards the zoo. I kept having the odd backwards glance, expecting to see Patrick haring after us any minute—but still no sign. Where could the idiot have got to?

We reached the bend in the path and entered the zoo, now brightly lit and not at all spooky. Bastar had quite a collection of animals. There were lions with youngsters, a couple of black bears, three wolves, two tigers and a bunch of other things, including a cageful of randy monkeys with embarrassing pink bottoms that looked sore as hell. I hurried the girls on from this cage because one dirty little sod, sitting close to the wire, had an enormous hard on and sat there playing with himself, chattering to the girls and flaunting himself. I could see the girls were dying to laugh but were pretending not to notice.

We moved on and came to the gorilla. Jeez, what a brute. He was no longer leaping up and down, doing his nut, but he *was* still gripping the bars and glowering at everyone like he wasn't overly fond of them.

'Good heavens!' I exclaimed. 'Patrick ...! How did you get in there!? Stop monkeying around and come out at once!'

The girls laughed. The gorilla switched its evil eyes on me and, by heaven, I swear it recognized me. It gave a deep rumbling growl and opened its mouth wide, baring its bloody great fangs at me.

'Oh, look!' exclaimed Consuela, 'it's smiling at you!'

'Yes, I have this way with animals. Don't know what it is but they seem to love me on sight.'

Now the gorilla was getting mad again, growling and grunting and beating its great black-leather chest and rattling the bars. It was said that Tarzan learned the language of the monkey world and could understand everything they said. Well, I've never done a course in gorilla but I knew exactly what this one was saying to me. He was saying, 'if it wasn't for these bars, you pasty-faced berk, I'd be out there ripping your fuckin' arms off.'

'Ah, isn't he sweet?' said Victoria.

'Sweet,' I said, 'bless his little pointed head.'

Just then we heard distant sounds of shouts and laughter from the direction of the bullring and another loudspeaker announcement was made. 'Ladies and gentlemen ... welcome to the Fiesta of the Little Bulls! As you can see, each bull has a rosette attached to its head. Anyone brave enough to detach a rosette will be rewarded with a handsome prize! Pedro and Miguel will now demonstrate how it is done ... then we want every able man here to climb into the ring and try his luck! Ladies and gentlemen . . . Pedro y Miguel!'

'Oh, come on, let's watch!' Victoria said excitedly.

We hurried across to the bullring. The barrier was crowded with people, leaning against it, sitting on it, and we squeezed in among them. In the sanded ring, which was now floodlit by the lights high on the poles, there were ten young bulls, very young, with hardly any growth of horn, yet heavy enough for the purpose, especially since they all looked very skittish, very alert and ready to butt anything in sight.

Over the tannoy system came a fanfare of trumpets, the opening bars of the Fiesta parade music. The gates opened and into the arena strode two dwarfs, dressed in full matador regalia, carrying ridiculously oversized wooden swords. In they marched, proud as peacocks, chins high, each man three feet six of Spanish arrogance, acknowledging the applause of the crowd with a wave of their hats.

Suddenly the entire, elegant scene disintegrated into graceless panic as one of the young bulls leapt into action and started hell-for-leather for the dwarfs. Whooopps!! they were off, tearing across the ring, their bandy little legs going nineteen to the dozen, two bulls now in hot pursuit. Down went one of the dwarfs, arse over tip across his ungainly sword, nose in the sand. A bull was on him, driving its non-existent horns into his bottom pushing the little fellow along face down in the sand. The second dwarf doubled round in a wide circle, ran up to the attacking bull and kicked it in the knee (as high as he could reach). The bull shot round and went after him. The first dwarf was up and bent over, dusting off his uniform. From the edge of the ring a bull sighted the target, locked on to it and charged. Biff! The dwarf shot ten feet across the ring.

'Oh!' the girls cried. 'Surely they'll get hurt!'

'Heck no, they know what they're doing. Their suits will be well-padded. Hey, look at that!'

One of the dwarfs was sprawled across a bull's neck, hanging on for dear life as the bull bucked and bounced and tried to shake him off. Then with an almighty twist of its head the dwarf shot into the air and landed on the bull's back and rode it backwards, holding the rosette in the air, shouting, 'Come on, you men, try your luck, test your valour!'

To supplement this encouragement, the tannoy emitted another announcement. 'Ladies and gentlemen ... now you see how it's done, every man in the ring to capture a rosette!'

Most of the fellas on the rail, squiffed as they were, couldn't wait to get in. They leapt the barrier in their scores, whooping and shouting, taunting their mates to get in with them. In seconds the ring was a riot, men making wild dashes at the bulls, bulls dodging and weaving and butting, some men making attempts at cape-work with their jackets. One man flew into the air and landed in the sand with a bump, his coat over his head. The bull whirled, tucked its muzzle under his legs and threw him backwards. He rolled over and came to his feet, then started running blindly, the bull in hot pursuit, butting him in the bottom. There were dozens of very funny sights. One mad ass had lost his belt and was haring across the ring with his trousers round his knees, trying unsuccessfully to dodge a bull. Another fellow was riding a bull backwards, holding its tail, but not for long. He arc-ed through the air with the greatest of ease and landed on somebody's back, and started riding him.

The girls were in pleats. Consuela, wiping her eyes, said, 'What about you, Russ—are you going in?'

'Consuela ... the name of Tobin has for centuries been synonymous with coward and I don't believe this is the moment to change tradition ...'

'Hey ...!' she grabbed my arm. 'Isn't that Patrick!'

'Where?'

'There ... just climbing over the barrier on the far side ... no, more to the right.'

By gum, she was right. And the speed and agility with which he cleared the barrier astounded me. He actually seemed *keen* to get in there. He dropped to the sand, looked quickly and, I thought, anxiously behind him—and was off, racing across the arena like his Y-fronts were on fire. He hadn't gone ten paces when a bull spotted him. It came at an angle, galloping flat out. Patrick glanced and saw it. His mouth flew open in horror. He ran faster, arms and legs pumping, coat flying. The bull cut in sharply, reached for him, caught him on the arm. Patrick shot round like a top, two complete pirouettes, hopped sideways three times and took a header into the dust.

El torito was on him, butting him in the bum ... booom ...

booom . . . booom . . .

'Oh, *do* something!' Victoria implored me, grabbing my arm. 'He'll get hurt!'

'Who—the bull? Nah, he's all right . . .'

'Ooh . . . stop acting the fool! Go on, help him!' She gave me a push. 'Go on!'

'All right, I'm going . . .'

'Well, go! Hurry!'

I took a leap at the fence and dropped down into the sand. Yes, Patrick was right. It did look different on this side of the barrier. I started to run towards Patrick who was still getting it up the rear. But what was I going to do when I got there! I slowed a bit, hoping the bull would have a change of heart and target by the time I reached it. But no! Ten yards . . . five yards . . . three . . . two . . . it was still going at Patrick, heavens hard. He was yelling curses through a mouthful of sand. 'Gerrof, yuh daft bastard . . .!' and trying to boot the bull in the nose.

I bent down to him. 'Need any help?'

'Yes, get this bloody . . .' then he recognised the voice. 'By Christ, about time, too. Get this bloody beefburger off me, for Pete's sake! Ow! Ooh! Russell . . .!'

'What do I do?'

'I dunno! Kick it in the balls or something!'

I had a look. 'It hasn't got any.'

'Well, kick it where they're goin' to be! Ow! Twist it's tail, then . . . anything . . . but do something! Ouch! Geeerrrofff, yuh dumb bugger . . .!'

Gingerly I approached the sturdy, angry little animal, tentatively reached for and grabbed his ear, hauled up its head and yelled, 'FUCK OFF!!' down its ear. The thing leapt about four feet in the air, lashed out with its hind legs and was off across the ring like it was caught short.

Patrick, moaning and groaning, scrambled to his knees and looked nervously around. 'Where is it? Where's it gone?'

'Disappeared, dear boy. One word of command from its master . . . well, two, actually . . . and off it trotted good as gold.'

'Huh! Might have known you could communicate with it, the amount of bull you talk all the time.'

'Now, there's gratitude. I come in here, risking life and limb

. . . Patrick, what are you looking like that for—it's gone. No need to be frightened . . .'

He was staring about him anxiously, peering into the crowded ring and particularly towards the barrier where he'd climbed over. 'It's not the bulls I'm frightened of right now—it's the gorillas.'

'The wha . . .?'

'The gorillas—Bastar's bodyguards. They're after me. Come on, we can't stand here, they're not far behind. They've chased me through the woods . . .'

He started off at a fast trot and I had to run hard to catch up with him. 'Patrick, what the hell have you been up to . . . where did you disappear to . . .'

'Later, let's just get out of here.'

'Out of the ring?'

'No—out of the grounds! They're really going to do me!'

'Ah, you're joking . . . aren't you?'

'The hell I am. They've already had one go . . .'

At this point we got separated by a bloke being chased by a bull. We let them both go through and then rejoined, still running, heading for the barrier on the side away from the zoo. We reached it. I clambered over but Patrick stood on it, searching the ring.

'Patrick, what *hap*pened?'

'Well, I was in the dressing room after you left . . . and . . . oh, my God, there they are—standing on the barrier on the far side!'

He leapt down and looked anxiously about him. All we could see ahead of us was more black forest.

'Did they spot you?' I asked.

'They're on their way, Russell. We've got to run!'

'Run! Where? In there!'

'Can you think of anywhere else?'

'Hey, I like this "*we've* got to run" business. *I* haven't done anything.'

'You're with me, aren't you? That'll be enough for them, they don't need too much excuse.'

'Then, come on, let's run!'

We plunged into the inky blackness, realising after fifty yards, as our feet sank to the ankles in the rotting undergrowth, that we'd more than likely, once again, done the wrong thing.

FOUR

'Oh, you're ...' squelch, squelch, 'beautiful, Holmes,' I panted. 'Just ...' squelch, '... beautiful. How in Christ'sname did you get us into this mess?'

'Ssh, keep your voice down, they'll hear us!'

'You know, I don't care! Phew, God, this stuff stinks ... aw, hell Patrick ...'

With each laborious step we took we disturbed a clump of stinking, soggy leaf-mould (at least I prayed it was leaf-mould) and all but gassed ourselves. We couldn't see a thing; it was total black-out in there—no moon, no stars—nothing. And added to the torture of the soggy undergrowth were the tricky little thorn brambles strewn across our path at varying heights, so the ones that didn't trip you got you across the hands or face and tried hard to gouge an eye. And in addition to *this* little lot there was the rainwater that dripped down our necks every time we touched a branch or a trunk. Within a couple of hundred yards I, personally, had had more than enough.

'Patrick ... how *did* you get us in this mess? What happened in the dressing room?'

'I ... ouch ... I was just putting me jacket on when those two gorillas came in and said Bastar wanted to see me.'

'Aye, aye ... I told you. That dive was daft thing to do.'

'All right, all right, maybe it was, but ... Oh ... HELL!'

'What's the matter!?'

'I've lost me left shoe! The mud sucked it off!'

'Well, feel around for it.'

'I'm feeling!'

'Ssh! Listen!'

We stopped breathing. Far off, perhaps a hundred yards or more, we could hear the cracking of the undergrowth. 'It's them!' I whispered. They've followed us in!'

'Of course they've followed us in. Haven't I been tellin' yuh they're dedicated to duffing me up!'

'But why, for Godsake! Not just because of the dive?'

'No, because I booted one in the kneecap and the other on the shin.'

'Oh, my God! Why!?'

'Because Bastar gave me a right bollocking and told them to see me off the premises.'

'Understandable in the circumstances ... come on, have you found that shoe yet?'

'Ah ... yes! No, it's a piece of wood.'

'Come on, they're catching up, man. So why did you kick these blokes?'

'You should have heard the way Bastar said "see him off the premises". He meant take me to the woods and thump the living daylights outta me. So I got a couple feet in first and ran. Ah, got it!'

'Well, put it on fast, I can hear them coming!'

'Yerk, it's full of mud.'

'I don't care, Holmes, just get it *on*! Hurry, man. I don't want a thumping for nothing.'

'O.K. it's on,' he grunted.

On we plunged, working our way away from the distant sounds of the bullring, sucking up mud, walking with protective arms in front of our faces, heading—where?

'Holmes, where the blazes are we heading?'

'No idea, but I reckon there must be a road somewhere in this direction. The property's got to end sometime.'

'Wanna bet?'

And ten minutes later we were still ploughing through the muck, apparently getting nowhere. By now we were wet through, up to our knees in stinking leaf-mould and scratched to the bone by brambles.

'Aah, is there ... no end ... to it?' Patrick gasped. 'I bet we're goin' round in circles!'

'Well, if we are then they are. The muscles are still behind us, I can hear them. Come on, we can't stop.'

'If only we could see the moon ... Gob, I could use one of those quadruplet scotches right now.'

'I could use a glimpse of the road right now—and a very fast car. Can you hear any noise from the bullring?'

We stopped squelching and listened. All around us the wet wind whiffled through the trees and raindrops plopped into the undergrowth. There was no noise from the bullring but far off I heard a man's voice calling and then heard the vague response.

'They've got reinforcements!' Patrick whispered. 'The Fiesta must have finished . . .'

'Ssh! Listen!'

'What to?'

'Listen . . .!'

Had my ears betrayed me . . .? No, they damn well hadn't! There, quite far off, came a sound borne faintly on the wind that turned my blood cold and raised the hairs on my neck. I heard Patrick's intake of breath and I was about to speak the awful words when he beat me to it.

'The dogs!' he gasped. 'My God, Russell, it's the Dobermans!'

We fled. In blind panic we ran, crashing through the thick undergrowth as though it was a daisy patch, heedless of branches, brambles, bog or bugger-all, just bulldozing a way through to heaven knew where, but going! Knees up, arms in front of our faces, we belted through, vaguely aware of tearing cloth and ripping skin and *very* aware that the fierce barking of the dogs was getting closer and closer.

Were they on chains—or on the loose! Surely Bastar wouldn't allow the monsters to track us down loose! And who're you trying to kid, Tobin—Bastar sounded just the fellow to allow it. It was right up his alley, and if we didn't find the road in the next two or three minutes those Dobermans would be right up *our* alleys.

They were getting closer! I could hear them plainly now, even over the noise of my hysterical breathing, not only their howling but the crashing of the undergrowth as they belted through it. They must have been coming like rockets.

I could hear Patrick just ahead of me, murmuring to himself, 'Oh, bloody hell . . . oh, bloody hell . . .' and I knew just how he felt. I hadn't been so running scared since I was chased by a cow when I was nine years old. I must have run a hundred yards in seven seconds flat that day, wetting me pants all the way.

Then, suddenly, an exultant cry from Patrick. 'Russell . . . the fence!' and in the next moment we were out of the woods and into a narrow clearing. Oh, no! There was the fence all right—dead ahead—but it was all of twelve feet high and made of two-inch mesh with an overhang of stranded sheep-wire on the inside and of barbed wire on the outside!

'We'll never get over it!' I cried, nevertheless haring across to it and sticking my toe in the mesh.

'Russell ...' Patrick panted, 'we either ... get over it ... or ...' He got no further. In the next instant the dogs cleared the last ten yards of undergrowth and flung themselves across the clearing at us.

Don't ask me how I climbed that twelve feet of two-inch mesh because I just couldn't tell you. The next thing I knew I was dangling by my hands from the overhang with two insane Dobermans leaping into the air trying to bite me legs off. Patrick had, miraculously, already negotiated the overhang and was lying in the Y-valley urging me on to greater effort.

'Swing your right leg up, Russell, go on ... higher ... take a swing at it!'

'The wire's cutting me fingers off!'

'You'll lose a lot more than your fingers if you drop down there ... come on, now, get your leg up ...!'

The dogs were now taking flying leaps at the fence, bouncing me around on the wire, trying to shake me loose. I swung my legs ... and again ... and on the third try hooked my foot over the wire, then not a knee up—and from thereon it was sheer bloody agony.

'Look, Russell, let go of that strand and grab for this one ... go on, I've got you ... good, now pull! Come on, what's keeping yuh?'

'I've got the bloody support stuck up my shirt! Hang on, let me drop back a bit ... a bit further ... O.K., it's clear now ... ow!'

'What's the matter?'

'Nearly knackered meself. Jeezus, this wire's like cheese-wire. Right ... I'm O.K. now ... thanks, mate.'

With a mighty heave I was up and joining Patrick in the Y-valley between the two overhangs, and as I got there the two gorillas burst from the woods and blinded us with powerful torches.

'Come on down, you two,' one of them shouted. 'You can't get away.'

'Knickers,' said Patrick. 'Just watch us.'

The bruiser turned to his fellow-ape. 'Carlo, take the dogs through the gate.'

That did it. Barbed wire or no barbed wire we were standing on the grass verge on the outside of the fence in ten seconds flat, shoving two fingers up the boys.

'Carlo! Quick! Don't let them get away!'

But we were away—flying down the road like the very devil was after us, heading, we hoped, towards Palma but not really caring so long as we put a lot of distance between us and those damned dogs. On and on we ran, full pelt, for maybe five minutes then exhaustion called a halt. We dropped down into a jog-trot, puffing like old men, still glancing behind us every now and again, then into a walk and finally we stopped altogether, bent over, hands on knees, desperate for air.

'My God, Patrick ... what a night ... *what* a night. Just see ... what women ... do for you.'

'You're right ...! Never again . . I won't look ... at another woman ... the rest of me life ...'

'It's not the looking ... that does the damage. It's the mad ... mad passion ... that goes with it. God, I'm shagged. Let's walk a bit, huh?'

We staggered on down the narrow road, neither knowing nor particularly caring where we were heading. We were surrounded by fields, we knew that. There was a glimmer of moon now and again that showed us there was an olive orchard on our left and a flat field on our right, but that was all. We might have been anywhere and in any country.

'By heaven, Patrick,' I panted, 'I do not believe it. I do not believe an evening that started so mundanely could finish like this. I have to hand it to you, you have a knack of turning simple, everyday activities into frantic high drama. About five hundred people went to that party ... and four hundred and ninety eight of 'em will be leaving in a civilized fashion through the front door. Only *we* have to exit over a twelve foot fence chased by killer dogs and a couple of thugs.'

For a moment we plodded on in silence, listening to the wind whistling across the fields, then he chuckled ... and I chuckled ... then he burst out laughing ... and I burst out laughing ... and we were helpless in the middle of the road when the car came from nowhere and caught us in its headlights.

'The ditch!' I yelled. And we jumped. Splat! And Ugh!! Straight into six inches of rainwater and mud. Discomfort unheeded, we fell against the bank, face down, and with pounding hearts listened to the whine of the car as it gathered speed along the straight.

'D'you think they saw us?' gasped Patrick in a whisper. I don't know why he was whispering.

'I dunno. But if they stop, we're over this fence and into the orchard—right?'

'Right!'

The car came on, too fast, I thought, to stop. It would shoot on by. I began to relax instinctively. But when it was almost level with us it suddenly squealed to a skidding halt. I heard doors open, footsteps on the road.

'Come on, Patrick ...!' and we were up, dragging our feet out of the mud, clambering up the slope, clutching the wooden fence, cocking one leg over ...

Then the powerful torchlight hit us. It *was* the muscle boys! Up, Patrick, and over ... and go ...!

'Parese!' A command rang out in Spanish. Stop!

'Get knotted!' I yelled.

'Stop—or we shoot!'

Eh? Now, that was a bit different. I hesitated, one leg over the fence and glanced back, blinded by the torchlight, but not so blinded I couldn't see the glint of two revolvers on the edge of the beams.

'Oh, bloody hell ...' gasped Patrick.

'I know,' I gulped.

'Come back here—slowly!' the voice commanded. 'Don't try anything or we will shoot you!'

'You blokes are mad!' I shouted, shaking like a jelly. 'You can't do this!'

'Try us,' said the voice, with threatening calm. It's the first time I've ever heard a trigger-happy voice. It is not a very nice sound. 'We will shoot you off the fence like a couple of pigeons if you make one bad move. Now—get down!'

We climbed back over the fence and stood at the top of the slope, arms raised, knees shaking, trying to see the faces behind the torches.

'You ... you men are crazy!' Patrick said bravely. 'We'll tell the police about this ...'

There was a curious silence for a couple of long seconds and I thought I saw the thugs glance at each other. Then one of them growled, 'Are you being funny?'

'No, I'm not,' said Patrick. 'The Spanish police take a very dim view of people chasing around their island waving revolvers . . .'

'Idiot,' the same fellow said. 'We *are* the police. Now get over here.'

FIVE

My blood ran cold and I'm damn sure Patrick's wasn't running all that warm either, and at that moment I wasn't at all sure I wouldn't have preferred to be in the clutches of the thugs than these cops. Both of us had had enough experience of the Spanish police to appreciate the wisdom of keeping well clear of them. These cops do not, repeat *not*, bear the slightest resemblance to your friendly London bobby who is inclined to stroll up, saying 'Nar, then, what's all this 'ere?' and proceed to take a few notes while you hold his flashlight for him.

Mind you, I'm not saying *all* Spanish cops are undisciplined, ignorant, hysterical, trigger-happy lunatics—quite possibly one or two aren't—but what I *am* saying is that it's much healthier to *assume* they all are and behave yourself accordingly.

So when this fella said 'get over here', we got—very carefully, and stood in front of them, shivering inside, blinded by the torches and fully expecting a crack on the head or a kick in the belly for openers.

'Who are you?' snapped the voice, while the other bloke stepped behind us and ran his hands over us for weapons. By gum, it was the first time in my life I'd ever been frisked.

'You!' He stabbed the torch in my face and I shot back a couple of feet. 'Stand still!'

'My name's Tobin—Russ Tobin.'

'English?'

'Yes.'

'Huh! What were you doing on this road at two o'clock in the morning?' he asked, still speaking in Spanish.

Well, now, how'd you like to have a go at explaining this lot! 'We ... we were guests at the house of Calvario Bastar and ... and ... we ... well, we ...'

The torch left my face and travelled slowly down to my shoes, what you could see of them. Only now did I realize what a mess I must have looked. I glanced at Patrick to see what his condition was like. Oh, brother ...

The torch came back to my face. 'You don't seem too sure, do you. I think you're lying.' He swung the torch on to Patrick's face. 'You ...! What's your name?'

'Patrick Holmes.'

'Also English?'

'God forbid. I'm Irish.'

'Irish? Where is Irish?'

Ha! Served the bum right.

'The country is Ireland, Chief Superintendent ...'

'Sergeant.'

'... sergeant. After Spain the most beautiful and civilized country in the world and populated, for the most part, with people like your goodselves—gentlemen and scholars.'

The silence that followed was awful. The big gump had put his foot in it again. The cop was obviously trying to decide whether or not Patrick was taking the mickey and I was filled with dread he'd come down on the 'whether' side. If he did, then Patrick would get the torch full in his lying teeth and maybe a steel-toed boot in the goolies for good measure. You daft bugger, you've smoothed yourself right into bother again and maybe me with you, for I knew that if they cut loose on Patrick they wouldn't miss the opportunity of filling me in too, explaining it in their report, no doubt, as 'action to thwart attempted escape'.

The cop must have stared hard at Patrick for a year and a half before he growled snidely, 'You have a smooth tongue, Irish man, and you'd better use it to explain what you are doing here hiding in ditches. And, for both your sakes, make it believable.'

I heard Patrick gulp. As cold as the night was, I was sweating.

'Well, we weren't actually hiding ... sir ... we ...'

'You weren't actually hiding ... sir ...' mimicked the cop.

'Then is it a habit of yours to stand talking to your friend in a ditch full of mud and rainwater—at two in the morning?'

'Er ... no ... you see,' Patrick released a long, disconsolate sigh. 'Sergeant, this is going to sound very *un*believable ...'

'Going to? It already does. Hold out your hands, both of you—close together.'

Well, this was turning out to be a night of 'firsts'—my first frisking, and now the first time I'd ever been handcuffed to Patrick. They shoved us in the back of the squad car and got in the front, one cop driving, the other, a hard-faced creep with dark brutal eyes, turned in his seat keeing an eye on us, his revolver peeping over the seat, also keeping an eye on us.

The gun terrified me.

Apart from a radio message to headquarters in Palma stating that they were bringing in two suspects for questioning the cops didn't utter a word the entire journey. Sorry—correction—they uttered two, they uttered 'shut' and 'up' when Patrick tried to say something to me. So in solemn silence we drove through the quiet city, heading for Palma police station, a building already familiar, inside and out, to Patrick and me. Oh, yes, we'd been arrested before. Last June we inadvertently got mixed up in a night club brawl between some American sailors and the local Spanish lads and we were all whisked off in a bunch to the station for questioning. *We* were released very quickly—after a mere three hours—probably because we were with two birds and could prove we'd been dancing and minding our own business. Even so, those three hours were more than enough.

Palma police station is a grim, glowering fortress, a frightening, threatening labyrinth of dank stone-floored rooms and corridors, a haunted mausoleum of ancient misery in which, with even modest imagination, one can hear the distant, subterranean cries of the tortured as the creaking rack tears limb from mutilated limb and the flesh sears and bubbles on the white-hot iron and I'd better shut up because I'm frightening meself sick.

I knew what Patrick had tried to say to me in the car. He was hoping the same lieutenant who interviewed us last time would be on duty this time though why being arrested a second time should be testimony to our lily-white characters, I wouldn't know.

My stomach lurched as we swung in through the massive

studded gates and into the courtyard of the police station. Briskly the cops had us out of the car and hustled us in a panicky half-run through a door and along a smelly stone-flagged corridor. The speed of the action disturbed me. It was so un-Spanish. It was as though they couldn't wait to get the first pinky in the thumb-screw.

The leading cop stopped abruptly at a wooden, iron-studded door and flung it open.

'In here!'

The door slammed behind us. Patrick and I stood rooted like a couple of Burton's dummies, looking around the room ... bare bulb dangling on eight miles of flex from the high, high ceiling ... grey stone walls and floors ... a long, wooden trestle table and four chairs ... and a drinking tap dripping in the corner. We ended our gaze looking at each other. Slowly a smile appeared on Patrick's face, more nervous than amused by a long chalk.

'Well, we may as well sit down. I've got a nasty feelin' it's going to be a longish night.'

'What if I don't want to?'

'Ha! you're right. It pays to be handcuffed to a reasonable man. But you'll have to cooperate while I take me socks off and wring them out. They're squelching something terrible.'

'So are mine . . . you go first.'

As he tugged off his shoes I said, 'Hey, what d'you think will happen?'

He gave a resigned shrug. 'Who the divil knows with this lot. We could languish here without trial for maybe two years—or at least until somebody misses us badly enough to make some enquiries—which could well *be* two years . . .'

'Thanks a lot, speak for yourself.'

'Or they could phone Bastar and clear the whole thing up in half an hour.'

A nasty thought occurred to me. 'Hey, what if Bastar lies—just for the hell of it. He's an influential guy. He could probably get us put away for twenty years!'

Patrick was nodding solemnly. 'The thought has already visited and disturbed me. The way I see it, our fate is resting in the hands of a vindictive man who has no cause whatsoever to show any generosity of spirit towards us.'

'But surely Bastar wouldn't perjure himself just to get back at us. He wouldn't deliberately lie to the police.'

'No, I don't think he'd lie—but he could do other things ... like leave the island. You know how the man travels around—maybe he was planning to leave tomorrow—I mean today. *Or* he could be purposely vague—tell the cops he had no idea what we were doing on the back road at two in the mornin' ... you know, just screw things up for us. Granted they wouldn't keep us in here two years, but, bedad, two *days* would be fun enough for Bastar and hell enough for us.'

I was nodding miserably. In the eyes of these cops we were already guilty of something or other—even if it was only standing in a ditch at two in the morning. We had now to prove our innocence—and for that we needed Bastar's wholehearted co-operation. We may as well have hoped for tea and hot buttered crumpets right then.

'All we can do, Patrick, is tell the truth and hope for the best. To tell another truth I don't much fancy spending Christmas and New Year in here.'

'You realize of course,' he said, wringing out the first sock, 'that they put garlic in their mince-pies.'

'It wouldn't surprise me. I can't stand garlic.'

'I'll have to stop doing this.'

'What? Ringing out your sock?'

'Mm. I'm dying for a pee. This is making it worse.'

'What does one do ...?' I said, looking round.

He shrugged. 'I suppose one knocks on the door, very loudly. Bejaze it's coming on hard ...'

He quickly pulled on his sock and shoe and stood up. 'Russell ... if you'd be so kind?'

He dragged me to the door and bashed on it. It was opened in an instant by a small, rat-faced cop with one ear. 'What is it?' he scowled.

'Por favor,' said Patrick, wriggling a bit, 'Dónde están los retretes?'

The cop jerked his head and like a couple of Siamese twins we followed him down the dimly lit corridor.

'This isn't the same part of the building as last time,' I remarked.

'No, it isn't. This wing is for serious crimes—like standing in ditches at two in the morning. The other section is for the petty stuff—murder, rape and plotting against the regime.'

The guard led us down a few steps to a smaller corridor, then pushed open a door and motioned us through. Inside was a grim little lav with two cubicles and a pong as thick as a bog fog. We took two steps in and three out, retreating as though from a wall of tear gas, almost gagging.

'Holy mother,' Patrick gasped.

'Cor, blimey . . . are you *sure* you want one?' I choked.

'Got to—believe me.'

I turned to the guard who was standing impassively there, probably wondering what all the drama was about. 'Look, can't you take these cuffs off?'

He shook his head. 'I have no key. Hurry up, don't be long. The lieutenant will want to see you in a moment.'

'But how's he supposed to have a pee tied to me?'

The guard shrugged. 'Work it out for yourselves.'

I turned to Patrick who by now was in quite desperate straits. 'You heard the man—work it out for yourself.'

'Here, give us your arm.'

There was not enough room for us side-by-side in the cubicle so I finished up behind Patrick with my face pressed against the wall, my left arm (which was manacled to Patrick's right) stretched towards him so he could undo his fly.

At last I heard his sigh of relief and all was going well . . . well, for about fifteen seconds. By that time my eyes had adjusted to the poor light in there and that was when I saw it. I happened to turn my eyes to the right and there, lurking in a crevice between the wall and the doorpost, not three inches from my nose, was the dirtiest, fattest, ugliest, hairiest black spider you've ever seen. It was monstrous! Legs at least a foot and a half long and its blood-red eyes staring at me on the end of their stalks. My blood deserted me. There is not a spider over an eighth of an inch long I can stand being in the same room with. I have been known to track down and slaughter, nay disintegrate, a largish money spider, pounding it into the carpet with a rolled newspaper or pulverising it with a hammer, before I can settle in that room for the evening. I have the worst case of spiderophobia I've ever heard of. I am casually contemptuous of cockroaches; invariably indifferent to insects; and react rather reasonably to rodents. BUT I HATE BLOODY SPIDERS!

With a yell that could have been heard in Madrid I shot out of the cubicle, jerking Patrick with me. He simply flew out of the loo, crying aloud with surprise, 'Heeeeyyyy!!' Then it was the copper's turn. His roar of disenchantment as Patrick swung towards him outdid even mine, yet this was as nothing when Patrick got him all down the front of his uniform.

'Fools! Imbeciles!' he yelled with rage, shaking his leg and stamping his boot on the floor. 'What are you playing at! Get out of here! Get out of here! Hurry! Finish!'

'I've finished,' Patrick mumbled with embarrassment.

'I should think so!' said the guard, banging his boot and shaking his trouser leg one more time. 'Now, move!'

As we trundled back down the corridor, Patrick said side-mouthed, 'What got into yuh? What did yuh do that for?'

'Spider,' I said, shuddering at the memory. 'A monster—not an inch from my nose and just about to crawl up it.'

'Wonderful,' sighed Patrick. 'Just what we need to secure a speedy release. I'm not too sure what the penalty is for peeing on a Spanish cop but I should think in the region of a hundred and eighty-five years solitary—hanging upside down.'

'Sorry, mate, but you know how I hate spiders.'

He gave me a grin. 'Well, at least I've achieved one great ambition in my life. Not too many fellas have done that and lived to tell of it.'

We were ushered back into the waiting room place and once again the door was slammed. We flopped down at the table and lit cigarettes. At least they hadn't taken our fags away.

'I see Niki Spiropulous was here, then,' Patrick said casually, wiping smoke from his eye.

'Who?'

'Niki Spiropulous.'

'Who's he when he's at home?'

'No idea—but the poor devil was here. July last year.'

The table had obviously been scrubbed at least once in that time but the indentation made by the ballpoint pen was very visible. We began searching for other names and messages, and having covered the top of the table we bent down and searched the underside.

'Hey, some good stuff here,' I said. 'Come on down.'

We crawled under the table and lay on the floor. Here the grafitti was prolific. There was a profusion of languages—German, French, Scandinavian and quite a lot in English. 'Franco is a fuck-faced fink' was contributed in green biro by W.S. of Stratford, England, three years ago.

'Will Shakespeare?' Patrick suggested.

'Mm, could be. The illiteration is Will's style though I'm a mite doubtful about the green biro.'

'He'd have hardly used a quill, Russell. In this position the ink would've run up his sleeve.'

'True. Yes, could've been Will.'

'Ah, now, here's a heart-rendering stanza if ever I read one. Written by Butch Harrison in '71. Lord, how it tears the heart.

"As I walked through town I saw a girl
Her hair was long and yella,
Her legs were long, her figure sleek,
I was so knocked out I couldn't speak
To ask her out it took a week
Then she turned out to be a fella." '

'Ah, the misery of it,' I said.

'There's a footnote by Julian Catchpole of Norwich. "Coo, lucky old you!".'

'Aha! Here's a riddle for you, Patrick, contributed by Muleprick Kitchener of London, Ontario. Answer it if you can. "What is the difference between Raquel Welsh and Annie Lasouq of 1299, Danforth Trail, Montreal, Quebec?".'

Patrick shook his head. 'Ashamedly, the solution eludes me. I give up.'

' "Answer: There is no difference. I have stuffed both of them 800 times except Raquel Welsh." Think about it, Patrick.'

Patrick had no time to think about that or anything else. The door suddenly burst open and a pair of brilliantly polished brown leather boots took three smart steps into the room, paused, gave an uncertain shuffle and swivelled violently. 'Venga rapido!' Two guards came at the double. 'Where are they!? What is this all about!?'

One of the guards began a stuttering explanation but was demolished before he'd got the first few words out. 'Find them, you imbecile, find them! If they have escaped . . .!' The boots flashed out of the room and thundered down the corridor. As soon as he was out of earshot the stream of accusations commençed, each guard blaming the other. Patrick and I were staring at each other, wondering whether we should crawl out and clear the situation but, before we could move, the guards were off, racing down the corridor, shouting warnings and instructions to someone else.

Then silence—and the door was open!

Patrick shook his head. 'Ah, we'd never get off the island, Russell. Besides, I've got to get back next year! And besides again, we've done nuthin' wrong, don't let's forget that small thing.'

'So—what do we do?'

'We sit back at the table and wait.'

So we sat. It was a full minute before we heard the clatter of boots in the corridor and a tall, spindly, splendidly uniformed young officer flashed past the door, glancing in as he went by. It took him half a dozen steps to pull up, then he reversed and was filling the doorway, staring at us disbelievingly. 'Where have you been!?'

'Mm? Nowhere,' I answered.

'But you weren't here a moment ago! You sneaked back in!'

I looked at Patrick and shrugged again. 'No, we haven't left the room.'

'But I was *here*—not two minutes ago—and *you* weren't!'

'Perhaps . . . perhaps you had the wrong room?' I suggested.

His eyes popped but before he had time to explode the two guards came trotting up. One began breathlessly, 'They haven't left the building, sir. The gate . . .'

The officer flung an arm. 'They're here! They claim they've been here all the time! All right, I'll have him first!' he said, pointing at me, then swept away.

One of the guards came in and unlocked the handcuff. 'Where did you get to?' he demanded. 'Were you trying to escape?'

'Why should we try to escape? We haven't done anything,' I said.

'We'll see. I want to know how you got out of this room.'

'We didn't. We were under the table. I . . . I dropped my cigarettes.'

He glared at me. 'You were trying to make fools of us. You were playing games ...'

'We weren't, I swear!' This bloke was looking for trouble, looking for a chance to stick the boot in. Maybe things were a little out-of-season quiet and they saw Patrick and me as a chance to practise.

'We've had clever punks like you in here before,' he said, gripping my arm with a hand like a bench press. 'Somehow they're never quite as clever when they leave—*if* they leave. Come on, the Lieutenant wants you.'

He pulled me out of the chair as though I was weightless and hurried me down the corridor to the fourth door on the left. With a knock he threw me in and left me to my fate and Bright Boots.

The room was cold and ugly, hardly better than the one I'd left. Boots was warming his bottom in front of a battered electric fire and when I entered he quit the fire and went to sit at a cluttered wooden desk, removing the remains of his last meal and sticking the plate in a drawer. He shuffled papers for a minute, took his time filling his fountain pen, then finally drew a piece of clean paper in front of him and shot his cuffs.

'Name?'

'Russell Tobin.'

'Address?'

'Er, ah, that's difficult ...'

'What's so difficult about an address? You live somewhere, don't you?'

'Er, yes ...'

'Then that is your address. Where is it?'

'Hotel Gran Canaria, Palma.'

'For how long have you lived there?'

'Well, I haven't actually lived there yet ...'

His lips compressed and he snorted.

'I only booked in this afternoon,' I said hurriedly. 'I'm only staying one night. Tomorrow I'm flying to London. I mean *today* I'm flying to London ... this morning ... nine o'clock ...'

'"Were ... were flying" is the phrase. You were flying to London at nine o'clock. Until this matter is cleared up you will not be flying anywhere at any time.'

'No, quite.'

'Who are you, Tobin? What are you doing in Majorca?'

'I've ... I ... I'm ... I mean I *was* a courier with Ardmont Holidays. I've been here since March—in Magaluf. This is our last night.'

' "Our" last night? Who is the other man?'

'Patrick Holmes. He was also a courier with Ardmont.'

'What were you and he doing hiding in a ditch on the outskirts of town at two o'clock this morning? And why did you try to escape when the patrol car disturbed you? What have you been up to?'

It took me twenty minutes, with constant interruption for questions, to tell him and at the end of the statement (which he'd taken down verbatim in flying scrawl) it was obvious from his attitude that apart from my name and address he hadn't believed a word I'd said—and he probably had the gravest doubts about my name and address.

I glanced at my watch. It was nearly four a.m. There wasn't a hope of being on that plane. Maybe it was tiredness that induced the pessimism but I suddenly had the awful feeling Patrick and I would still be waiting in that room when the first tourists arrived in March.

'You will go back to the room and wait,' said Boots, screwing the top on his fountain pen. 'Your statement will be checked but it will take some time. Señor Bastar is one of our leading citizens. It would be in no way polite or politic to wake him at four in the morning to corroborate your ... your story. We must wait until a respectable time.'

'May I ask what *is* a respectable time?'

'No, you may not. That is entirely up to me.'

'Er, lieutenant, what happens if Señor Bastar refuses to corroborate my story?'

He looked at me, frowning. 'Is it likely?' He was annoyed.

'I believe so. I believe he'd refuse just for spite.'

'How can he refuse? He can't refuse.'

'Say, then, he's gone away. He travels a lot.'

'In that event you will have to be patient while we find him, won't you?'

'But ... our plane! It's due to leave at nine o'clock!'

'It will still leave at nine o'clock ... but unless your story is corroborated in every detail, you will not be on it . . .'

'But, lieutenant, I've got an appointment in London . . .'

He pressed a button on his desk and instantly the guard appeared. 'Take this man back and bring the other one.'

'Lieutenant . . .'

'That is all, Tobin.'

The guard seized my arm and put an end to all discussion. When I arrived back in the room I was surprised to see Patrick was not alone. Sitting on the floor in the corner was a weirdie—a formless, white, pinched face surrounded by a frizzy Afro mass of flaming, carrot-coloured hair. His long, twig-thin legs were clad in the filthiest jeans and his skeletal frame in a tattered tartan shirt and a greasy-fringed leather cowboy jacket. He didn't bother to look up as I entered. He seemed fascinated by his right boot.

I raised a brow at Patrick who made a face, meaning, 'We got a character,' and said, 'How d'it go?'

'Wonderfully well. He's just got to check out the story with Bastar and we can all go home. I reckon September ought to see it through.'

'Hey, you're kidding . . . mm?'

'Nope. I got the impression he'd had enough of the English for one year.'

Patrick threw a glance at the hippy on the floor. 'Can't say I blame him.'

'English?' I mouthed.

He nodded.

'Come on, you,' said the guard, getting hold of Patrick's arm.

'See yuh,' said Patrick. 'And don't worry—garlic ain't so bad when you get used to it.'

'But in mince-pies?' I winced.

The door closed. The hippy still hadn't looked up or moved in any other way. He appeared hypnotized by the boot, a battered job with a crater in the sole. I edged over to the table and sat down, nervous of this guy. I didn't like the look of him at all. He looked high on something or other. His eyes were sunken and bloodshot, his mouth listless. It was a weak, dissipated, dangerous face. I sat at an angle, so I could keep an eye on him without actually looking at him, and began working on a plan of self-defence if he started anything. I reckoned the best bet was to hit him with a chair and yell for the guards. You could never tell with these people. I'd met up with quite a few of them in London, particularly around the all-night chemists in Piccadilly, and they terrified me. It's their unpredictability. They lack coordination, reason. You just don't know which way they're going to jump, what they'll do next.

It was three or four minutes before he realized I was in the room. He raised his pale, formless face and focused on me with difficulty. It was probably the scratching of my match that attracted his attention. His head and shoulders began to weave and jerk, lacking all coordination. He was uptight all right.

A corner of his loose mouth lifted in a gesture of recognition. 'Hi, man, where ya get to?' Then began the laborious process of getting to his feet. My heart began to pound. I smelled danger. He never did make it to his feet and finally abandoned the effort in favour of crawling towards me on his hands and knees. He paused half-way and raised his head to make sure he was still on course; then he lowered it again, shook it from side to side and murmured, 'Oh, man . . . oh, man' and began crawling again.

I decided I would clobber him with the chair if he tried anything; question was—how soon should I do it. He reached the end of the table, stopped as though marshalling his strength to kneel upright, then did so and flopped his arms down on the table and stared at me, his idiot face two feet from my own.

I was repulsed, frightened. He was ugly, emaciated and filthy, blown out of his mind. I got up immediately and sat in a chair on the opposite side of the table and was tempted to bang on the door then. The cops had no right to put this guy in this room. They should have locked him in a cell or the hospital wing. Still, why should they give a stuff. I glanced at my watch. Unbelievably Patrick had only been gone seven minutes. It seemed like seven weeks.

The thing opened its mouth with difficulty and mumbled, 'Hey, c'mon, Cowley, give us a fix, man. You gotta fix. I need one real bad, man.'

'I haven't got one . . . and I'm not Cowley.'

'What's that you're smokin'?'

'Straight virginia, nothing more.'

'You're a lyin' po-faced fucker, Cowley. You're turnin' on, man.'

My heart was thumping. This bloke was going to get violent, I could feel it. He was probably suffering from withdrawal symptoms and for some of these junkies the sky was the limit. They'd do anything for a fix. I had to get to the door and call the guard. Jeez, there was a turn-up for the book—me shouting for police protection in a cop station! What an unbelievable night.

He was staring right through me. Maybe he was watching pretty patterns or whatever they're supposed to see. Maybe I could humour him until Patrick got back.

'Where ...' cough, 'where d'you come from?' I asked with quaking nonchalance.

He just stared, his head and shoulders jerking like an epileptic, fidgetting his filthy fingers.

'Do you ... come from London?'

'Fix me, man, f'Chrissake!' The words bubbled out with a trickle of saliva that ran unheeded down the side of his mouth. 'You gotta fix, yuh lousy bastard. Hit me, Cowley!'

'Look, I haven't got anything. I don't use it ...'

'You *got* it!' His face twisted angrily and he slammed his fist into the table. 'Y'bought six pieces an' we only used *two*! Now c'mon, Cowley, or I'll *kill* yuh!'

He smashed the table again, gaining strength, massing energy. He levered his elbows on the table and tried to get up. He half made it, slipped back, then tried again. This time he made it. God, he was tall—six four or five, thin as a pole. I was out of my chair and back against the wall, all plans for hitting him with the chair forgotten.

'Look!' I shouted, 'I'm not *Cowley*! You've got the wrong man! I haven't got any stuff!'

'You're a lyin' *bastard*!' he screamed. 'I'll fuckin' *kill* yuh!'

He made a lurching grab for me, caught the corner of the table with his thigh, stumbled sideways, bounced off the wall and started moving in the wrong direction, spun off another wall and came straight for me, hands outstretched, clawing for me.

'C'm here, Cowley, I'll fuckin' kill yuh! Yuh got four pieces, yuh bastard!'

I dodged, weaved and ducked under his outstretched arms and ran to the opposite side of the room. He didn't even know

I'd gone until he slammed into the wall, smacking his head, and he didn't even know about that. He rounded and came on fast, flaying the air with his fists and making insane gurgling noises. The poor guy was completely off his chump. I had to get to the door!

'Socorro!' I yelled. 'Policia! Open the door! Abra la puerta!'

I heard footsteps in the corridor. The hippy was almost on me. I leapt towards the door, ducking beneath his arm. This time I didn't make it. Wompf! His flashing fist caught me on the back of the neck. I stumbled across the room losing balance, went down on my knees in front of the door and hit it hard with my back, winding myself. The hippy was on me, grabbing at my hair, trying to haul me to my feet, mouthing obscenities and I was yelling bloody blue murder. Bash! The door swung in and cracked me in the small of the back. The guard was shouting, 'Que hace usted! What are you doing?'

'I'm being murdered!' I yelled back. 'This guy's a junky! Get in here—quick!'

The guard heaved against the door, trying to push the two of us away from it so he could squeeze in. Snowflake was pressing me against it, ripping at my pockets trying to find the stuff, whatever that was. Zzzziiiipppp! My breast pocket parted company with the jacket. He staggered backwards. Sock! He hit the table, sat down hard and bashed his head on the table top. I rolled over, trying to clear the door and the cop, who must have been in mid-charge, flew in, tripped over my outstretched legs and fell, sprawled over Snowflake. Snowflake, now completely out of his mind, mistook the cop for me and rolled over on him, tearing at his uniform with one hand and squashing his face into the stone floor with the other, yelling, 'I'll kill yuh, Cowley, I'll *kill* yuh!'

Well, as much as I disliked tangling with Snowflake I felt duty bound to help the cop who was being very efficiently smothered. Besides which, if the cop snuffed it, I'd be hung on sight for complicity in the crime so there was no choice. I crawled to my knees, got behind Snowflake and whipped an arm around his neck, hauling him off. He twisted sideways and threw himself full-length, taking me with him and the next thing I knew I was looking up at the bewildered, frightened cop who was struggling to get his gun out of its holster with every intention of filling Snowflake full of little bullets.

'No ... no!' I yelled. 'Don't shoot him! He's on drugs! Lock him up!'

The cop's eyes were mad with fright. He jerked the gun out and levelled it at Snowflake and I just don't know what would have happened next if at that moment three other cops hadn't come charging into the room, guns at the alert. I reckon in the next five seconds Snowflake would have been very dead. And if it hadn't been for the presence of mind of this same cop, the cop I'd rescued, I wouldn't have given much for *my* chances. The three police who'd rushed into the room read the situation all wrong and hauled me up and had me slammed face against the wall, guns rammed into my spine, before you could say Juan Robinson, and with cool reasoning comprising such a small part of their character, it wouldn't have surprised me if I'd been shot full of holes ... well, it would, if you know what I mean.

But such misery was prevented by a shout, 'No, not him! He helped me!' and three pipes of cold steel were removed from my spine.

Poor Snowflake. He was carted away like a shot boar, a cop at each corner, and as his demented cries faded down the corridor, Patrick returned with his guard. He entered walking backwards, looking at the luckless Snowflake.

'What ...' he enquired as the door slammed, '... has been going on in my absence? God, the sight of yuh! I can't leave you alone for five minutes without yuh gettin' into trouble. Have yuh no sense of decorum, Russell?'

'You, mate,' I said, wincing with pain as I bent to pick my pocket up off the floor, 'should be more choosey about your houseguests. That junky nut tried to kill me.'

'The divil he did! He was as nice as pie with me—apart from gettin' me name wrong, kept callin' me Cowley. But quiet as a lamb.'

'How did you get on with the lieutenant?'

'Aw, like a house on fire. Charming fellow. Said he'd get around to calling Bastar just as soon as he could ... and in the meantime hoped we wouldn't be too uncomfortable spending the night in these chairs. What time is it now?'

'Nearly half past rotten four.'

'Mm, well, I think we can kiss the plane goodbye. He'll not

call Bastar until mid-mornin', I doubt. So ... bedad, I'm bushed, Russell. It's all beginnin' to catch up with me. I think I must try to get me head down for an hour.'

'Where? Y'mean sitting up in a chair?'

'Can yuh think of an alternative?'

I thought. 'Yes, lying on the stone floor.'

'That's the one that came to me. So ...'

We flopped in the chairs, elbows on the table, heads on our arms, now utterly fatigued. I suddenly felt very tired, very cold, very hungry, rather hung-over, somewhat dejected and in addition my back was beginning to hurt. In truth I was not too happy.

Patrick, obviously feeling the same, turned his face on his arm and gave me a weary grin. 'Well, now, how about *that* for a last night in Majorca. Yuh must admit it was memorable, Russell.'

'Oh, I do, Patrick— as were all the other great disasters—*The Titanic* ... the San Fransisco earthquake ... the day you were born ...'

'Ah, a week from now we'll look back on it and have a good laugh, so we will.'

'Provided that a week from now we're not still sleeping on this table.'

He laughed, though with not the whole-hearted confidence I would have liked.

'The men the world forgot ...' I droned, feeling my eyelids dropping. 'Eighty-seven years in a Spanish waiting room ... because the lieutenant died of food poisoning during the night ... and didn't call Calvario Bastar ... think of it, Patrick ... you'd be ... one hundred ... and eleven years ... old ...'

I awoke with a terrible fright as the door banged open.

'Right, out you come, you two ... hurry it up!'

I staggered to my feet with no idea where I was and followed a weaving Patrick in bewildered half-sleep. Cold and shivering we sent down the icy corridor in the wake of a guard who seemed to be in a terrible hurry to get somewhere. We turned corners and went through doors and finally stepped through a door into the cold fresh air of the courtyard. I panicked. We were going to be shot! It was dawn! We were going to be shot at dawn!

At a stiff march we crunched across the gravel, my heart thumping in time with my stride. I glanced at Patrick. He was marching like a zombie, vacant eyes glued to the ground. The poor devil didn't realize!

We came to a halt at a narrow door in the wall of the yard. The guard jerked it open and beckoned us through. I went through first, Patrick followed, and we kept on marching. It was ten strides later that I heard the door slam behind us. I turned, expecting the guard close behind. I stopped, bemused. There was no guard. I looked at Patrick. He stared at me, beginning to come round.

'Russell ...' He spun round, staring wide-eyed at our surroundings. 'Russell ...'

We were in a side-street, outside the station walls. We were out! We were free!

'Russell ...!'

'I know! We're ... we're ... HEY TAXI!'

The cruising cab squealed to a halt at the top of the street and we took off like madmen.

'Gran Canaria Hotel!' Patrick shouted. 'Wait there ten minutes and then out to the AIRPORT! As fast as you like!'

It was sleeting in London. As we stepped down from the plane a bitterly cold north wind cut through our thin clothing, chilled us to the bone, drove the freezing wet muck into our ears and down our collars and turned our fingers blue on the baggage handles. A really beautiful day.

One of the most beautiful days I've ever known.

SIX

Yes, it was good to be back in London, despite the weather. After a break of nine months the magic of the city was new all over again. I'd forgotten just how big and busy it was, and how exciting, especially now, just before Christmas. Maybe this is the way to live in huge cities, the way to get the most out of them—by visiting them only now and again. The noise and the bustle can be very stimulating when taken in small doses.

Nothing much had changed in nine months, of course. The headlines in the papers were almost identical to those last March. Wilson was still heckling Heath; Heath was wigging Wilson. The cost of living was still soaring. London Transport was still regretting delays due to staff shortages. The telephone service was still abominable with eight out of ten public phones either vandalized or just plain out of order. And London was choking itself with ever-increasing efficiency with its traffic. Comforting normality all round.

As my plans were still fairly vague I decided to establish headquarters in a small, very modern and very comfortable hotel, the Phoenix, jut off Bayswater Road, about a mile from Marble Arch. And Patrick, who had decided to say in London for two or three days to see the sights and meet up again with our mutual pal, Tony Dane, also booked into the Phoenix.

Tony, if you remember, has a flat in Stanhope Place, very near to Marble Arch.

So, there we were. By two o'clock on the day of our return, November 5th, we were esconced in the Phoenix, bags unpacked and rarin' to go.

I phoned Cane at his flat, using a phoney American accent.

'Mr. Dane?'

'Yes.'

'Mr. Tony Dane of T.V. fame?'

'Who is this?'

'Hollywood, Mr. Dane. This is Hyram N. Fyram of Nauseating Films Inc. You've been recommended to us for the lead part in our latest blue film extravaganza entitled "Azure Father—All right?", a neat little transvestite story based on a true-life romance between those two kinky bodysnatchers, Berk and Hair. We'd like you to play the former, Mr. Dane, because a big man is required and we've been reliably informed we won't find a bigger Berk in London than you . . .'

'Tobin, you bastard . . . !'

'Took your time, didn't you, Dane. Is your ear slipping or is my accent improving?'

'You've got your hanky over the mouthpiece.'

'No, I'm eating a ham sandwich. How are you, you old bugger?'

'Fit, fit. Where are you speaking from?'

'About four hundred yards down the road. We're in the Phoenix, just got in.'

'Why didn't you let me know you were coming, for God's sake?'

'Because neither Patrick nor I like a lot of fuss and all that business of press photographers and the military band at the airport would have embarrassed us . . .'

'Patrick's with you! Oh, well, that's it, isn't it . . .?'

'That's what?'

'That's an end to my plans for a quiet week.'

'Dane, are you *sure* you're all right? Since when have you ever planned a quiet week?'

'Since I was ten. I was going to start, come what might, tomorrow night.'

'Ah ha! Why not tonight!?'

'Because I've got a little thing going tonight, baby, a little thing.'

'Dane, there is never anything little about your things.'

'Cheeky, you've been peeking.'

'All right, where's the party and what time do we get there.'

'You're a cheeky sod, Tobin.'

'Look, we've been hibernating in Majorca since you left in June. So help me, not a moment's fun or excitement have we had. We're counting on you, Anthony. Patrick's only got three days here and we've got to show him a sight or two—and I'm out of touch.'

'Where's he going then?'

'He's going to die in Dublin for the winter.'

'How about you—how long will you be staying?

'I've no idea. Remember Frank Chappell of Centaf Tours . . .?'

'Sure, sure, he offered you a job . . .'

'Well, I'm going to call him and see if it still stands. If it does, I'm going to buzz off to Africa for a few months. I can't stand this weather.'

'You don't say! That sounds like a ball.'

'I'm hoping. Now, what about this thing tonight. We could do with a party for openers.'

There was a small thoughtful silence. 'Give me ten minutes,

I'll see what I can do.'

'What and where is it?'

He laughed. 'It's a firework party that promises to be more fun than the original Guy Fawkes' rave up. You've heard of Albert Chutney, of course, well ...'

'No.'

'I met ... hm? You putting me on?'

'I believe I would've remembered the name.'

'You haven't heard of Albert Chutney!' He sounded quite outraged. 'Tobin, where have you been for the past six months —Siberia?'

'No need to be insulting, Dane, just get on with it.'

'Russ, I can't believe it! Albert Chutney is the biggest thing to hit the pop scene since Tom Jones. Hey ... you *have* heard of Tom Jones ...?'

'Dane ...'

'Russ, Chutney's got two records in the top ten right now and one of them is currently number one! You mean you haven't heard of "Alpaca Jack"!?'

'Now, who's *he*—another newcomer?'

'No, you berk, it's the number one sound—Chutney's record. It's been number one five weeks running.'

'Tony, nothing is allowed into Majorca unless it's six months old, remember? So none of the discos would be playing it and as I never listen to the crummy radio, there is no way I could've heard it. Sorry to disappoint you, but ...'

'Jeez, you amaze me. I'd have thought the whole world would've heard it.'

'Where did Albert Chutney orig ... Dane, I can't *believe* that name ... where did he originate?'

'Why, that breeding ground of so much other genius—Liverpool.'

'Aha! I might have known! Good old Chutney. So—the genius well has not run dry yet, we are still pouring south.'

'Oh, I love the way you fellas from the North jump on the bandwaggon when one of your contemporaries makes it. Tobin, you are not even *from* Liverpool, you're from Cheshire!'

'A minor technicality, Dane. As a matter of fact, I'm from the Liverpool *side* of Cheshire.'

'Well, don't get too smartarse about it. I've met Albert Chutney—whose real name incidentally is Horatio Death . . .'

'Aw, come on, Dane . . .'

'I kid you not—Horatio Death.'

'Come to think of it, I like it better. He should have kept it. Go on, what were you saying about our Albert?'

'Just that I've met him. He's a nice guy and voice he has, but he's not too abundant in brightness. He's a big handsome dope, Russ, an ex-docker with muscles in his spit—all the ingredients for a manufactured money-making machine which he has become in the past six months. And, following the undeviating pattern for overnight pop successes, Albert has bought himself a monstrous big pad, a 30-room Gothic job slap in the middle of the ever-so-swish Bentley Park—which is deep in the heart of filthy-rich-stockbroker-belt Surrey.'

'Yes, I know Bentley Park.'

'You do?! Thank God you've heard of something. I was just about to ask you if you'd heard Mafekin has been relieved.'

'Yes, I had heard. Mrs. Mafekin was responsible apparently.'

'Oh, fun-nee. You've had too much sun, son.'

'How did you meet up with Albert, Tony?'

'At a recording session. As soon as "Alpaca Jack" hit the top ten and looked like heading for the top, an enterprising overcoat firm that uses alpaca leapt in quick and paid a pop-star's ransom for the track to use in a T.V. commercial. Albert came down to record some new lyrics and I was doing the voice-over tag line. We spent the day together.'

'Sounds cosy, dearie.'

'Oh, Albert's all man, man. And he pulls more birds than a team of pheasant pluckers. You should've seen them outside that studio . . . ten deep on the pavement!'

'You're sure they were waiting for him, Dane. Maybe they'd heard you were there?'

'Hell, Tobin, now don't get nice to me and spoil a beautiful relationship. Sure they were waiting for him. And I know who tipped them off he was there—his manager, Mickey Pink.'

'Dane, will you *stop*!'

'Swear to God, it's his real name. Russ, this guy's too much—or not enough, depending on how you look at it, 'cos he's only five feet two—in his cowboy boots, that is. He's a twenty-five year-old Mickey Rooney with a cigar. You meet the cigar first and ten minutes later you get to Pink. But what a manager! We should be so lucky. Anyway, instead of me rabitting on, why don't I get on the phone and see if I can get you two an invite?'

'O.K., mate. Listen, how about birds—do we need to take any?'

I heard him sigh exasperatedly. 'Boy, you really don't know Albert and Mickey Pink, do you. No, Russell, I promise you there will be no need to take any. Call you back.'

I replaced the receiver and whirled on Patrick. 'How much of that did you get?'

He grinned. 'Enough. Sounds good.'

I slapped my hands together. 'Not a bad start to the festivities, Patrick.'

'Are you sure Tony can pull it, though?'

'Consider it pulled. Tonight we hobnob with the nouveau riche. It's got to be good. I just gotta see Albert and Mickey Pink. Now, what time is it? I wonder if Frank Chappell works Saturday afternoons? I think I'll give Centaf a call and put Africa firmly in or out of my mind for the weekend.'

I phoned. Frank Chappell's secretary answered. Mr. Chappell was on another line, would I hold? I held. Frank came on in three minutes.

'Mr. Chappell, this is Russ Tobin. We met in Majorca in June ... at Harry Onion's party ...' puzzled silence. '... we talked about a job as courier in Africa ... I was with Ardmont Holidays ... you gave me your card ...'

'Oh ...! Oh, yes, I'm sorry, Mr. Tobin, yes, of course. How are you? Are you back in London?'

'Yes, just arrived, flew in this morning. I was wondering if the job was still open ...'

'Well, yes ... it is ...' He didn't sound too sure. 'But I have a small problem. Our rep out in Nairobi, Jim Fuller, won't be leaving for a couple of months yet—he's getting married and moving down to Cape Town in the New Year—so I couldn't take you on for about a month. That would give you about three weeks or so with him before he left. How does that fit in with your plans?'

Mm ... that meant kicking my heels around London in the snow for a month and I didn't want that. Tony would be working; Patrick would be in Dublin. I'd be bored blue inside a week. Still, I was sure I could solve the problem somehow.

I said to Chappell, 'I could make it fit, Mr. Chappell. I'd like to talk to you about the job, if I may.'

'Sure, like to see you. How about . . . let's see, how about this Monday—say eleven o'clock?'

'Fine. Eleven on Monday.'

I put down the phone and was about to speak to Patrick when it rang again. It was Tony.

'O.K., men, you're in. Bentley Park, ten o'clock. Got any transport?'

'Legs.'

'Right, I'll pick you up at the Phoenix at nine—but I can't guarantee the return trip, know what I mean?'

'Of course. There are always mini-cabs.'

'Sure. And get some sleep, you'll need it.'

'Will the party be over by eleven on Monday? I've got an appointment with Frank Chappell?'

'Who knows—but you can always leave early. See you at nine. Must dash, I've got something on the boil.'

'What colour?'

'Red—this week. She's out of this world.'

'You mean like nothing on earth?'

'Tobin, you want to walk to Bentley Park?'

'Ciao, Anthony.'

SEVEN

Between the time Tony rang off and the time he picked us up, Patrick and I had heard 'Alpaca Jack' eight times on the bedroom radio, and even after the eighth hearing we were still at a loss as to what the song was all about. Even if the written lyrics made any sense, ridiculous supposition, our Albert made damn sure none of it came through in the singing. His diction was so appalling neither Patrick nor I could distinguish more than six words in the entire piece—other than 'Alpaca Jack' which must have been repeated nine hundred and forty-two times and comprised the last two minutes of the song. But who cared? It's the beat, man, the beat. And of that there was plenty. What a production! So many tracks had been overlaid on other tracks to achieve that sound, the final tape must have been eight inches thick. It was pure manufactured hysteria.

Give Albert his due, though, he had a big voice—powerful, strident and resonant, ranging from low tenor to hight falsetto scream, and on 'Alpaca Jack' it was mostly the later.

Patrick, Tony and I discussed the matter on the drive out to Bentley Park. Tony had borrowed a white Jaguar 420 for the occasion, believing, quite rightly, that it would be a shade more comfortable for the three of us than his two-seater Lotus. Smart fella.

'Rubbish,' commented Patrick. 'And my heartiest congratulations to Albert for making number one. He deserves it. Anyone clever enough to make number one with rubbish like that deserves to succeed.'

'Albert, of course, had little to do with it,' said Tony. 'It's all Mickey Pink's doing. He's dynamite. He's already landed Albert a series of six T.V. spectaculars in the States worth half a million.'

'Dollars?' I enquired.

'Pounds,' he replied.

'Live shows, hm.'

He laughed. 'Not a chance. They'll all be magnificently manufactured, just like "Alpaca Jack". Albert wouldn't last five minutes with an American audience, they wouldn't understand a word he said. *I* don't understand a word he says. You might be able to pick up a word or two, Russ, you can translate for us.'

'Is he really that broad?' I asked.

'You wouldn't believe it—well, maybe *you* would, coming from the North. It's the thickest scouse I've ever heard. I catch about one word in seventy-four which is about par for the course.'

'Will we be meeting Albert tonight?' I asked, quite chuffed at the prospect of meeting a pop super-star.

'Sure, if you can get to him through the birds. They really go for this kid.'

'Why—is he supposed to be sexy or something?'

Tony shrugged. 'Who knows what birds go for? They go for

Tom Jones because he's a rugged, good-looking charmer and built like an athlete—besides having a great voice—but they also went for Sinatra when he weighed three stone six and looked like a hat-rack. Who knows? I'd say they go for power—you know, the number one. I don't know ... how the hell should I know? You'll have to ask them.'

'I will,' I said, quite chuffed at *that* prospect, too.

Bentley Park comprises two thousand acres of the most expensive and most exclusive residential property in the south of England.

There are four entrances to The Park, each having a white five-barred gate which is closed once a year to comply with local by-laws regarding the continuing viability of the park as a private estate governed by its own Residents Association.

There are, as it were, two main roads intercommunicating these entrances, plus dozens of twisting minor roads leading off them to the houses, these minor roads invariably terminating in cul-de-sacs.

The minimum size of plot permissible in the park is one acre, though many homes have much more land than this. And as the current buying price of one acre (if it can be found) is in the region of twenty thousand pounds, it is safe to assume that the minimum price of a completed house would be at least twice that.

Invariably, therefore, when you make The Park, as it's known locally, you've made it big.

There are about four hundred houses in The Park, all individually designed. They vary greatly. Some, though comparatively few, are ultra-modern creations, long, low and handsome, built of glass and timber and acres of slate. The majority, by far, are more conventionally English—Georgian, Elizabethan, cottagey, some expensively thatched. Others are downright conventionally English, square, unimaginative boxes, albeit enormous square, unimaginative boxes, ten up and five down with bathrooms en suite and kitchens the size of an airfield.

Then there are the monsters, the dark museums, the Gothic (to my way of thinking) nightmares with their high-pointed arches and clustered columns, such, it would seem, as our Albert had bought.

Each of The Park houses lies well within its own grounds, protected, for the most part, from the prying public eye by high fences and thick hedges, for it's a popular Sunday afternoon pastime for locals and outsiders alike to 'cruise The Park', trying to catch glimpses of the homes and their magnificent gardens.

I've driven through a couple of times in the past and while readily admitting the houses are quite something to see, I honestly find The Park too wooded for comfort. Fine on a bright, sunny day when there's bags of light reflecting off the leaves; but drive through on a grey, rainy November afternoon and then the overhanging mass of towering, dripping trees becomes oppressive and depressing. Without being facetious, if I could afford to live in The Park I'd have second thoughts about it. Mind you, the houses and the size of the gardens and the privacy they give is only one reason for living in The Park. The other, perhaps greater inducement is—the Prestige. If one is somebody who has pretentions of being anybody, one simply *has* to live in The Park.

In a count of 'Park heads' published in a recent Sunday colour supplement there were revealed: twelve titled families (including, naturally, a Ruritanian princess); twenty-four millionaires; fifty-two company chairmen; sixty-three managing directors; eleven merchant bankers; seven internationally-known actors; four ditto actresses; four best-selling authors; three pop-stars (one female); and three managers of pop-stars.

And now there was Albert. And presumably Mickey Pink.

Quite a place The Park.

The big headlights on full beam picked up the open white five-barred gate swung back against the tall laurel hedge, and as we drove slowly past the gate I read the sign on it: BENTLEY PARK—PRIVATE ROAD—NO THOROUGHFARE FOR TRAFFIC. PLEASE DRIVE WITH EXTREME CARE—MAXIMUM SPEED 20 M.P.H.

Immediately inside the gate, on the grass verge, was a mounted, illuminated map of the entire Park, giving the names of all the small approach roads and the names of the houses served by them (there are, naturally, no house *numbers* in The Park, only names).

Tony stopped the car and we all got out.

'Now,' he said, consulting a piece of paper, 'we want Cornish Road which leads off South Road which leads off High Road.'

'We're on High Road now,' I said, pointing. 'And there's South Road ... and there's Cornish. What's the names of the house?'

'Mango.'

I peered at the list of houses on Cornish Road. 'There's no Mango listed here.'

'There's got to be,' said Tony. 'Oh ... ah, no, hang on, is there a Mandalay?'

'Er ... yes, there is.'

'Well, that's it, then. They changed the name.'

'From Mandalay to Mango? What for?'

Tony looked at me. 'Mango ... Chutney? Mango Ceutney? Would you believe Mango Chutney, Russe ... Russell, don't you *dare* be sick over my party suit!'

We climbed back into the car and I was glad to do it. Despite my heavy winter coat I was freezing. The sleet had stopped but the wind was right out of the Arctic. After nine months in Majorca I was feeling the cold keenly. As we drove slowly along the poorly-lit, tree-hung length of High Road the prospect of half a year in Africa suddenly became immensely appealing to me. I am simply not a winter man. Never was and never could be. Drop my enveloping temperature below fifty-five and you've got misery on your hands. Africa ... yeh.

'Mango,' Patrick muttered pensively. 'Well, it could have been worse. It might have been "Piccalilli" ... or ...'

'Albert's Memorial?' suggested Tony. 'Good job he changed his name. It might have been "Death House".'

'How about "Chut's Hut"?' I offered.

'Jeez, this is a creepy road,' said Patrick. 'I bet they filmed *Gaslight* in here.'

'South Road coming up on your left, Tony,' I said.

He turned into South, lighting up the high, impenetrable hedges that pressed in on both sides. They were all evergreen—laurel, yew, cypressus or holly.

'They guard their privacy jealously,' remarked Patrick.

I said, 'At these prices they're entitled to. Cornish on your left, Tony.'

At the corner of Cornish there was a post bearing a dozen house signs. 'Mango' was the newest and the biggest. It was also the only one painted luminous pink.

We knew we were approaching the house yards before we reached it. The girls gave it away. There must have been a hundred of them, all shapes and sizes, filling the road, crowding the grass verges, standing on each other's shoulders to look over the high brick wall that presumably surrounded the property. The wall was black and old, though one aspect of it wasn't so ancient. It was the barbed wire. Six strands of it forming a nasty overhang impossible to climb, though several of the girls appeared to be having a good try, nevertheless.

As we reached the first of the fans they suddenly turned their full-blooded attention on us. They crowded in, forcing Tony to a halt. They peered in at us, thrusting their faces up to the windows, smearing the glass with lipstick, implanting lip-shapes in a dozen different colours—blue, green, purple, orange and white. As the crowd behind them pressed in for a look the faces of these girls became weird, distorted masks pressed against the glass. The car began to rock. We were now totally surrounded by a sea of faces. Even with the windows tight-closed we could hear the clamour of shrill, silly noise. An ugly red-head stared at me insolently six inches to my right and yelled through the glass, 'Are you anybody important!?'

I'm not too sure what happened next. Either some of the girls recognised Tony from his T.V. ads or quite possibly the red-head recognised me from the White Marvel series, but in the next moment the so-far fairly contained excitement erupted into something close to hysteria. 'It's *him*! It's *him*!' they shrieked, rocking the car violently, screeching hysterically. They hammered on the windows, screaming to be let in. And then they were on the bonnet and the roof.

'Holy God,' gasped Tony, 'they'll wreck the bloody thing!'

'Get moving, Tony,' I urged. 'They'll break the windows! They'll have us over!'

Patrick was sitting stiff and glassy-eyed. 'Bejaze, they're not human. Tony, you've got to get movin'.'

'How *can* I? I can't see! I'll run some of the stupid bitches down!'

'Just keep crawling forward, they'll have to move.'

But they didn't have to, because they couldn't. The word had obviously flashed round the entire crowd that there was 'somebody' in the car and they were fifteen deep round us. There was nothing to see through the windows but line upon line of faces, faces that bore no resemblance to pretty teenagers. They were monstrous faces with bared teeth and flattened noses, staring eyes and distorted cheeks.

And then the inevitable happened. Crump! A girl's face was pushed hard against the windshield. Blood spurted from her nose and streamed thickly down the glass. She began to cry, in panic, and her face became an even uglier mask of pain and tears and blood and running mascara.

'Oh, my Christ, this is awful,' whispered Tony. 'How do we get *out*!'

The rocking of the car was now frighteningly dangerous. Tony had to cling to the wheel, Patrick and I to our armrests to save ourselves being thrown from side to side. Suddenly a group of girls on my side fell away as a girl on top of the car fell off on to them. I used the opportunity to lower my window a couple of inches and yell, 'Let us through! We're nobody important!'

Lowering the window was a mistake. A hand snaked round from the rear of the car and through the gap, clawing for me. It was as terrifying as a triphid. I would never have believed the hand of a young girl could frighten me. Then her other hand shot in . . . then the hands of a second girl. They began heaving, trying to break the glass.

'For Crissake, wind it up!' yelled Tony.

'I can't man, I'll cut their fingers off!'

'Well, frighten them!'

I began winding. The young devils were as tenacious as octopuses, they wouldn't let go.

'It's the White Marvel fella!' one shouted. 'Give us your tie! Give us your hanky!'

Gladly I stuffed my dress handkerchief out through the gap and the hands disappeared in a wild scramble for it. Zip! Up went the window.

'We can't just sit here all night!' said Tony. 'Oh, my God, there goes the windshield wiper . . . hey, you bitches . . . oh, my God, they've ripped off a wing mirror. We've got to move, they're taking the bloody thing to pieces!'

He began edging forward slowly. In the light of the dash I could see he was sweating. Suddenly there was a bump and he slammed the brakes on hard. 'I can't . . . I can't! I'll kill somebody.'

Patrick said solemnly, 'Is this what people like Albert go through all the time. Bedad, it's no wonder they sometimes get nasty with the fans. I'd shoot the buggers.'

How long we'd have been stuck there if the other car hadn't arrived behind ours, I hate to think; and I also hate to contemplate what would have eventually happened to the Jaguar and to us. At least we'd have been turned upside down. But suddenly the inside of our car was lit up like day as the powerful headlights swung up behind us. And just as suddenly we were alone, deserted. The seething mass of distorted humanity disappeared as though by magic, leaving the road clear. Patrick and I turned to look through the rear window. It was difficult to see much because of the blinding headlights but we saw enough to tell it was a Rolls Royce—and, even more horrifying—a convertible.

'Oh, my God,' whispered Patrick. 'Can you imagine what the creatures could do to that with a pair of scissors or a nail-file . . .'

Tony hit the accelerator then and took the Rolls out of our sight.

We reached the main gates quickly. They were wrought iron, ten feet high, topped by spikes and newly added barbed wire. They were also locked and guarded. Two uniformed men with Alsatians were standing inside the gates and were the obvious reason why there were no fans around the gates.

They opened the gates when Tony waved an invitation card and as he drove through he stopped and said to one of the guards, 'We had trouble with some fans . . .'

The guard was grimacing at the car. If the rest was like the bonnet, it was smothered in lipstick.

'Yes, bad do, this,' he said grimly. 'Beats me how the news gets out about these parties. It was kept as quiet as possible. When you leave, don't come out this way, sir, there's a rear entrance.'

'There's a Rolls Royce right behind us. I reckon he's in big trouble.'

'I'll give the police a call, clear the young bastards away. Straight on, sir, you'll find the house.'

As we drove slowly along the twisting gravel drive, bordered by a towering screen of rhododendron bushes, Tony breathed a sigh and said, 'All this for a bloody firework party. I sure hope it's worth it. I reckon those kids have done a couple of hundred quid's worth of damage to the car. Ralph will go beserk. He was taking off on Monday for a week in Scotland.'

'Birds,' snorted Patrick. 'Y'know it's a wonder the other people in The Park haven't complained about this. What about the other people living in Cornish Road. Do they have to run that gauntlet all the time?'

'I believe they're all show-biz folk,' said Tony. 'I think that's the only reason Albert got into The Park, provided he lived in the leper colony.'

'How can *he* stand it?' I asked.

Tony smiled. 'I doubt if Albert really notices crowds. There were twelve kids in his family and he was the last. I imagine he's always been surrounded.'

'By people wanting to tear him to pieces?'

He laughed. 'Could be. Wait till you see Albert.'

The gravel drive ended in an immense courtyard in front of the house. There must have been fifty or sixty other cars there already, a lot of them Rolls and Bentleys. There were D.B.S.s and Ferraris; Jensens and Jags and a flush of fast-looking foreign jobs. They all looked quite unscathed and it occurred to me their owners all knew of the back entrance to the house.

Tony parked the Jag alongside a California-green D.B.S. that was so clean and gleaming it might well have been kept in a chamois fob during the day and slipped out for the night.

We got out and studied the house. It was immense. Lights blazed from a dozen rooms and yet another dozen were in darkness. What, I wondered, did Albert Chutney from Liverpool want with a monstrosity like this.

'Welcome to Wuthering Heights,' said Tony. 'Come on, I need a drink bad.'

As we entered the arched porch I felt I'd walked into church. Even the musty smell was there and the wrought-iron lantern in the roof. The front door wouldn't have seemed out of place on Windsor Castle. It was the type built to withstand seige—six inches of solid oak studded with iron bolts. Tony twisted the iron ring and we walked in—into warm, cozy, noisy, jovial, comfortingly ostentatious theatrical bedlam.

EIGHT

In former circumstances the oak panelled hall with its walk-in fireplace, solid oak staircase and minstrel gallery would have been a ponderous, depressing place, despite the huge log fire that blazed in the wide iron dogs; but not tonight. Who noticed the room when it contained no fewer than twenty very beautiful young women? Tony's eyes lit up. Patrick caught his breath. The cold disappeared from my bones. I grew more erect. Spring returned to my step. Off came the overcoat.

Patrick turned to me and gasped, 'It's the Wildcats!'

'You're telling me!' I murmured back.

With bated breath I flashed a look around the crowd, spoilt for choice, there was so much to look at. I recognized many faces. At least half a dozen of the girls were members of the famous Wildcats dance group, a fabulous group who had established themselves two years ago as the best dance team ever to hit T.V. Their routines were outstanding, always immensely well-rehearsed, frequently brilliant and always wildly sexy. The girls had been chosen for their height and slenderness. There wasn't one under five seven and every figure was perfect; long-legged and willowy.

A face turned and I caught the devastating profile of the group leader, Tania Marechal. Lord, what a fantastic-looking girl. She was a French negress, very lightly coloured, with skin like beige satin. And her eyes! They were amber. The eyes of a tiger. An incredibly beautiful girl.

I stood rooted, watching her, disbelieving the dress she was wearing. It was full length, in deep Royal blue velvet, and slashed from the hem to the waist, exposing, as she moved, her entire leg and thigh. And as though that weren't heart-stopping enough, there were vents in the bodice that exposed more coffee-coloured flesh. Come to think of it, there wasn't too much of Tania Marechal I couldn't see.

There had been more publicity about this girl in the press than all the others in the group combined. She had, it was reported, an I.Q. as impressive as her looks and a talent for painting to match. A formidable bird.

As I watched her a man broke from the group and approached her. I knew him, too. Whispering Jimmy Christmas, a pop singer who didn't, he just whispered hoarsely into the mike. He was supposed to be sexy. He was a big lad, broad of shoulder, with a shock of fair hair. He was wearing silver lamé trousers, a purple shirt and beads, and right now he was also wearing a snide leer like he was whispering sexily to Tania Marechal, obviously on the make.

I left them and looked around the others in the hall. There stood Tony Jackson, disc jockey and comforter of lonely housewives—and not only over the radio if the rumours were true. And there, Freddie Rich, T.V. compere of panel games ... David East, well-known impressario and talent manager ... and so on ...

The place throbbed and sparkled with well-knowns and lesser knowns, each, by the looks of things, determined to be clever, witty, gay, beautiful—and noticed.

I followed Tony slowly across the hall, slowly so we could get good close-up looks at the birds. Oh, what a night. I turned to Patrick and raised a brow. He grinned like an idiot and nodded. He was in happyland.

We entered a huge room that had a bar covering all of one wall and jungle music blasting from eighteen antique loudspeakers. To our left was another room, serving as a cloakroom. We dumped the coats in there and crossed towards the bar where five white-jacketed barmen were working themselves to a frenzy providing the stuff.

Patrick gave me a hand on the shoulder and a silly grin. 'All right?' he asked, indicating the room, the house, the party.

'Just what the doctor ordered.'

'Y'know ...' he said, scratching his nose. 'I've got the strongest feelin' I'm going to get well and truly laid tonight.'

I grinned. 'You, too?'

He laughed. 'And you, too?'

'It must have been with seeing the Wildcats or something.'

'Yeh, or something. It's been a long time, Russell.'

'An eternity, son. Must be . . . heck, it must be a week!'

'Can it be! I was wondering what was wrong. A week! Bedad, that's terrible. I'll be comin' out in spots or somethin'.'

'We *must* take care of ourselves, Patrick.'

'You're right. Consider it put in hand.'

'Mm? Well, whatever turns you on. Here, have a drink.

By gum, I'll say one thing for Albert, he was generous. Or his barmen were. The booze flowed like they were desperate to empty a reservoir of it somewhere. We stayed at the bar for a couple (the equivalent of ten small ones in a pub), surveying the scene, digging each other in the arm as the talent rolled by, and then, by mutual consent, we split up.

We never have operated as a wolf pack. That gets no one anywhere. The chances of three fellas meeting three totally compatible birds is as chancy as winning the pools, so we always go solo, though we did agree to try to meet up at the bonfire at eleven thirty in time for the firework display.

So I wandered off, carrying a lifetime's supply of vodka-and-tonic in a glass large enough to have doubled as a tulip vase. And, being normally nosey, I began opening doors to rooms and having a peek inside. Without realizing it I wandered away from the heart of the party to an extreme end of the house, and there, crossing a deserted drawing room, I pushed open one half of a pair of tall oak doors and looked in.

It was a billiards room.

The room itself was in darkness but the magnificent full-sized table was brilliantly lit by the low-hung overhead lights. The balls were all set out for snooker—a sight to stir the heart of any snooker enthusiast.

It's the colour, I suppose, and the symmetry of the balls in their positions—green, brown and yellow standing like open-order troops along the baulk line at the bottom of the table; blue in dead-centre; stalwart pink protecting the perfect triangle of reds at the top end; and the big boy, black, head of the clan, lurking behind the reds. The colours looked beautiful against the bright green baize, especially as the baize had been ironed and brushed to perfection. The room was silent and still, yet the prepared table evoked an atmosphere of expectancy, as though a great game was about to start. The balls invited play. I stepped into the room and closed the door behind me.

I'm not much of a player, believe me. I used to enjoy a game up at Slash Lane Cricket Club in Liverpool back in my sewing machine days and I've had the odd game in London with Tony, but fair-to-mediocre would describe my talent—much more enthusiasm than skill. Fred Davis could accomplish forty times more with an umbrella than I could with a cue, but as a game I love it.

I wandered over to the table and stroked the baize appreciatively. Twelve feet by six, it stretched away like a manicured football field under nightlights. Compulsively I reached for the green ball, rolled it across the table and watched it glide back, smooth and silent. I was returning the ball to its spot when the voice out of the darkness frightened the life out of me.

'D'ja play den, la?'

With pounding heart I peered into the gloom, seeing nothing. I heard the creak of a chair. A tall, broad-shouldered lad in an open-necked, dark blue satin shirt approached the table and walked towards me, hefting the white ball in his right hand. He was big, six feet two and strong-looking, with huge hands and arms. His face was almost very good but somehow not quite. All the pieces were there—strong jaw-line, generous nose, firm mouth, but the eyes let him down. They lacked brightness, intelligence. He looked like a big, soft lad—but big. I wondered if he was a bodyguard for Albert. It was possible I was about to be chucked out.

'Er, sorry if I intruded,' I grinned. 'I was just wandering around and spotted the table. Afraid I couldn't resist a closer look.'

'Sorlright,' he said, slurring the word with a Liverpool accent as thick as treacle. I smiled to myself. It had been a long time since I'd heard such pure scouse. 'D'ja play, den?' he repeated and I had another inward grin. This was the accent of the Liverpool slums, of Scotland Road before the developers bulldozed it flat. It gave me a big kick. It was like coming home.

'Not much,' I said, 'but I'll give you a game if you're stuck.'

His face lit up like a child's. 'Will ya! O.K., yer on. Grab a kyew in da corner, der.'

I walked over to the wall and chose a cue from the rack while he went towards a dark corner and came back with what was obviously his own special cue.

'That your own?' I asked him.

He grinned, revealing white tombstone choppers. 'Yeh, me da gib me dis f'me sixteenth birthdee,' meaning his father gave it to him for his sixteenth birthday. He *must* be Albert's bodyguard, I thought . . . or a relative . . . maybe even a brother. From what Tony had said about the accent and there being twelve kids it seemed very possible.

I took a coin and tossed it. 'Shout.'

' 'eads.'

It was heads.

'You break,' he said.

I pushed the white down the table, barely touched the triangle of reds and brought the white back off the cushions to nestle right behind the green, almost touching it. What a fluke! A snooker first shot!

'Ah, 'ell,' he grinned. 'Eh, I thort you sed you cudn' play!'

'I can't. That was pure luck.'

'Ah, reck.'

It was a very awkward shot for him. He had to stretch across the table and play the white back off the bottom cushion and try to hit a red off a side cushion. He didn't make it. He muffed the shot and the white trickled ignominiously towards the cushion and didn't even reach it.

'Der yar, la, yor four up,' he said, moving over to the scoreboard and sliding the 'spot' tab along four points.

I made my next shot, again barely touching the reds but in doing so I disturbed one red that moved away from the pack. He pounced. Before he'd finished his break he had thirty-two points on the board. He was beautiful to watch. He moved around the table as fleet as a ballet dancer, giving full concentration to the game, chalking his cue automatically after each shot, working out his next shot or next two shots before he potted a ball and controlling the white masterfully.

I followed him around, lifting and replacing on their spots the colours he potted, enthralled by his skill. Oafish he may appear but at snooker he was nobody's fool.

At last he missed a pink by a gnat's whisker and stopped scoring.

'Hey, that was terrific,' I said.

He shrugged modestly. 'Well, not bad, y'know, bur I shud 'ave 'ad dat pink. Go on, I've given yus a gift.'

He'd left me an easy pink over the hole and a good red to go with it. I put down the red, sank the pink, doubled a flukey red into centre, trickled down the blue, smacked in another red and cut in a good black—twenty-one points—twenty-five counting the four already on the board. The game was now nice and tight.

'Bluddy good black, dat,' he said, nodding approvingly, replacing it on its spot.

I missed the next red and he took over. The game continued to be tight. He made ten in his next break. I made fourteen in mine. By the time all the reds were down and only the colours left to pot, there were only six points in it, him in the lead, and it stayed that way until only the pink and the black were left.

Now if he got the pink the game was over, he'd be twelve points in the lead and I couldn't touch him—the black being only seven points. So I wanted both the pink *and* the black to win.

Well, the game of shrewd cunning began, the object being, of course, that if you couldn't pot the pink you put it nice and safe so *he* couldn't pot it. Shot after shot after shot was taken. And then ... he left me a diabolical chance. The white was positioned in the worst place imaginable—right hard against the bottom cushion, leaving very little of the ball to hit with the cue. The pink was up at the top end, near a pocket, but at such an angle to it that it needed a very fine cut to put it down. Well, there was my choice—if I put it down I had an even chance of winning. But if I pushed the badly-placed white to the left I could go in-off and give six away to him; and if I pushed to the right I'd miss the pink altogether and *still* give six away to him. Some choice.

'O.K.,' I said, 'here goes for the "men-from-the-boys" shot.' I chalked my cue carefully, got down behind the white, splayed my fingers on the edge of the table, got my angle, felt comfortable ... even confident ... and drew back my cue ... and ...

At that very moment the door behind me burst open. 'Albert for Chris*sake*, man, what are you hiding in here for! You've got a party on ... the goddam *press* are out there waitin' for an interview and you're in here fartassin' around playin' pool!'

The shock I'd got from the crashing door had caused me to skewer the ball across the table, six feet from the pink. I stood up and faced the intruder. It had to be Mickey Pink—five feet two, cowboy boots, red hair, floral shirt and the cigar, a foot and a half long.

So! I'd been playing snooker with none other than Albert Chutney! I turned to him. His face was a picture of disappointment. He was gazing at the still-rolling white with anguish. 'Ah, eh, Mickey, look wha ya dun!' he groaned. 'He wus on dat pink wid a black ball fight cummin' up. Ah, reck, the best bluddy game I've 'ad since I cum down 'ere . . .'

Little Mickey Pink strode into the room, puffing smoke. 'Look, kid, when are ya gonna get it inta ya thick head you're a fuckin' *star* not a fuckin' pool-playin' docker any more! This is *your* party, man. There are three hundred goddam people out there all screamin' for ya and you're in here playin' hermit with this guy. Who is he anyway?'

Albert shrugged. 'Dunno, Mickey, burre plays a good game a snook . . .'

Mickey whirled on me. 'Who are ya—Press?'

'No, afraid not. My name's Russ Tobin. I came with Tony Dane.'

'Oh, yeh, well, no offence Tobin but Albert has ta mingle, know what I mean? Come on, let's get goin', Albert.'

Albert gave me a lopsided grin. 'We'll finish it sum uvver time, eh, Russ? Good game, la . . .'

'Sure, glad to.'

'Come on, come *on*,' urged Pink. 'Jeez, some goddam star . . .'

'You cummin'?' Albert asked me.

'Look, never mind him,' Pink cut in. 'Just get yer ass outta that door and into the bar!'

I followed them out, feeling spare, very much in the presence of big, big business that has no time for anything except big, big business. Well, I couldn't blame Pink. It was this drive that had brought Albert from the Liverpool docks to number one in the hit parade and T.V. series in the States. I supposed it needed this sort of ruthlessness, though the understanding of it didn't make me like it any the more.

I followed them through to the room with the bar to replenish my drink. The room was packed to the walls, as was the hall, the staircase and the minstrel gallery. The noise was absolute. Whether by chance or judgement 'Alpaca Jack' started up as Albert entered and what with this noise and the racket the crowd was making it was Deafsville in there.

Mickey Pink barged through the crowd, clearing the way for Albert and inadvertently for me too and we all finished up at the bar, and my first action was to have a mild heart attack because sitting on a stool not an inch away to my right was the incredible Tania Marechal.

'O.K., Albert, in here, on this stool between Tania and Jennie,' ordered Mickey, thrusting and pushing. 'We're gonna get some shots of the three of ya later.'

Albert settled in between the girls, Jennie being a blonde Wildcat and also quite something. Albert grinned at both of them, totally perplexed, and Mickey said brusquely, 'Albert, these gen'lemen are from the States. This is Paul Godbere from "Music Scene" in New York and this is Dale Ryden from "Top Disc" in L.A. Now, look, they're flyin' out tonight. They want some background stuff, y'know, your life in Liverpool as a kid, Kay?'

Albert nodded dumbly. I was sure he'd much rather have been playing snooker. He looked petrified, hemmed in by the crowd and I wondered why Mickey Pink hadn't arranged the interview in quiter surroundings.

'Kay, it's all yours,' Pink said to the two men standing in front of Albert.

Paul Godbere was a small, dark, Jewish-looking man with a big nose and weary eyes. Ryden was younger, light ginger hair, freckles. Both of them had pads and pencils at the ready.

Godbere started the questioning. 'Albert, where did you spend your childhood—where were you born exactly?'

The pencils were poised, ears were attuned, cutting out the surrounding noise, and Albert began to speak. I watched the faces of Godbere and Ryden. The first ripples of dismay appeared after ten or fifteen seconds. Their pencils quivered but nothing was written. A deep frown appeared between Godbere's black brows. Ryden openly winced. Godbere looked up from his pad, as though taking a good second look at the man he was interviewing and wondering why he'd mistakenly believed that Albert was English.

It was all I could do not to laugh. They couldn't understand a word Albert was saying.

Mickey Pink was watching the situation closely, not, I

thought, unduly perturbed. After a while he said to the Americans, 'Look, gentlemen, we have all that information on handouts, you know ...'

Godbere said, 'Yes, so we understand, Mr. Pink, but we did want to get this first-hand from Albert. Albert ... could you please repeat that bit about "being born in a playschool for Zachary" ...?'

Albert gave an embarrassed grin and shook his head. 'No—norra "playschool for Zachary"—a place call' F'zachley—y'know.'

Godbere stared. Ryden was biting his pencil and surreptitiously glancing at his watch. Finally Mickey Pink was about to intervene when one of the barmen stretched a hand over the bar and tapped him on the shoulder. Pink turned. The barman held aloft a telephone receiver in his other hand and mouthed something. Pink looked quickly at his watch and turned anxiously to the Americans, 'Gentlemen, I'm sorry, but I've got the States on the line, I'll have to leave you to it.'

'Sure, go ahead,' said Godbere, in a tone that implied that with or without Pink the interview was washed up anyway.

Pink disappeared into the crowd. Ryden seemed determined to have one more go. 'Albert ... perhaps if we took it just a *frac*tion slower ...?'

Albert took a deep sigh and began with ebbing confidence, confused that he couldn't communicate with them. 'Well, y'see, me da an' me ma 'ad to moove ta justoff Scotty Road wen I was a yeer ode, y'know ...'

By chance I was looking at the completely mystified Godbere when he happened to glance up and caught my eye. Whether he thought I was part of Albert's entourage because I was standing so close, I don't know, but he offered me an expression of hopelessness and regret with a slight shake of his head and began closing his pad.

'Scotland Road, Mr. Godbere,' I said. 'Albert's father and mother had to move from Fazakerly—that's a district in Liverpool—to Scotland Road when he was one year old ...'

Suddenly everybody was looking at me ... Godbere and Ryden with surprise and relief; Jennie Durant and the incredible Tania Marechal with delight; and Albert with an expression that said 'well, heck, isn' that what *I* said?'

'Well, thank you,' smiled Godbere, beginning to write. 'Excuse me, are you, er, associated with Albert?'

Albert laughed, for the first time. 'Yes, 'e's me mucker ... 'n 'e plays a bluddy good game a snooker ...'

Godbere's wry grin broadened. 'No offence, Albert, but translation, please, Mr. ... er ...'

'Tobin. Russ Tobin. Albert said I was his mucker, his mate, and that I play a good game of snooker ...'

I was very aware that Tania Marechal was watching me closely—and I do mean closely. She was three inches away on my left, perched on the stool. I could smell her perfume, feel the warmth of her body, and it was doing my composure no good at all.

'Have you known each other long?' asked Ryden.

I grinned at Albert. 'How long would you say, Albert?'

Albert made a big thing of looking at his watch, 'Er, rabout forty-five minutes.'

'We've just played our first game,' I explained. 'I wandered into the billiards room and found Albert there.'

Godbere asked, 'Mr. Tobin, we're grateful for your help. How come you can understand Albert's regional dialect so well?'

'Because I'm practically a scouse ... a Liverpudlian myself.'

Albert's eyes lit up. 'Are yer!? 'Ey, I din know dat, la. Y'don sound like a scouse.'

'Well, strictly speaking I'm not one, Albert. I was born in Cheshire but I worked for a long time in the Pool.'

'Did ya!?' he said, obviously delighted to renew contact with even the name of his old home town. 'Where dja werk, den?'

'Oh, several places. I worked for a firm near Sandon Dock ...'

'Did dja! Blinkin' 'eck, *I* used to werk der ...!'

'Er, gentlemen ...' Godbere cut in, 'sorry to interrupt this Liverpudlian reunion, but Dale and I have a plane to catch ...'

'Oh, yeh, sorry,' laughed Albert. ' 'ey, we'll 'ave a natter after, Russ, O.K.?'

'O.K.,' I grinned, and turned to Tania who was laughing. It was the first time she'd looked directly at me. The impact of her amber eyes sent a thump right through my body. Blood rushed to my head. My eyes lost focus. And she knew it. Her eyes stayed on mine just that fraction too long for a casual glance, then with a slight, amused flicker of her mouth she turned to look at Godbere who was asking Albert how he started singing.

Well, that was me slaughtered for the night. I was conscious of her closeness every second of the interview from there on, conscious of her breathing, the movements of her hands, the way her dress lay open at the side exposing her thigh, of the vents in her dress that revealed her body, of her low-cut neckline and her breats, her small, firm, satin breasts. Whenever I could I turned to look at her, captivated by her profile, her small pussy-cat nose and wide, sensuous mouth, and her hair, short and loosely curled, fitting her head like a neat Afro-cap. And again she knew it. Of course she knew it. She had been used to men looking at her most of her life. But she didn't respond.

Albert was saying, in reply to Godbere's question, 'Ah, well, y'see, I wus wid dese free mates wun night, skylarkin' around an' we gorrinto a bittova scuffle up a jigger wiv a scuffer ... well, dis scuffer blows 'is pipe, y'know, an' we run like 'ell and 'id in a werkinmen's club ...'

'Woa woa woa ... !' laughed Godbere. 'Help, Russ ...!'

The group burst into spontaneous laughter at Albert's barrage of scouse, with Albert laughing as hard as anyone, perhaps at last seeing the daft humour of me having to translate for him. The girls were in pleats. Tania, laughing hard, turned towards me, shaking her head, 'Isn't he *gor*geous!' and touched my arm in a gesture of helplessness, then took her hand away. That was all, but it was enough. Contact had been made. 'Oh, Albert, that was *so* pretty ...'

Godbere, wiping a tear from his eye, said, 'Russ ... would you mind?'

She had a wonderful voice, low, confident, unmistakeably French, more of a caress than an instrument for words.

'Not at all,' I said, shaking inside. 'Albert said he was out with three pals one night and got into a scuffle with a cop in an alley. When the cop blew his whistle for help the four of them ran into a workingmen's club to hide.'

So the interview proceeded. Albert went on to tell them that as they entered the club the M.C. was calling for volunteers from the audience to do something in the way of entertainment, and with the cops hard on his heels Albert leapt on the stage and sang the only song he knew 'Roll Me Over Lay Me Down And Do it Again'. It was such a hit with the drunken audience he went back the next night *and* the next and so became a favourite at the club . . .

Godbere and Ryden were scribbling happily away. 'Yeh, great . . . great,' said Godbere.

Ryden was looking anxiously at his watch. 'We gotta go, Paul.'

'Yeh, sure. Albert thanks a million . . . you, too, Russ. Now, let's get some shots of you, Albert, then some with the girls, huh?'

Ryden lined them up and took a dozen flash shots of the three of them. 'Fine . . . great . . . that's it, then.'

Albert looked at me and grinned. 'Ah, 'ey, fellas, warrabout Russ, den? Ya gorra get one of 'im!'

Ryden laughed. 'Yeh, sure. Get in there, Russ. Albert and interpreter, yeh, great . . .'

'Cum in, mate,' said Albert, releasing Tania and holding up his arm. 'Squeeze in 'ere.'

Oh, you doll, Albert.

I moved in, slipping my arm tentatively where Albert's had been, hardly daring to touch her, going wild inside as my hand touched warm flesh through one of the vents. I can't even remember them taking the photograph. The next thing I knew they'd packed up their equipment, were shaking our hands and making an exit.

With a big sigh of relief Albert said, 'Jeez, I cud do wid a pint, I'm sweat'n. 'ey, tanks a million, Russ, I won't ferget dat.'

I grinned at him. 'Pleasure, Albert. We'll call it quits for a drink, hm?'

'Right, yor on. Cum on, now, gerls, wotcha 'avin'?'

The barmen were obviously keeping an eye on Albert and leapt to attention when he gave them a nod. We got drinks instantly.

'Well, tank God dat's over,' said Albert, gulping half his pint hungrily and smacking his lips. 'I 'ate those bluddy interviews.'

Tania said with a smile, 'Aw, Albert, you were beautiful.'

'I was byootiful! Worrabout me mate, 'ere?' He pointed a

thumb at me and Tania turned and looked at me. 'Yes, he was ver' beautiful, too,' she smiled. 'Haven't I seen you somewhere before? Your face is very familiar.'

'Probably on T.V. I do the White Marvel ads.'

Her eyes widened. 'Yes, of course!'

Jennie, a very good-looking bird with long blonde hair and very blue eyes, said, 'I *told* you, Tania, when he first came in.'

'You didn't say White Marvel—you said that biological thing ...'

Jennie shrugged and laughed at me. 'Oh, well, you know ... they all sound the same, don't they.' She turned to Albert. 'Albert, what time are the fireworks? I don't want to miss them.'

Albert looked at his watch. 'Yeh, any time now, luv. Tell ya wot, you two go'n get your coats and we'll go'm seeum, eh?'

'Shall we meet you back here?'

'Yeh, sure, Russ 'n me 'll wait for ya.'

They finished their drinks and went off towards the cloakroom, joining the crowd that was now shuffling out towards the hall, heading for the garden. Tania was barely lost to view before I suffered the first pangs of loss.

'What a beautiful girl,' I found myself saying.

Albert drained his pint and nodded. 'Tania? Yeh, she's a belter, i'nt she. You ... er ... a bit keen den?'

I grinned at him. 'More than a bit, Albert.'

'Well, get stuck in, la, before sumbody else does.'

I laughed. 'Who—me? With Tania Marechal?'

'Well, why not?'

'Well ... you know. She's a big name ... and with all these celebrities around ...'

'So what?'

'Isn't she with anybody?'

'Not as far as I know. She's very pertiklar, Tania.'

'That's what I'm afraid of,' I laughed.

'Why? You seem t'be doin' orlright.'

'You reckon?'

'Sure. Bluddy 'ell, she's only a bird, y'know. Go on, get stuck in.'

I had to laugh at him, he was so uncomplicated. Maybe that's why he attracted the girls, they liked his simple, guileless approach.

At that moment Mickey Pink pushed through the exiting crowd and dashed up, puffing away on a new cigar.

'Eh up,' muttered Albert. ''ere comes trouble. Can't even gerra quiet pint down.'

'O.K., Albert, how'd it go? Come on, we've got three big wheels from New York ta meet. They're outside, warmin' their fat asses by the bonfire. Grab your jacket an' let's go.'

Albert turned to me and grimaced, 'See whar I mean. I'll see ya out der, den, Russ. Bring da gerls out, 'ey?'

'Yes, sure. See you by the bonfire.'

They shot off and I slipped on to a stool to finish my drink and think about Tania. Nah, it just wasn't possible, not with all these celebrities here. She was here to be noticed, to be photographed with other big names. She wasn't going to mess around with the White Marvel man. These parties weren't just parties, they were opportunities to advance a career, to meet influential people, to be seen rubbing shoulders with the 'in' people, and by no stretch of the imagination could a presenter of soap powder be regarded as 'in'.

I became aware of passing time. I checked my watch. They'd been gone five minutes. They should have been back by now. There was still quite a crowd around the cloakroom and the doorway to the hall, but even so, they should have been back by now.

I gave it another five minutes. There were now only six people left in the room and five of them were barmen. To escape their curious glances I got off the stool and headed for the cloakroom, fearing the worst. I got it. There wasn't a soul in there.

Aw, buggerritt . . .

As I collected my overcoat the whole house was suddenly shaken by a terrific overhead explosion. This was followed by the machine-gun crackle of dozens of smaller explosions and the distant cheer of an awful lot of people. By gum, Tobin, you've certainly got life nicely in hand, son. Not only have you lost out on Tania but you're probably the only guest in the place missing the fireworks! Well, sod it, there was nothing I could do about Tania but I could do something about the fireworks.

I went out into the deserted hall and into a drawing room whose french windows were wide open to the rear garden. Now I could see the gigantic bonfire. It was some distance from the house and set on a lower level of lawn. It was enormous, twenty feet high, and sitting on top was a costumed guy in a wooden chair. As I crossed the rear patio and began descending to the lower level, the roaring, crackling flames reached the guy and set it on fire and the crowd cheered as the guy exploded into a firework display. Simultaneously a salvo of a dozen huge rockets swished skywards from a long wooden stand erected to one side of the bonfire. In rapid order they exploded, lighting up the sky with green, red, blue, yellow and white tracers, and as they descended and faded, a very comprehensive firework display began on the wooden stand.

As I walked towards the display I spotted Tania. She was standing with Jennie and two men. One man was Tony Jackson, the amorous D.J.; he had his arm round Jennie's waist. The other man was, of course, Whispering Jimmy Bloody Christmas. He wasn't actually touching Tania but was standing close enough to her to make no matter. Ah, well, I was right. I didn't blame her for a moment. Christmas was big business. Move on, Tobin, it was wonderful while it lasted.

I moved to one side and stood alone, watching the firework display. It lasted quite a while. Catherine wheels spun, crackers cracked, aeroplanes zizzed and howled and rockets shished away in their scores. Then, finally, the piece de resistance—a battery of six enormous rockets were fired simultaneously. They exploded very high, lighting the night like day, filling the sky with a huge umbrella of silver stars that hung suspended for a while before drifting to earth in a great curtain of shimmering spirals. A dramatic finish to an excellent display.

The crowd applauded. I wandered towards the bonfire, unable to resist a look at Tania. Over the fabulous dress she was wearing a floor-length cape in the same Royal blue velvet, the high collar lined with white, framing her fabulous face. I held the look until my neck hurt, hoping she'd look across, but she didn't. She seemed too engrossed in what Christmas was whispering to her.

I sauntered around the bonfire, glad of its intense heat because the night was very cold. Then, on the far side of the fire, I saw the bar and the barbeque fires. Four uniformed chefs were cooking chicken, chops, steaks and sausages on raised charcoal troughs and dispensing the food on paper plates. At the trestle-tabled bar, four barmen were ladling out the stuff that keeps the pneumonia at bay. It was all highly organized.

The drifting aroma of cooking food reminded me of how hungry I was, so I walked over and joined the line of people waiting to be served. I'd only just arrived when Albert, Mickey Pink and, presumably, the three American business men strolled up. Pink was in earnest conversation with the Yanks and Albert looked perplexed and lost. But he beamed when he saw me.

' 'ello, mate—'ey, where dja get to? Where're the gerls?'

I nodded. 'Over there. They didn't come back, Albert. I waited in the bar for ten minutes and they didn't show up. They're over there now with Tony Jackson and Jimmy Christmas.'

'Oh, that bluddy creep.'

I laughed, pleased by his opinion. 'Is he?'

'Pain in de ass,' he said, looking across to the bonfire. ' 'Ey up, they're cummin' over now. 'ey, don't that Tania look sumthin' in 'er cloak?'

'Yes, something,' I said. 'Does she, er, have a thing going with Christmas?'

He looked at me, aghast. 'Who—'er, wid 'im!? Nah, she wudn't go fer a bloke like 'im. 'E's a cunt.'

I felt a hundred pound weight fall off my shoulders.

The foursome came up to join the queue for food.

'Oh, I'm so *cold*!' groaned Tania, stamping her feet and huddling into her cloak. 'The bonfire is lovely, Albert, but you can only warm one side at a time.'

'Why don't you go and stand by the barbecue fire,' I suggested. 'I'm sure no one would mind if you jumped the queue.'

'I've got a better idea,' said Christmas, and slipped his arm around Tania's waist, pulling her to him. 'How's that, gorgeous?'

She turned her face to him, eyes flaring, and made a movement to escape his arm. 'No thank you, Jimmy, I'm all right ...'

But he clung on, laughing. I could see now he was quite high. 'No, you're not, sweetheart, you're freezing, come on, cuddle up here ...'

She twisted away more violently. 'Jimmy, let go . . .!'

'Aw, come on, I'm warm, baby . . .'

'Get off me!'

I was blazing. I wanted to flatten the bastard. The words were out before I could stop them.

'Leave her alone, for Chrissake, Christmas!'

There was a deathly hush. He froze, as though he hadn't quite heard right, then slowly he turned to me with a puzzled frown that turned into a threatening glare.

'I beg your pardon?'

'I said leave her alone. You heard.'

His arm dropped from Tania's waist and he turned fully to me. 'Do, er, I know you, then?'

'No.'

'Do you know me, then?'

'No.'

'So what did you say that for?'

Tania snapped at him. 'Jimmy, stop it, you're drunk. Why don't you go away . . .'

He silenced her with a hand, saying to me, 'Who d'you think you are to tell me anything. Who the hell *are* you?'

'I'm one of Albert's guests, Christmas—and so are you. You'd do well to remember it and cool it . . .'

'You cheeky goddam bastard . . .!' he shouted and came at me, lunging forward. Albert's hand flashed out and grabbed his arm, and Christmas stopped so abruptly he might have run into a brick wall.

'Lissen, la,' Albert said quietly, 'will ya do me a favour an' go 'ome? Will you go 'ome before yuh get 'urt?'

Christmas glared furiously at Albert, right into his face, and I thought for a second he was going to take a swipe at Albert.

'Are yuh goin'?' Albert asked with venomous quiet, teeth clenched. 'Or 'ave I got ta send ya? If I do, I'll break ya fuckin' arm.'

Christmas winced at the vice-like pressure on his arm and slumped in defeat, and as Albert released his arm he turned away quickly and disappeared across the lawn.

'Phew', I gasped, releasing my breath. 'Thanks, Albert.'

Albert shrugged and grinned.

Mickey Pink darted in. 'What's the matter—you got trouble?'

'Nah,' said Albert, surprised at the suggestion.

'Sure?'

'Sure. It was only Christmas doin' 'is party piece.'

'O.K.,' said Mickey, rejoining the Americans.

Tania smiled at me. 'Thank you. He's a bore and a bit drunk. We're rehearsing together for a T.V. show and he thinks it gives him the right to be familiar.' She looked from me to Albert and back again. 'So what happened to you two? You disappeared.'

I laughed. '*We* disappeared! I waited in the bar for ten minutes for you.'

'But ...' she turned to look at Jennie, 'but Jennie and I saw Albert leaving with Mickey and we assumed ... you weren't with them?'

'No,' I grinned. 'I was doing a solo in the bar.'

'Oh, I'm sorry. We collected our coats and followed Albert out and then lost sight of him.'

By now the queue in front of us had diminished. Albert said, ' 'ere y'are, gerls, now wot would ya like—a birra chickin ... a steak ...'

Tania hugged her cloak more closely round her and said, 'Darling Albert, I'm sure I'm too cold to eat anything. I really am freezing.'

'Not surprisin',' Albert grinned, 'wid da dress you've gorron. Lissen, why don't ya go on up to de 'ouse. There's stacks of food in de kitchin—loads of it. Russ'll take you up, won't ya, mate. 'e suffers badly from the cold, y'know.' He turned on this last bit and gave me a wink. 'Don't ya, la?'

What a luvly bloke, playing Cupid in return for my help.

'Badly,' I said, nodding at Tania. 'So help me, I'm freezing.'

She gave Albert a sly smile to let him know she'd missed nothing of this exchange and said to me, 'All right, let's go.' She said to Jennie, 'You staying?'

Tony Jackson answered for her. 'Yes, we're staying. Jennie's hot blooded, aren't you, darling?'

From the look she gave Jackson I didn't doubt it.

I said to Albert, 'How about you, though?'

He shrugged and indicated Mickey and the three Americans. 'Nah, I gorra stock around. Bizzness, y'know. I'll catch up wid youse later. Go on, push off, the bird's freezin' ta death.'

So Tania and I took off for the house. I felt suddenly nervous. Tobin alone with Tania Marechal. Yet was I really *with* her? I still had a feeling it had to be a very temporary thing. Any moment now a photographer or a manager or a P.R. man would leap out of the bushes and whisk her away for something or other. Anyway, make the most of it. Even a sandwich and a coffee alone with her was something to remember.

We went in through the french windows, teeth chattering. 'Oh, I really am *free*zing!' she gasped.

'What you need is some very hot coffee.'

'What I need,' she said, scurrying in, 'is some *very* hot coffee.'

We found the kitchen and a huge lay-out of cold food and, more importantly, four glass coffee percolators bubbling away on an electric burner. The kitchen was deserted.

'Obviously,' she said, throwing open her cloak and sliding on to a stool, 'all the other guests are hardier souls than I. I feel the cold terribly.'

'So do I. I've just come back from nine months in sunny Majorca and I'm feeling it badly tonight. I don't function too well in anything under seventy fahrenheit.'

'Et moi,' she laughed, showing perfect white teeth.

'Black or white?'

'White, no sugar, thank you.'

I put a cup before her and took a stool facing her, then for a while we drank in silence, hands cupped around the coffee, sipping it and gasping, sniffing from the cold.

Suddenly she laughed, 'A couple of tender hot-house blooms, aren't we? There was Albert, wearing just a thin jacket and an open shirt as though it was the middle of August, not noticing the cold . . . and we're trussed up like Eskimos . . .'

'Ay, he's a tough lad, Albert.'

'He's adorable. I love him. I felt very sorry for him tonight at that interview, he looked so bewildered. It was very good of you to help him.'

'I'm very surprised at Mickey Pink letting him suffer it. He must know Albert's practically incoherent, especially to Americans.'

She shrugged. 'I think Mickey does it purposely—to bring Albert out, get him used to talking in public. Mickey's job can't be an easy one—trying to turn no more than a wonderful natural voice into an international star.'

'No, I'm sure it isn't. Y'know, I'm ashamed to admit it, but I only heard about Albert today . . .'

Her eyes widened.

'. . . oh, I know, I must be the only person in Britain that hasn't. But Majorca's something of a hit-parade backwater. Nothing reaches there until it's six months old.'

'What were you doing in Majorca—T.V. work?'

'No, I was a courier for a travel firm . . .'

We spent half an hour in the kitchen, virtually alone, apart from the odd head that popped in looking for somebody or a cup of coffee. I was completely knocked out by her. She was captivating. She told me something of her background, of her early life in Paris, and she talked about dancing and painting. She was very good to be with.

The privacy didn't last. People began pouring into the kitchen, shivering, searching for coffee, laughing and making a big noise. The stereo started up in earnest in the bar and the party was on again.

'I hear music,' Tania said. 'Would you like to dance?'

'If you promise not to notice I've got seven feet on the end of each leg.'

'Don't worry, there'll be no room to move in there. It's more a matter of keeping warm.'

We went through and deposited our coats in the cloakroom and took the floor. The instant she started dancing an incredible transformation took place in her; she became liquid, sensuous grace, flowing and undulating with lazy rhythm, hypnotic and magical. At once she became the centre of attraction, though unwittingly. Couples all around us stopped dancing and watched, captivated by her animal litheness, the sexy undulation of her wonderful body. My own movement slowed to no more than a gesture, because I felt I had no place in the arena. I melted into the crowd around me, more than content to watch.

She danced for no more than a minute, aware, of course, of what was happening and the exhibition she was giving and yet her performance was in no way exhibitionism; it was simply a spontaneous theatrical moment that was exciting, and fun and right. Then she threw up her arms and laughed. The crowd applauded and whistled and it was over. She smiled at me and held out her arms for me to join her, saying, 'I'm sorry, that was a bit wicked but it just sort of happened.'

'Aw, don't apologise, please. It was gorgeous. I feel very honoured dancing with you.'

'You underestimate yourself," she said, watching me. 'You move well. Come on, we're not here for dancing lessons or exhibitions, we're here for fun.' And she put her arms round me and slid into close contact, stopping my breath with the warmth of her body.

We danced maybe three or four numbers before finally breaking away. I don't know how many . . . how should *I* know how many? I wasn't listening to the music. I was listening to my thumping heart, wondering if she could feel it through her almost non-existent dress. And I was thinking about her body in my hands and pressed against mine. And I was thinking about her cheek against mine and the smell of her perfume in my head. And I was thinking about how I was being turned on like I'd never been turned on before and what a damn great shame we couldn't go on dancing like this all night . . . and all next day . . . and all that night . . .

'Thank you,' she said, smiling, breaking away.

'And thank you,' I said, wiping my face with my hanky. 'Phew, I'm warm now.'

'Me, too.'

And I'm trembling, too, I wanted to say. I'm shaking like a damn jelly because you've turned me inside and upside down and I fancy you something awful. But I didn't say those things. I just looked at her and smiled and she smiled back at me and then I knew I didn't have to tell her all those things. Because she knew.

NINE

My mood from then on varied according to whether, at the time, Tania was in my sight or out of it. We danced some more and I was treading clouds, then she danced with some big punk actor and I stood at the bar seething, not for a moment listening to a tall, long-haired bloke going on about filming in Antarctica, then she came back and the sun came out again, they she disappeared for a quarter of an hour and I was close to suicide.

During this time I encountered Albert, or rather he encountered me. I felt a thump on the shoulder and turned to find him.

' 'ow ya doin', wack? Gorra drink?'

'Yes, thanks, Albert. All the business finished for the night?'

He pulled a face. 'It's never bluddy finished. I've, er just seen Tania. You're doin' orlright, aren't ya?'

I shrugged despairingly. 'I don't know, Albert.'

'Well, ya shud do. She says she likes ya.'

'She did?'

'Yeh ... says you're ... you're ...' his face crumpled in a frown, 'wot the 'eck was it ... sim ... simp, somethin'.'

'Simple?'

'Nah,' he laughed. 'Nah, simpat, somethin'.'

'Sympatico!'

'Yeh, that's it. What's it mean?'

I grinned. 'It's the very best, Albert. For a girl like her it's the essence of life.'

'Ya wha'?'

I laughed, on top of the world. 'Can't explain, but it's not bad news.'

'Oh ... well, that's orlright. I gotta go, see ya around. Don' do anything' I'd do, you'll get arrested. Tarra.'

I stood there, gazing round the crowd, not seeing them, only hearing what Albert had said. Then Tony was suddenly passing me and waving frantically, snapping me out of my trance. He appeared to have landed a tall, glam-looking red-head with dreamy eyes and a figure that left no doubt in anyone's mind as to her sex or her capacity for it. He gave me a hell of a wink that confirmed my suspicions and I reckoned there and then I wouldn't be travelling back to town in the Jaguar.

I'd spotted Patrick a couple of times in the past two hours and he'd been looking quite delighted with a nice little bird with long black hair, big green eyes and a bosom that would've supported a tray of cups. But I didn't get a chance to have a word with him until I entered the gents shortly after Albert left me.

Patrick, eyes down, zipping his flies, bumped into me as I went in. 'Oh, sorry,' he muttered, without looking up.

'Goddam clumsy Irishmen!'

He glanced up, puzzled by the abuse. 'Russell ...! By the saints, I've missed yuh. The evening has been an event of utter misery without yuh.'

'Same for me, you lying swine. Hey, you're doing all right. See, I told you my training over the past nine months would pay off, didn't I?'

'Isn't she somethin'? She's from Cork, Russell—Irish as Mick's shallelah and as hot as a curry butty. Aw, the agony of it. I had to come in here for a bit of a rest, she's knocking corners off me.'

'You'll, er, be finding your own way home, no doubt?'

His eyes twinkled. 'If I don't make it by dawn, tell them to lock up and go to sleep—though by the looks o' things, you'll not be disturbin' any hotel sheets yourself tonight.'

I grinned. 'I don't know. She lives on the river near Chertsey. It'll be a long drive from there back to town. I may be forced to accept temporary accommodation for the balance of the night and who am I kidding? I'll be lucky to shake her hand good-night.'

He looked aghast. 'Why so? Sure, she would be sayin' that herself—*the* Russ Tobin ... trained by *THE* Patrick Holmes ... my cup runneth over. How can a girl land so much luck.'

'Patrick, your undying faith is heartening, but tonight I'm a man of modest expectation. However, I'll see you when I see you and whatever happens I'll be at the airport Wednesday to see you off.'

'If I *get* off on Wednesday, Russell. My little dumpling's got a few days off next week and is nipping over to Paris for a break. I may just be nipping over there meself—y'know, to help her on with her French.'

'And off with everything else. Well, bonne fortune, son, and keep a stiff upper lip.'

'Funny you should say that,' he said with a wave, walking away in peculiar, straight-legged fashion.

When I got back to the bar, Tania was talking to Albert. As I approached them, he said to me, ' 'ey, Russ, talk to this naughty gerl, will ya, she sez she's goin' 'ome!'

My heart sank. '*Are* you! But it's only early . . . well, it's only just after two.'

'I need sleep, Russ, really. I've been rehearsing all day and we've got heavy rehearsals all next week.'

'Sure, I understand.'

'Oh, 'scuse me,' said Albert, looking across the room. 'Mickey wants me body. Don' go widout sayin' goodbye, now.'

As he left us, I said, 'How did you get here?'

'By car.'

'Your own?'

'Oh, yes. I never rely on lifts to a party. Too many plans go awry.'

'Yes, I know,' I smiled.

'Oh, has it happened to you?'

'Sort of, but I was prepared. I was going to get a mini-cab back to town.'

She looked at me closely, smiling with her eyes. ' "*Was* going to"?'

'Mm. I'd . . . I'd like to take you home—in *your* car.'

She laughed. 'Well, it's novel.'

'May I?'

She gave a little pause then nodded. 'Mm, mm.'

'Would you like one more dance?'

She shook her head. 'No, thanks . . . I think I've done enough for one day.'

'I'm sure you have. I'll go and get the coats.'

We said goodbye to Albert. 'Well, tarra,' he said, 'an' lissen, Russ, give us a ring any time ya fancy a game of snooker, eh? 'ere . . .' he fished a card out of his back pocket and handed it to me. 'Dat's me private number. Don' spread it around 'cos the bluddy birds give me no peace, y'know. Bur any time . . .'

'Thanks, Albert, and thanks for a great party.'

He shook hands with me and pecked Tania on the cheek and we made our way through the crowd to the front door. As we crossed the courtyard to her car, she said, 'I'm sure it's too early for you. Wouldn't you rather . . .'

'No, I wouldn't,' I answered quickly.

'Mm, a man of quick decision,' she laughed. 'There are plenty of girls there . . .'

'Were there?'

'. . . who will be staying most of the night . . .'

'Will they?'

'Mm, I can see there's no reasoning with you.'

'None at all.'

We reached the car. It was a gleaming white Lotus Europa, very low, very fast, an exciting car for an exciting girl, exactly right. We squeezed into it and the first thing she did was release the cloak fastening and throw it from her shoulders, then with a confident deftness I fully expected from her she started the car, flicked on the lights, heater and stereo tape machine and zoomed out of the car park, taking a gravel drive that led to the rear of the house.

'Ah, so this is how you get in without being lynched,' I said. 'We ran into trouble with a crowd of fans out front. They bruised the Jaguar I came in pretty badly.'

'Oh, did you hear about the Rolls Royce convertible! she said, aghast. 'It belonged to those three American businessmen who were with Mickey and Albert at the barbecue. They almost ripped the top off.'

I groaned. 'Oh, my God, they must have been right behind us. The mad animals left us to attack them. That's terrible. I tell you, we were very frightened. We thought they were going to tip the Jag over.'

'It's madness,' she said, shaking her head. 'You just can't believe that young kids can do such damage. You know, a man I know started a car-hire firm a couple of years ago. He was an ex-actor and was able to get some good contacts through the business. He bought four Rolls Royces and landed some marvellous contracts with the pop people, you know, driving stars like Albert to their theatres, particularly visiting American stars. He was out of business within six months. The fans did eight thousand pounds worth of damage in one month alone. Can you understand the mentality of a fifteen-year-old girl who runs a screwdriver down the bodywork as the car drives off?'

'I can from what I saw tonight. How have you made out—have they inflicted any damage on you?'

She gave me a wry smile. 'Not to my car. My punishment comes in a different form—filthy letters and telephone calls.'

'Really! What do they say?'

'Oh,' she shrugged, 'the obvious things . . . what they'd like to do to me in bed. One perverted soul sends me regular drawings of me and him in the weirdest positions. It's a shame he wastes his talents on that stuff, he's really a very good artist.'

'And you should know, hm?'

She smiled and kicked in the clutch, doubling down for a corner with the slickness of a racing driver. Out of The Park and on to the main road we went ... brooom ... brooom ... brooooom! and every time she hit that clutch I got an eyeful of that naked thigh, in ... out ... in ... out, sleek as a velvet piston.

It was on the Chertsey by-pass, after she'd changed gear about forty times, when she said matter-of-factly, 'Do you like them?'

'Mm, do I like what, Tania?'

'My legs.'

'I ...' I laughed, embarrassed at being caught out. 'Sorry, I didn't mean to stare.'

'Yes, you did.'

'Yes, I did,' I nodded. 'You've got fabulous legs and I did mean to stare at them. That the most incredible dress ... I mean—wow!'

'It disturbs you?'

'Well, not so much *it* as what's in it. You.'

She smiled. 'Do I disturb you?'

'You know you do.'

'Why—how?'

'Well, you just *do.* It's just you—everything about you—your looks, your body ... your style ... the way you move. You've ... you've had my heart beating like a drum since I stood by you at the bar.'

'I know, I felt it when we were dancing.'

'I'm not surprised. It's doing it now.'

'Why now? Is it the dress ... I mean my legs?'

'Well ... yes, but not only that. It's you—in the car with me ... it's ... it's incredible this chemistry business, isn't it? How is it that with all those girls there tonight only you turned me on?'

She glanced at me, smiling, enjoying herself. 'I can't answer that—anymore than I can tell you why you turned me on with all those other men there.'

'I did?' I gulped.

'You do, Why d'you think you're here in the car?'

I grinned. 'Sure. Well, why, d'you think?'

'Oh . . . I think it started when you helped Albert out. I began to look at you then and the more I looked the more I liked. Then, of course, you did your Sir Galahad bit down by the barbecue . . . well, a girl's *got* to be impressed by a man who's ready to fight for her. Then . . . the way you talked to me in the kitchen . . . it was nice, relaxed . . . you're a very easy person to be with, you know.'

'So are you,' I said.

'Others wouldn't say so. I can be a bit of an ogre when it's called for. With ninety per cent of the men in showbiz on the make one learns to be forthright or succumb. I didn't feel the need with you. Even when we were dancing. That's when it usually happens. Their greasy little hands start to wander . . .'

'I, er, I must admit the temptation was there. I mean, with a dress like that . . .'

'Oh, I knew what you were thinking, of course.'

'You did?'

'Of course,' she smiled. 'Just as I know what you're thinking now.'

I swallowed hard. 'You do?'

'Hm, hm, naturally. You want to go to bed with me.'

The blood rushed to my face. Boy, talk about straight from the shoulder.

'Well?' she said, teasing me. 'Don't you?'

'Well, yes, I do . . .'

'But? There's something else?'

'Well, yes, there's a lot else. I mean, I *like* you . . . I want to talk to you . . .'

'Do you? Before or after you make love to me?'

'I . . . wow!' I laughed.

'Do I embarrass you? Are you shy?'

'Well, no . . . not exactly, but . . .'

'Do you mind talking about it?'

I laughed again. 'No . . . it's just, well, it came as a bit of a surprise.'

'I wonder why it should.'

'It's all right,' I said, 'I'm settled now—fire away. No, I'll answer your question. I want to talk to you both before and after.'

'And tomorrow morning? How will you feel then?'

'I shall want to talk tomorrow morning, too.'

'You sound pretty sure. How can you be sure you won't want to flee at the first light of dawn?'

'Because I have never flown at the first light of dawn. If I felt it was likely, I wouldn't go to bed with the girl in the first place.'

She nodded approvingly. 'Well, now, that's refreshingly different.'

'Well, it's the way I'm made, Tania. Sex is only dirty when it's selfish, a quick release with no affection. That's whoring and I've never whored.'

'You've never been with a prostitute?'

'No, never.'

'You've never had a girl because you fancy her purely physically?'

'No. There's always been fun . . . and respect. Or at very least she's had as much out of it as I've had—maybe more. Hey, does that sound twee? Don't tell the fellas I said so. It's supposed to be the manly thing to lay anything we can get our hands on, isn't it? Numbers being everything?'

'Don't ask a woman for an opinion on that. Well, if that's supposed to be manly, how come *you're* doing so well?' She glanced at me, her amber eyes hooded, lazy, yet excited. 'I know why you do so well.'

I could hardly speak for the constriction in my throat. 'Oh, why?'

She didn't answer. She turned her eyes to the road, smiling, nodding slightly and said quietly, 'We'll see.'

Her hands were gripping the wheel harder than they ought, considering what a damn good driver she was.

In a while she pulled off the dual carriageway and turned into a narrow, winding, flat-cobbled street of tiny white cottages, a few shops and an ancient pub. In the lights of the car, brass doorknockers and ships' lanterns gleamed and the white paint sparkled. There was a wondrous, peaceful, settled, ancient, almost villagey atmosphere to the street, so close-to yet a world away from the thundering traffic of the highway.

As we drove slowly along the little street, I said, 'Oh, boy ... this is beautiful. How ever did you find an oasis like this?'

'I looked for it.'

'Yes, of course you did. This must be old Chertsey.'

'Old old. It's heaven.'

'Mm ... I can almost smell tarred rope and hear the slap of the water.'

'Well, I can't promise you tarred rope, but there's plenty of slapping water. Here we are, over the shop.'

We drew up outside a ships' chandlers, a two-storey building faced with white-painted ship-lap timber, its framework crooked with age. I glanced up. Only one window was visible, a bow window that protruded just a few inches over the narrow pavement. Elegant and very beautiful, the architecture of a sadly bygone age.

We got out and I followed Tania down an alley at the side of the shop. At the end we came upon the river and its cindered towpath. At the rear of the shop we climbed wooden stairs and stood for a moment on the platform outside her door, looking at the river. It was black with night yet sprinkled with the reflection of the lights on the distant highway, and it was deserted, though dozens of motor boats and cabin cruisers, canvas-covered for the winter, lay moored along both banks, fast asleep.

'In the summer it is very beautiful, very colourful,' she said, as though apologising for its appearance.

'Yes, I know. I used to come down here quite a lot to a riverside pub in Egham. It was so close to the water you could sit on the wall and paddle—if you were given to that sort of thing.'

After a tiny pause she said. 'I'm glad you like the river,' then she turned and opened the door with a key.

She reached for a switch just inside the door and bathed the room in warm lighting. I felt at home instantly. It was a painter's room, colourful, full of texture. The brick walls were painted white and hung with a dozen paintings. There was an easel by the window holding a half-finished canvas of the river, and against the wall there were stacked a score of canvases. There was a fireplace and a glowing coke fire in the centre of one wall, and placed around the fire—a big brown couch, a couple of deep armchairs and a low table. These were set on a white sheepskin rug which half-covered the polished wood floor, the colour of chestnuts.

'Come in,' she said, leading the way. 'And welcome to my soul. This room is me. Not too many people come here.'

'I'm honoured.'

She turned, smiling, removing her cloak. 'Give me your coat. Would you like a drink?'

'Mm, if you would.'

'A small one—with coffee. Are you hungry?'

I thought about it. 'Hey, yes, I am. We didn't get around to eating at Albert's, did we?'

'What would you like?'

'Tempt me.'

'Well ... I can give you some fabulous ravioli—from a fabulous tin ... and hot buttered toast ...'

'Say no more, that's it exactly.'

'Then come into the kitchen—you can do the toast.'

On the way through she stopped at a stereo set and put on some quiet piano. The kitchen was small and neat. She got some drinks then worked around the stove while I cut the bread and filled the kettle. In a few moments the bread was under the grill, the ravioli was warming in a pan and the kettle was humming.

'There,' she said, handing me a vodka, 'see what a little teamwork can accomplish.' She raised her glass. 'Here's to ... to what? Here's to love.'

'O.K., to love ... but love of what?'

'Oh ... everything—life, colour, people, warmth ... to love of love.'

She was standing very close. I leaned towards her, watching her eyes watching me, and with eyes open placed a kiss softly on her mouth, and stayed there, sensing her lips.

'I like that,' she said, barely removing her lips. 'That's nice.'

'Mm.'

'Is it nice for you?'

'It's lovely for me. You have a wonderful mouth ... soft and warm.'

'Don't you think it's too big?'

'No, I don't. It's perfect.'

'Thank you. Russ ...?'

'Mm?'

'I've . . . I've got something to tell you . . .'

My heart tumbled. 'Oh?'

'You're . . . not going to like it.'

'Oh? What is it?'

'Your toast is burning.'

'Oh, hell . . .!'

I sprang for the grill as the black smoke began to rise, saving it in time. Tania, laughing at me, ladled the ravioli on to plates as I buttered the toast and made the coffee. Then we took it into the back room and sat on the rug on either side of the low table in front of the fire.

'How's the ravioli?' she asked.

'Superb. You're a wonderful cook. Is there *nothing* you can't do . . . hey, you know, you should sit right there, all the time. The fire light does incredible things for you. You look as though you were moulded in copper.'

'Sounds nice. I'd like to paint that.'

'You paint a lot, don't you. I'd like to see some of them.'

'Mm, you can if you want.'

'How long have you been doing it?'

She laughed, 'Since I was born. My mother is very talented. She brought me up with a brush in my hand. Have you ever painted, Russ?'

'Of course! Let me see, now, I once painted a cycle shed for my mother . . . well, she didn't actually commission the job. I was four at the time. Then at six I painted the kitchen windows . . . not the frames, the windows.'

She laughed and reached for the coffee pot. 'But nothing serious?'

'Oh, I was deadly serious. No, nothing serious. Do you have any favourite painters?'

'Lots of them. Perhaps I'm a little biased but I like the French painters—Lautrec, Braque, Matisse, Modigliani . . . oh, all of them. Do you know anything about the French painters?'

'But of course!' I said, beginning now to feel the soporific effect of the hour, the meal, the fire and the vodka. 'Ask me anything you like.'

'All right,' she laughed, 'an easy one for a start. Who came first—Ingres or Braque?'

'Oh, please, not so easy. Braque, of course.'

'Ooh, almost right. I'm afraid it was Ingres—but only by a hundred years—you were very close.'

'Well, one can't know absolutely everything. Go on, ask me another.'

'Er ... who said "A painter paints to unload himself of feelings and visions" and "People who try to explain pictures are usually barking up the wrong tree"?'

'Er ... you?'

She laughed, wrinkling her nose. 'No, it was that other genius, Picasso. Again you were very close.'

'Do you agree with him? Do *you* paint to unload yourself of feelings and visions?'

'Yes, I suppose I do, though I've never stopped to analyse why I paint. I just do it because I love it.'

'I'd like to see them.'

'What ... now?'

'Mm, sure.'

'All right.'

We left the fire and went to the end of the room. She removed the canvas from the easel and one by one lifted those stacked against the wall on to it. They were very, very good. Her paintings—of the river, of Kingston market place, of London—were bold, colourful works, free and confident. One of them was breathtaking—an action study of the Wildcats in performance at a T.V. studio. All the zip and sexy freedom of the girls was captured there, all the colour and noise and excitement of the studio.

'Oh, what a talent,' I said, shaking my head. 'That is wonderful. Just look as you go, there, moving like a tiger. You remind me of one ... you have the eyes of a tiger. You paint as you dance, don't you—with style and passion. You're a very passionate woman.'

She removed the canvas, smiling to herself. 'Yes, I am. The French are passionate people ...' She placed the canvas against the wall and turned to me, looking at me, calmly, softly. 'I want to go to bed, Russ.'

I nodded, smiling at her, and she turned and walked down the room to turn off the stereo and the lights.

We entered a passageway. She indicated a door on the left.

'I won't be long,' she said, and went on to the bathroom as I entered the bedroom.

Her bedroom was, like the lounge, strong and interesting, nothing fluffy, flouncy, frilly. A turquoise and white woven counterpaine covered the double bed and a white carpet warmed the floor. There was a built-in wardrobe on one wall and a dressing table beneath the curtained window. That was all, apart from the many paintings on the other walls, the dominant one being a large print of Gauguin's *Tahitian Mountains* above the bed.

I took my clothes off and lay on the bed, looking at the paintings by the dim light of a small orange-shaded bedside lamp. I was involved in an upside down study of Gauguin and didn't hear the Tiger enter. When I looked towards the door the sight of her standing in the doorway gave me a start, not only because I hadn't heard her arrive but also because she was completely naked.

I stared at her, my heart pounding, and she looked at me, as I sensed she'd been doing for some moments, then she walked into the room and stood at the foot of the bed, very relaxed, completely unselfconscious, smiling slightly, inviting me to look at her. Her body was perfect, slender and lithe, her breasts small but full and firm with large brown nipples that were erect with excitement. It was a beautiful body and she was proud of it.

'What do you see?' she asked, watching my inspection, without a trace of embarrassment.

'I see a very lovely woman. I believe Gauguin would have loved to paint you, just as you are, now, in this light. It would take someone like him to do you justice. You know, skin is often compared to satin but it probably rarely is—except in your case. Yours looks exactly like it.'

'You're . . . in no hurry, are you?'

'No.'

'I knew you wouldn't be. I knew from the way you've behaved all evening . . . from the things you said in the car. I knew it would be good.'

She came around the bed and lay down beside me, on her back, not touching me, her hands behind her head, lifting her breasts high. 'Funny,' she smiled, looking at the ceiling, 'how one can feel so comfortable . . . so uninhibited with a certain person. I feel I've known you all my life.'

'Me, too. I can be quite shy at times, believe it or not.'

She nodded. 'I believe you. So can I.' She turned her head and looked at me, wanting to be kissed. I leaned towards her and did it gently, hearing her quick intake of breath. She made to remove her hands from behind her head but I said, 'No ... stay like that ... relax.'

She fell back against the pillow, breathing erratically, chest heaving. 'What are you going to do?' she laughed.

'You worried?'

'No ...'

I started with the lightest touch of my finger on the inside of her thigh, down by the knee. She gave a start and a quick, fleeting smile. 'Hey ...'

'Ssh, relax. Just lie there and enjoy it.'

'I can't, it tickles.'

'How about here?' I had reached mid-thigh, travelling up very slowly, very gently.

'Mm ... that's nice.'

'Close your eyes and concentrate.'

She did so, then flinched as my finger skirted her heart-shape of black, curly hair and ran up over the flat plane of her stomach. She smiled as I circled her small, neat navel and drew in a quick breath as I travelled up to her left breast, skirting it, round and round, closing in on her nipple but not touching it ... then she relaxed as I moved on, down along one arm to her finger tips and up again to her neck ... her ear ... she chuckled and squirmed ... 'Hey ...!'

'Relax.'

'How *can* I!?'

Down again to her breast, watching the change in her expression, her mood as this time I gently caught her nipple between thumb and forefinger and squeezed. Her eyes flew open. 'Hey ...' Her eyes closed again and she rolled her head on the pillow. 'Oh, my God, that's wonderful ... oh, that's beautiful ...'

Her breathing was passionately erratic. Her body was tensed, braced. She began to writhe, eyes still closed, her face contorted in a frown, mouth open, almost snarling. 'Oh, my God ...' she breathed.

Now I released her breast and took it in my mouth, transferring my hand to her other breast. She gasped and her eyes flew open. 'Russ . . . !'

Her hand came behind my head, holding me firmly to her as she tossed and writhed, her legs now parting in need, hips rising from the bed. 'Russ . . . !' she whispered. 'Russ . . . I'm coming . . . oh, my God, I'm coming . . . ! OHHH! OHHH!' She jerked violently, crushing my face to her breast, and brought her knees up tight to her stomach. 'Ohhhh . . . ohhhh' she groaned, holding hard, stroking my head, panting for breath. Slowly she calmed and released the pressure on my head, raising my face to look at me, still panting and moistening her lips, shaking her head. 'My God . . . I don't believe it.'

I grinned at her. 'What don't you believe?'

'That . . . ! It . . . ! You . . . ! You . . . didn't even touch me!'

'No.'

'It's never happened before—nothing . . . like that.' She smiled, still shaking her head in wonderment, then gave a laugh, 'Now, that . . . is what I *call* a turn-on.'

'*I*'d call it compatability—incredible chemistry.'

'You . . . you don't sound too surprised it happened.'

'No. You're a very sensuous and sensitive woman . . .'

She gave an amused laugh. 'I'm sensitive all right. You've done funny things to me. I feel all floaty. You know, you may be the answer to the drug and alcohol problem—with you, who needs them!'

She lay still for a while, eyes closed, her breathing returning to normal, a curve of pleasure on her lips. Then she murmured, 'I knew, you know . . . I knew something like that would happen. I knew it in the car. That's what I meant when I said I knew why you did so well.'

'Why?'

'Because you care about the girl. You care about me.'

'Yes, I do.'

I reached for her and began again, slowly, with all the time in the world.

She groaned softly and shifted her legs. 'If you do that it will happen again.'

'I hope so. And maybe again after that.'

'Don't you mind? I'm doing nothing for *you*.'

'Yes, you are. It gives me pleasure to please you.'

She smiled and shook her head. 'Incredible . . .'

'What is?'

'I've actually met an unselfish man.'

'The Freudians would dispute that. They claim there's no such thing as unselfishness. They'd say I am selfishly enjoying giving you pleasure.'

'Then they're sad people. A selfish man couldn't wait to get inside a woman and have his orgasm. What you're doing is for me.'

'Yes.'

'I appreciate it . . . oh, that's beautiful. Russ . . . it's going to happen again, I can feel it. It's there. Do you . . . think there's any limit?'

I laughed. 'I think exhaustion would take over eventually.'

'When, though—after how many?'

'That would depend on the woman's stamina.'

She chuckled. 'I've got a lot of stamina.'

'Mm, so I imagined.'

'Russ . . .?'

'Mm?'

'Can you spend the day with me?'

'Yes, I can.'

'Will you?'

'Yes, I will. What would you like to do?'

She smiled. 'Ask me when we wake up.'

'All right.'

'It . . . may be very late . . . because in a moment *I'm* going to start being Freudianly selfish . . . ohhh! . . . I'm going to . . . oh, my God . . . ohhh! . . . Russ . . .!'

'What . . .?'

'It's . . . OHHH!'

And so the loving night began.

TEN

I awoke cocooned in the scent of her body, her warmth in my arms. I felt wonderful, quite restored, although my watch, which said ten o'clock, reminded me I'd had less than five hours sleep. It was five o'clock before Tania, with a disbelieving shake of her head, had said, 'Don't you think we've had enough? I've got a feeling we're about to cross the boundary of plenty into the territory of greed.'

I'd laughed at her droopy-eyed portrayal of exhaustion. 'It's up to you.'

'In that case,' she'd said, collapsing into my arm, 'we've had enough.'

We didn't sleep immediately; she nestled close and talked.

'I don't believe it, even though it's happened,' she'd said. 'I've never known anything like this. I wonder if people know it can be so good? I can't believe anybody else has ever enjoyed it so much. You know there are women who never enjoy it at all?'

'So I've read.'

'Woman who have had children and never had an orgasm. I think it's very sad. What do they feel when they get into bed with their husbands? Weariness ... resignation ... dutiful ...? Perhaps even revulsion. I wonder how many rush to get into bed first and pretend to be asleep when he climbs in and starts "messing about" as they call it. And if they can't pretend, what do they do? Take a deep breath and open their legs and think about the next day's shopping, the washing, the kids ... isn't it sad? ... hoping he'll be quick and roll over and go to sleep, leaving her sticky and totally unsatisfied.'

'It goes beyond sadness, Tiger, it's a sinful waste. It can be so very much more than just physical release.'

'As we've just proved,' she'd said, snuggling even closer. 'I love your body. It's warm and clean and hard.'

'And I yours. I could eat yuh.'

'What d'you mean "could", she chuckled. You did. I loved it.'

'You're a sexpot.'

'Mm mm,' she agreed. 'And look who's talking. I guess we turn each other on, hm?'

'Ha! The understatement of the century. And if you don't stop doing that . . .'

'You couldn't . . .! Not again . . .'

'Tiger, I don't believe you even begin to realize your powers. You're a living breathing match to my touchpaper . . . Tiger . . . we've *got* to get some sleep . . .'

'All right,' she said, kissing me, 'we sleep . . . and see what the morning brings.'

Then she'd turned to snuggle backwards into me and hadn't moved all night.

Now, on Sunday morning, I lay looking at her, looking closely at the texture of her satin shoulder, the soft curl of her hair. A beautiful sleeping animal, breathing gently and rhythmically, totally relaxed. Curious, I thought, how people meet and attract and love and part. I had lived so many years without knowledge of this girl, she without knowledge of me. Then . . . woomf. A word, a smile . . . and the magic begins. Now I was sharing her bed, her body, her mind, living and loving a few days with a spirit so kindred she gave me joy just looking at her.

In that moment I felt so warm towards her I hugged her close, my hand on her breast, and kissed her shoulder, her neck. She moved in sleep, straightened her legs, and pressed my hand that held her breast. I felt her wake. She stopped breathing for a moment, then relaxed, releasing the breath.

'Good morning,' I murmured.

She smiled. 'G'morning.' Her voice was sleepy, lazy. 'Who are you?'

'I'm the man from Slap 'n Tickle. I've come for your order. How much today?'

'Don' want any today,' she murmured into her pillow. 'Had a fellow round yesterday—he left me a month's supply. Come back at Christmas.'

'How are you fixed for coffee? Would you settle for coffee?'

She turned her head quickly. 'You wouldn't!'

'I would.'

'In bed!'

'Or a cup, whichever you prefer.'

She rolled over on me, flattening me, and kissed me. 'Oh, what a find. What else do you do?'

'I cook the most incredible bacon and eggs.'

'Ah, now, come on ...'

'True, so help me.'

'Nobody can be that perfect. You'll have to prove it, y'know.'

I shrugged. 'O.K., so I just suckered myself into making breakfast.'

'I'll help, I promise. I'll ... I'll make the marmalade ...'

'Gee, thanks. No, all you're required to do is sit there and look beautiful ... which you do ... right now ... very beautiful ... up there.'

'So do you, down there.'

'I need a shave. I'm spiky.'

'I love you spiky. It's butch.'

'If you don't remove your lovely body this instant, there'll be no coffee ... and no breakfast ... and maybe no lunch ...'

She laughed and rolled off me. 'Hurry ... I need it badly. The *coffee* ...!'

I skipped out of bed and went to the chair where I'd put my clothes.

'Hey!'

I looked at her. She was peeping over the sheet, inspecting me with blatant candour.

'Mm?' I asked.

'Nothing. I just wanted to make sure he wasn't just a gorgeous dream.'

'Satisfied?'

Her eyes crinkled in a wicked smile above the sheet. 'Hurry back, hm?'

'Yes'm.'

We sat up in bed drinking the coffee.

'What's it like out?' she asked.

'It's beautiful—brilliant sunshine. Probably very cold.'

'My favourite days. The river is wonderful on a sparkly day. We'll take a walk along the towpath, if you like. There's a pub about a mile along.'

'I'd like it. Do you like Sundays? What do you normally do on Sundays?'

She shrugged. 'I walk ... and look ... and paint. I usually paint in the afternoons.'

'You can paint this afternoon if you want to. I'd like to watch. Or I'll read or something.'

'We'll see. This has the makings of a nice floppy, play-it-by-ear day, I think. I want us to do whatever comes to mind ... and you can get that look off your face for a start. We're going out *some*time today ...'

'I ...' I protested.

'I know exactly what you were thinking, Tobin. We need fresh air. We're not going to lie in this disgusting environment all day.'

'Yes'm ... whatever you say 'm.'

She finished her coffee and put the cup on the bedside table, then slid down in the bed, stretching luxuriously. 'Oh, this is *gor*geous. How I love Sunday mornings ... no alarm clock ... no dashing to rehearsals ... it's beautiful ... beautiful ... beautiful ...'

I finished my coffee and slid down beside her, on my back. 'You work very hard, don't you?'

'Hm mm,' she nodded. 'You've got to if you want to be the best, no matter what you do.'

'And you Wildcats are the best. I think you're wonderful. I admire hard work and talent ... hey, what're you doing?'

'I'm lying here playing with you.'

'So I see.'

'You're all warm and gorgeous ... heaven, it doesn't take you long, does it?'

'Well, what d'you expect when you do that. You're getting randy.'

'I've got. I always do when I lie late in bed.'

'I thought it was supposed to be the fellas that got randy.'

'Huh! Why should you have all the fun?' She turned into me, burrowing her nose into my neck. 'You like that?' she murmured.

'It's wonderful.'

'I want you.'

'Do you?'

'Mm, right now ... quickly.'

It was well after noon before we made the door. We stood on the platform of the stairs, me in my overcoat, Tiger—appropri-

people are mostly a sailing crowd, healthy and hearty, but despite that, very nice. It's one of the few places I can go without being pestered.'

'Pestered—how? You mean autographs?'

'Yes ... and a lot worse. The boys can get a bit naughty at times.'

'The price of fame.'

'Do you suffer from it?'

I looked at her, and laughed, surprised, 'Me! God, I'm not famous.'

'Yes, you are. I knew your face as soon as you came into the hall.'

'Oh, my face ...'

'Do you realize you're seen on tele far more often than I am? You're as well known as Wilson and Heath.'

'Oh, go on ... good Lord, I suppose I am. Hey, ma, I'm famous!'

'You mustn't be so self-disparaging. They're very good commercials.'

I smiled. 'Well, thanks, but they *are* only commercials. Compared to what you do ... perhaps if I starred in Captain Marvel instead of White Marvel ...'

'A job is a job,' she said. 'And I'm not too sure some of the commercials aren't more entertaining than some of our shows.'

We mounted the steps that led up from the towpath to a patio set out with wrought-iron tables and chairs, all of which were occupied by young people in sweaters and slacks, the Thames jet set. There were several calls of 'Hi, Tania!' which she acknowledged with a wave, and the eyes of every male followed us to the open door of the saloon bar.

The bar was crowded, noisy and smokey. As we pushed through, several more people recognized her and called a greeting, and a great many eyes were on me, the fella with her, wondering, speculating.

We squeezed through to the bar. Beside me stood a tall, portly colonel-type in a navy blue seaman's sweater. Tiger glanced at him and squeezed my hand, telling me to get a look when I could. He was beautiful, so typically ex-Raj, sparse white hair, a bulbous, almost puce nose, pink scrubbed complexion.

As we waited to be served, he began to hum, a nondescript

tune, in deep, rumbling bass ... oom ... poom ... poom poom poom ... pooom ... then turned to look at me ... then at Tania. He smiled, rather severely.

'Good morning to you, sir ... and to you, miss,' he rumbled. 'A wonderful morning.'

'Wonderful,' I said.

'Are you boating, sir?' he enquired, very much aware of his fine, resonant voice, his immaculate diction.

'No, sir, just strolling. Are you boating?'

'No, sir, I'm painting—at least, not at this precise moment. At this moment I am drinking ...' and to prove it he raised his silver tankard and downed the remainder of the pint, then wiped his bushy grey moustache with deft flicks of his hand.

'What have you been painting?' I asked, aware that Tania was studying him intently though inconspicuously. 'Your boat?'

He laughed, shaking the glasses on the bar. 'No ... my wife's bedroom. Bit of a disaster, really. You see, I started two months ago by painting my study—nothing too elaborate, just a lick of emulsion to brighten it up ... but then I discovered it was showing the hall up in very bad light, so I painted the hall. Now, blast it, I find the hall is showing my wife's bedroom in bad light, so I'm having to paint that. In short, sir, I'm painting the entire blasted house. I say, would you care for a drink, I'm just about to order the other half, then I must go. The wife's got a handsome piece of pork in the oven ...'

'Well, that's very kind of you. I was about to order one for my ladyfriend and myself ...'

He turned to Tania and studied her, embracing her with a smile. 'May I say, m'am, that beauty such as yours is extremely rare. Truly you put the day to shame.'

Tania smiled delightedly. He ordered drinks for us and when they were served raised his glass and said, 'Now you two must wander off and be by yourselves. I'm an old bore and would not wish to spoil your time together.'

But we didn't wander off. I left it to Tiger and she was obviously enjoying him, his charm, his extravagant manner. And he was no old bore. He kept us entertained, making us laugh with accounts of hilarious pig-sticking sortees in India, talking as though it had happened yesterday instead of forty years ago. And when he finally left—'Heavens, is that the time! The old gel will murder me'—we left with him, parting company on the towpath.

With my arm around Tiger we strolled back towards her flat.

'Wasn't he lovely, the colonel?' I laughed.

'Gorgeous. I felt very sorry for him. What a come-down from the life they led. It doesn't seem right he should be painting his house out, climbing on a chair, waving a brush about. It seems so undignified somehow. I see him on a splendid horse, leading his troops out of the fort, the fierce sun glinting on their brass and the pennants on their lances fluttering in the desert breeze.'

'Aha, a true romantic.'

'All women are romantic—and you must admit it's a prettier sight than an old man in baggy pants painting a ceiling.'

'Infinitely.'

'Anyway, that's the way I shall paint him—in uniform.'

'Yes, I knew why you were in no hurry to leave him. I saw you studying him.'

'He has a wonderful face. In that face was the once great Britain. I *will* paint him.' She cuddled closer. 'It's getting colder. The sun is cold, now. Let's go in, hm, we've had enough fresh air.'

'Anything you say, it's your day. What will you do—paint?'

'Mm,' she demurred. 'Don't know yet. Let's see when we get in.'

Once again inside the warm flat, I stoked up the fire and made coffee, and when I brought it into the lounge the stereo was playing and Tiger was sitting on the rug by the fire.

She looked up at me and said, 'I wish, I wish . . .'

'What do you wish?'

'I wish I could put this day on canvas. I wish I could put you there . . . and the nice things you do and say . . .'

I began to pour the coffee. 'That's very nice.'

'. . . I want you, Russ. Now. I want to hold you in bed, now. And I want to stay in bed all afternoon . . . where it's safe and warm . . . and then later on we'll get up and watch television and have a drink and something to eat . . . and then I'll take you to bed again—to sleep . . . Russ!'

'Mm?'

'The cup is *full!*'

I drew the bedroom curtains against the cold and turned to find her naked. Like a fleet brown deer she plunged between the sheets and drew the bedclothes over her head and rolled herself into a squirming ball. 'Quick, quick!' she squealed, her voice muffled by the blankets. 'I'm freezing to death!'

'Patience, your little hotwater bottle is coming.'

She flung back the clothes. 'My *what* hotwater bottle?'

'Little?'

'Ha!'

As I leapt in beside her she attacked me, fell upon me, wriggling to get closer. 'Ohh, that's better ... oh, that's beautiful ...'

Soon she relaxed and just lay upon me, her breathing subsiding, and gradually the nonsense died. I held her and ran my hands lightly over her silky back, down her spine to her buttocks. She drew a quick breath and flinched, bracing her pelvis against me.

'You know all the little places, don't you?' she murmured. 'All the secret little places.'

'Don't you?'

She nodded, grinning mischievously. 'Mm mm, one or two.' She began to kiss my face, lazily, teasingly, working around my ear, then down to my chest, pecking, tickling, and this time I flinched as she laid a trail of fleeting kisses across my stomach. Then in one smooth sudden retreating movement she disappeared from my sight and I went through the ceiling at the touch of her warm, moist mouth. It was many moments before she raised her head and came up quickly, saying excitedly, breathlessly, 'I *want* you,' and straddled me, gasping, her eyes bright with excitement. After a while, when she was more relaxed, she looked down at me, smiling.

'Hi.'

'Hi,' I laughed.

'You look awfully good down there. Very sexy.'

I raised my hands and traced the perfect contours of her body. 'And you look exquisite. I wish I could put this moment on canvas.'

'I love you.'

'And I love you.'

'For a week we shall love each other—then go our separate ways—but I will remember it all my life.'

'And so will I, Tiger. I don't need a canvas.'

'No, nor do I.' She came down and kissed me, very softly. 'Nor do I.'

ELEVEN

Monday, 7th November.

I only just made Frank Chappell's office on time due to an understandable reluctance to leave Tiger's bed and an equal reluctance on her part to let me go.

'Oh, this is *ter*rible!' she gasped, collapsing against the pillow.

'Awful,' I agreed, fighting for breath

'We can't keep this up—we'll kill ourselves.'

'At least.'

'I'll probably fall down dead at rehearsals this afternoon and there'll be an embarrassing post-mortem diagnosis . . .'

'Too much lovin'.'

'Too much lovin',' she nodded. 'Miss Tania Marechal, lead dancer of the famous Wildcats, collapsed and died today from an over-abundance of love.'

'This unusual expiration . . .' I continued, 'could well be linked with the equally premature demise of Russell Tobin, of White Marvel fame, who was found in a crumpled heap in Oxford Street, his face wreathed in a delighted smile. Post-mortem revealed that Mr. Tobin's heart had recently undergone a strain equal to running up Mount Everest six times carrying a fully grown bullock.'

She laughed and flopped an exhausted arm upon the bed. 'You must go, you're going to be late.'

I nodded. 'I know. It's half past nine. I've got exactly ninety minutes to wash, dress and get to London.'

'So—go!'

'I will . . . I will.'

'That . . . is not going,' she said, removing my hand.

'*Please* kick me out of bed, Tiger.'

'I will . . . any day now. And *I* must go! I've got rehearsal at Elstree.'

'So—go.'

'I will. Everybody out on the count of three—all right? One . . . two . . . three . . .'

'Mm . . . nobody moved.'

'And nobody's likely to while you continue to do *that*!' she said, removing my hand again. 'Russ, we *must* be strong.'

'Ruthless.'

'I'm seeing you tonight, for heaven's sake.'

'An eternity! Hey, what would you like to do tonight.'

Her chuckle was quite obscene.

'Ohhh,' I groaned. 'I must leave for Africa, I must, I must . . . while I still have the strength to climb on the plane.'

'Well, of course, I left it to the very last minute and the mini-cab driver was knocking on the door before I'd got my trousers on.

' 'bye, love,' I said, giving her a kiss. 'See you tonight,' then fell down the steps and into the taxi, waving to her in the window overlooking the street.

I got to Chappell's office with two minutes to spare, badly in need of both sleep and a shave. Chappell saw me on the dot of eleven.

He's a medium tall, middle-aged, quiet-looking man who exudes an air of intelligence and dependability. With his permanent tan, iron grey hair and short grey beard he looks a little out of place in a city office, clad in a dark grey business suit, and much more at home in the bush khaki he wore as a hunter in Africa. There was a photograph of him dressed this way on his office wall, a rifle slung on his shoulder. I was studying it when he came in from the outer office.

'Hello, Russ, nice to see you again. Have a chair. Like some coffee?'

'Love some, Frank,' I said, taking his 'first name' cue.

He pressed a button on his intercom and ordered it. I pointed at a dozen magnificent framed colour photographs, each three feet by two, of wild animals in various poses and moods, that decorated his office walls.

'These are beautiful, Frank. Who took them?'

'I did,' he said, sitting in his chair.

'You mean you've been that close to charging elephant!?'

He laughed. 'A darned sight closer. That brute was a wounded rogue. The ivory poachers had poisoned him with arrows but hadn't finished him off. I went out with two other hunters and took that picture as he swung to attack. A couple of seconds later the poor old fellow was dead—literally at my feet. A bit close for comfort.'

'Wow, the size of him!'

'Yes, he was big all right. I don't think it's generally realized just how enormous and terrifying a full-grown elephant is when you meet him in open bush. A tame, docile elephant in a zoo or a circus is one thing, but to come upon a wild tusker in thorn-bush is quite another. He's as huge as a Chieftain tank and four times as deadly, capable of monstrous damage. Tembo is trouble by the ton.'

'Tembo? Is that the African name for elephant?'

'Yes, Tembo is elephant. Lion, as you probably know, is simba. Leopard is chui, the rhino is faro and the buffalo is mbogo. Those are the animals regarded as the Big Five.'

'Which is the most dangerous, Frank?'

'Well,' he smiled, 'you've just put your finger on the oldest argument in big-game hunting. It quite possibly depends on one's own experience. If you've had the socks shocked off you by a leopard and uneventful experience with the others, naturally you'll plump for the cat. Personally, I'd come down in favour of tembo, there. In terms of murder, malice and mayhem there isn't a creature on God's earth to touch him. If he's peeved with you he'll come after you remorselessly until he's got you. And there's not much chance of escape. If you climb a tree beyond his reach and he can't pull you out with his trunk, then he'll shake the daylights out of you until you fall out. And if that doesn't work he'll whistle up a couple of his pals and push the tree down. From then on it's curtains all the way. If you're very fortunate he'll pick you up and slam you headfirst into a rock straight away, considerably reducing your concern for what he does to you afterwards ...'

I winced and fought a creeping temptation to have second thoughts about Africa.

'If you run for the river and hide in the reeds, he'll tear up a small tree and beat around until he flushes you out ...'

'Oh ... really?'

'And having got you out he might decide to play with you a little. There are several amusing games tembo enjoys. One is to stomp on you with a foot the size of a dog-basket until you resemble a hundredweight of minced beef ...'

I gulped, wishing the coffee would come.

'Another game is to attempt to drive you into the ground like a stake, using his trunk as a pile-driver ...'

Majorca, I remember, was so *safe.*

'Or he may simply decide to roll on you. Great fun, that. You've no idea how six tons of pachyderm can alter a man's appearance.'

Yes, I have ... truly, I have.

There was a tap on the door and a trim brunette in white blouse and tight-fitting navy blue skirt brought in the coffee on a tray. She placed it at Frank's left hand, gave us both a nice smile and departed. She had very good legs.

'How'd you like it?' asked Frank.

'Gorg ... oh, white with two, thanks.'

He grinned as he spooned in the sugar. 'Well, I don't see why one shouldn't surround oneself with beauty as well as efficiency, hm?'

'Totally agree.'

He handed me the coffee and pointed at a cigarette box. 'Help yourself.'

'You obviously have quite a love affair going with Africa,' I smiled, lighting up.

He relaxed in his chair, stirring his coffee, looking around the photographs on the walls, smiling nostalgically. 'Yes, that's true, Russ. There's no place like it on earth. It has changed a lot, of course, since I first went out there thirty years ago. What with so many of its countries getting independence ... jet travel ... a lot more spending money for a lot more people. But there's still a lot of the old savage Africa left. Leave the big cities and towns behind and you don't have to travel too far to tingle with the sense of danger. The bush will always be the bush and the sight of any one of those animals roaming free ... the scream of an elephant ... the rattling roar of a lion at night ... they can still send shivers of fear shooting through you.'

He pointed to one of the photographs. 'There's a sight, Russ, one of the loveliest and most exciting I've ever come across—a herd of twenty elephant swinging through the daum-palms on the bank of a Kenya river. I took that one early morning, just after dawn, with the sun rising and the air as cool and sweet as you'd find in the Scottish Highlands. And that one there . . .' he pointed to an incredibly beautiful photograph of a lone giraffe, standing in low bush, alert and curious, against a backdrop of a soaring snow-capped mountain.

'Kilimanjaro,' he said, with awe and nostalgia softening his voice. 'The snow-covered peak is called Kibo. What a moment that was. A day to take your breath away. I've known countless days like that, but every one was new and different. I can smell it now. There's a wild, exciting earth smell to Africa that no other country or continent has. I'm sure if I was put to sleep and dropped in foreign parts, I could tell when I woke whether or not I was in Africa.'

'You make it sound very exciting, Frank.'

He laughed. 'I only hope I don't bore you. I remember when we met, Harry Onions warned you not to get me going about Africa or we'd be there for a week. I'm afraid I do tend to get carried away. But it's not my intention to influence you one way or the other about this job, Russ. It's entirely up to you. You may not *like* Africa . . .' he grinned and shook his head, 'Y'know, I just cannot imagine anybody not liking Africa. However, if you decide to join us we'll be glad to have you. As I said, Jim Fuller will be moving down to Cape Town in January, so I'd like you to be out there around the first of December—that's what . . .? three weeks from now. How does it fit in with your arrangements?'

I replaced the cup on the desk. 'Not badly, Frank. I'm foot-loose at the moment and would've preferred to fly out in a week's time . . . you know, I'm living in a hotel and it means messing around London . . . but I'll find something to do . . .'

He was plucking his lip thoughtfully and staring at his blotter. 'Russ . . . I remember when I offered you the job, you told me you were planning to do quite a bit of independent travel with the money you'd earned—see a bit of the world . . .'

'Yes, that's right, but I hadn't made up my mind where.'

'All right . . . why *fly* to Nairobi from here?'

'Mm?' I looked at him.

'Why fly? Why not go by boat? Do you fancy the sea?'

'Well, yes, sure, very much.' I laughed and shrugged. 'Y'know, it just never occurred to me. I suppose I took it for granted you flew your reps out.'

'Yes, we do. Going by boat is very much the long way round, much more expensive. But if you were willing to pay the difference yourself Centaf would contribute the normal jet fare *and* get you a good discount on the sea booking and the flight from Durban to Nairobi. It's just an idea.'

And by heck *what* an idea. It excited me immediately. Ever since my impecunious days in Liverpool when I spent so much time down at the docks I'd wanted to ship out on one of the big liners.

Frank was smiling. 'I can see by your face it appeals to you.'

'It does appeal to me, Frank. How long does the trip take?'

'Well, if you went by Union Castle . . .' he opened a drawer in his desk and took out a cardboard file and from this he took a sailing schedule. 'Now . . . Union Castle have five boats. The *Windsor Castle* is the biggest—36,000 tons. Then there's *The Vaal*, the *Pendennis Castle*, the *Edinburgh Castle* and the *Oranje*. Take your pick.

'I fancy the biggest. Let's say the *Windsor*.'

'All right . . . *Windsor Castle* . . . there's a sailing leaving Southampton on November 11th—that's this Friday coming.'

My heart leapt. This Friday!

'It calls at Las Palmas on the 14th . . . Cape Town on the 23rd . . . Port Elizabeth—25th . . . East London—27th . . . and you arrive in Durban on the 28th. Sounds perfect for time.'

'Absolutely spot on.'

'Then you'd fly from Durban to Nairobi—probably via Johannesburg—and be there for 29th or 30th. We'd do all the bookings for you, get you a good price.'

'How much would it cost, Frank?'

'Well, it would depend whether you wanted to go First Class or Tourist. First Class costs about double the Tourist price. It's up to you.'

I thought about it. Hell, I hadn't had a holiday all year, why not do it properly. I said to Frank, 'I'll go First. If I'm going to be seasick I'm going to do it in comfort.'

'All right,' he grinned. 'We'll fix that for you. Now, with regard to the job, we'd require you to sign with us for six months, the contract to be extended six months at a time thereafter, is that all right with you?'

'Yes, fine, Frank.'

'All right, I'll get the paperwork completed, book your passage and flight and if you could drop in tomorrow afternoon . . .?'

I shook hands with him and left. As I crossed the outer office the secretary bird called, 'Er, Mr. Tobin?'

'Yes, m'am?'

She gave me a beautiful smile. 'Welcome to Centaf.'

'Thank you . . . er . . .'

'Cynthia.'

'Thank you, Cynthia.'

'I'm going out to Nairobi myself in January. I'm taking over as private secretary to our manager there.'

'Really! How very nice.'

'So . . . I'll be seeing you there.'

'How *very* nice. See you tomorrow afternoon.'

'Yes. 'Bye.'

'Goodbye, Cynthia.'

I took a cab back to the hotel in Bayswater and was surprised to see Patrick heading for the door as I walked into the foyer. He looked terrible.

'Well met, man,' I said, peering at him. 'Apart from grossly discomknockerated, how are yuh?'

'Wey hey!' he grinned, forming venetian blinds under both eyes. 'Did you see Chappell? When do you leave?'

'This Friday! Come into the bar and I'll pour it in your ear. When are you off to gay Paree?'

We straddled a couple of stools and ordered lagers. I gave him a side-long inspection and he grinned like a man who'd just done himself the world of good. 'Wow!' he whispered, shaking his head. 'What a week-end.'

'What happened, cock?'

'Precisely.' He was still shaking his head. 'And by the looks of things that was only openers! We're flyin' off to the city of love this afternoon.'

'Tell me all.'

'Ach, she's incredible, Russell. Here capacity for affection knows no bounds. It *feeds* upon itself . . . the more it consumes, the more it needs. Sure, I didn't see daylight at all yesterday and it's so long since food passed me lips me belly thinks its throat's cut.'

'Pills,' I said. 'You must take pills, Patrick—and try to get some sleep.'

'Sleep! Jaze, the woman refuses to admit its existence. She has some infernal internal clock that goes off every hour on the hour and must be sexually wound or explode. Russell, it's a terrible itch I've engendered, quite awesome in its aggravation. It's the dadblasted chemistry, y'see . . . we're absolutely compatible.'

I grinned. 'And so say all of us.'

He beamed with delight. 'I knew it! Yuh looked so right together. Tell me about your Sunday.'

The beers came and I told him—well, bits.

'Gorgeous,' he sighed. 'Obviously a day of days.'

'How did Tony make out—have you seen him?'

'No,' he said, wiping lager from his mouth, 'not a sight nor sound. The last glimpse I got of him was of the two of them tearing out of Albert's courtyard in the Jag as though a gun had gone off.'

'Probably had. Ah, it's nice to know the world is full of love, Patrick.'

'Tell me about the job now . . . what's this about Friday?'

I told him about the interview and of my decision to go by sea. He nodded approvingly and sighed, 'Ah, the thought of it. Seventeen days on the briny and all that sun greetin' yuh when you get there. You'll have a wonderful time—all that eating and boozing and forn . . .'

'Oh, no,' I protested. 'Women are out.'

'Yes, of course.'

'This sea trip is for a rest . . .'

'Yes, naturally.'

'. . . a chance to recuperate from a hard summer in time to take up my responsibilities in the new job.'

'As you say, Russell, as you say.'

'It'll be good food . . . fresh air . . . a bit of gentle excercise . . . and seventeen early nights . . .'

'But what else! Faith, knowin' you as I do, it'd never enter my head to think otherwise. But yuh'll be droppin' me a long postcard from Durban, no doubt, confirming the truth of the matter.' He smiled then, suddenly serious. 'I'll miss yuh, Russell, sure I will. Next summer won't be the same without yuh. But keep in touch and maybe one day we'll meet up again. Sure, I wish I was coming with yuh. Africa sounds a good place for us.'

He left shortly after that and I saw him just once more as he came down into the foyer with his cases to pay his bill. It seemed strange that after nine months of the most easygoing relationship with him that we should suddenly feel awkward. I could strangle the guy that invented goodbyes. It's a hell of a way to part.

He tucked his wallet into his overcoat pocket and turned and held out his hand. 'Good luck, old son. So help me, if yuh don't write I'll have it spread around Nairobi that yuh haven't got one.'

'I'll write, I'll write!' I gripped his hand. ''Bye, Patrick. Be happy. I'll catch up with you one day. I'll have to, you owe me a beer.'

I watched him go, struggling through the swing doors with his cases. Outside he dropped one case, gave me a last wave and his old familiar grin, and was gone.

I stood there for a long moment, feeling suddenly bereft, realizing just how much a part of my life the big lug had become in the past nine months. It seemed impossible I'd never see him again, hear his blarney, swop an insult with him. I was really going to miss him.

Ah, well, this wouldn't do, life had to go on . . . and I had to shave and take a bath and change and get some lunch . . . But despite a big effort to rally my spirits the feeling of emptiness persisted. I took a good long soak in the bath and spent an unhurried hour getting ready and was all set to leave my room when the unattractiveness of eating alone overcame me. Instead I lay on top of the bed feeling suddenly very tired and a bit lonely and a bit lost. It was the tiredness that was doing it, of course, and after some minutes of lying there I knew there'd be no fighting off the depression until I'd had some sleep, so I ripped off the clothes I'd so carefully put on and got between the sheets.

I was away in seconds, dreaming of life on the ocean wave. Patrick was there, poncing about in white naval uniform ... and Tania ... and Albert was singing in the band ... Dirty Dick was serving drinks behind the bar and Calvario Bastar was leading his gorilla around on a chain, impressing the birds.

When I awoke at five the room was dark and for a moment I didn't know where I was. Strange hotel-type sounds filtered to me from the corridor and somewhere close a telephone was ringing. It turned out to be closer than I thought—like in my room.

I leapt out of bed and fumbled for the light, swaying with sleep.

'Hallo?'

'Hi—it's me. You sound dozey.'

It was Tania. I came awake immediately. 'Hi, love ... yes, I am. I've been to bed.'

'Oh ... with whom?'

'With youm.'

'Was I nice?'

'You were lovely.'

'You sexy pig, don't you get enough?'

'Nowhere near enough. I think you're a nothing no-time bird.'

'I'll try harder, I promise. Are you coming out?'

'What's the time now?'

'Five.'

'Let's see ... it's twenty-five miles ... I'll be there at ten past.'

'Why so long?'

'I have to get dressed.'

'Hey, now *there's* a novelty. When you get here, knock three times, hm?'

'Eh ... what for?'

'So I'll *rec*ognise you with your clothes on. Hurry!'

TWELVE

The realization that I was going to Africa really hit me forcibly for the first time when I picked up the sailing tickets from Frank Chappell the next afternoon. There, in my hand, was tangible evidence that I was on my way.

'It's a good cabin, Russ,' he said, spreading out a deck-plan of the *Windsor Castle* on his desk. 'Here we are ... it's a W1 grade, Outer single cabin with bath ... number B60 ...' He traced his finger over the deck-by-deck plan searching for the cabin. 'B deck ... even numbers on the port side ... here it is—right opposite the ladies' loo.'

'Smashing.'

'Well, at least there'll be lots of female traffic past your door.'

Excitedly I ranged over the plan. It was headed 'R.M.S. *Windsor Castle*— First Class.' Then there were some details of the boat: Length overall: 783 feet 4½ inches. I loved the 4½ inches! There's meticulousness for you. Breadth: 92 feet. Tonnage: 36,123 gross tons. Fully air-conditioned throughout all passenger spaces.

Beneath a cut-away side view of the ship, with its numbered legend explaining the accommodation, were overhead views of each of the decks—Bridge deck, Promenade deck, Boat deck ... then, descending—A Deck, B Deck and C Deck. The First Class accommodation didn't descend below C Deck, except for the dining room. My cabin, on B Deck, was roughly amidships —or as they say in the navy—near the middle of the boat.

Surrounding the drawn plans were several coloured photographs of some of the accommodation—there was one of the wildly expensive suite sitting room, then a De luxe cabin, a double cabin, the lounge, the dining room etcetera. The decor wasn't exactly my tot of rum; a bit too floral chintz, but it looked very comfortable. The people featured in the dining room photograph produced a small doubt as to the wisdom of travelling First. They all looked elderly, grim and stodgy.

'What's it like in First Class, Frank, any idea?'

'Yes, I've travelled First, though not on the *Windsor*. I did a trip on the *Edinburgh* some years ago. First is extremely comfortable, the service is excellent—and of course there aren't so many passengers to fall over. In the *Windsor* it's ... let's see ...' he consulted the 'Fares and Sailings' brochure. 'She carries 238 First Class and 585 Tourist Class. That's quite a difference. It means more deck space ...'

'No, I really meant what were the passengers like in First Class. They look nice and fuddy in the photograph here.'

'Well, you generally get older people travelling First because they're the ones who can afford it. As a rule the younger stuff travels Tourist—unless of course it's the colonel's daughter ... and then the colonel's usually with her.'

'Mm. D'you reckon it's going to be lively enough for me in First—or will it be Snoresville after din-dins?'

He laughed. 'Why worry—you've got the run of the boat.'

'I have?'

'Oh, yes. The Tourist passengers aren't allowed in First, but you can pop down to Tourist.'

I shrugged. 'Problem solved. We live in F—and play in T. She looks a monstrous size, Frank.'

'She is a monstrous size. You don't realize until you stand on the dock and look up at her. It's a floating city, Russ. I'm sure you'll get a tremendous thrill when you first step on board.'

'I'm getting one now, just thinking about it.'

I spent another half hour with him, signed on the dotted line, received details about clothing and things and it was all done.

He stood up, offering his hand. 'Welcome to Centaf, Russ. I know you'll do well. Jim Fuller is a good man. He'll give you a thorough grounding before deserting you. Any problems afterwards, our Nairobi office will set you straight. I'll be over in March, so I'll see you then. Best of luck and a good trip out. Don't miss the boat, hm?'

Groundless fear. I left the office, said tata to Cynthia, and reached the street. On the pavement I converted 783 feet into yards and began pacing them out, using a lampost as a starting point. Two hundred and sixty-one yards is an awful long way. Adding the 4½ inches for fun I looked back to the lampost. The *Windsor Castle* was a heck of a lot of boat.

I killed the remainder of the afternoon with a quick visit to my agent, Mike Spiring, to let him know my plans; then to Philip Ardmont to thank him for my season in Majorca. It was nice to hear that anytime I wanted to go back to them I was welcome. Then I hired a Cortina for a couple of days, did a bit of shopping and that was Tuesday shot.

Africa was getting very, very close.

Wednesday passed . . . and Africa came closer still.

Thursday, weatherwise, was a mixed day. It began in brilliant sunshine but by mid-day the sun, like the shopkeepers, had closed up and gone home. An arctic iciness crept in with a front of thick white cloud, promising a lot of snow.

Tania deserted me during the morning for the final rehearsals for the big Friday night spectacular and wasn't due to return until nine at night. The day promised to hang heavily until an idea came. I'd phone Albert.

He was in and he was bored. He'd practised singing all morning and his aesthetic soul was now screaming for a game of snooker. I went out and lost to him four games to five but had a ball (no pun intended).

I left him at five o'clock with his warmest good wishes and a promise to look me up if ever he played Nairobi, then I drove to my hotel and phoned Tony who had just got in from a day's shoot on Nescafé. He told me to go round and have a drink with him so I packed my bags, paid the bill and checked out.

My actions were, I realized, now becoming an exciting series of 'lasts' as I went through the revolving door of the hotel for the last time.

Tony greeted me with an effusive bow. 'Welcome to my humble kaya, bwana. Your dearest wish is this poor wog's command.'

'You couldn't do it, Tony, it's physically impossible.'

'Fun-nee. Hey, Patrick wrote to you care of me, thinking the card might not reach you in time. It's on the table.'

While Tony built us a couple of drinks I read Patrick's card. It said: 'Have not wasted an aesthetic moment. Have seen the Louvre, the Seine, the Eiffel Tower and the Palace of Versailles—all on T.V. (There's one at the bottom of the bed!) Bon voyage, old buddy. Take care, Patrick. P.S. What's the French for "please send up an iron lung, a couple of crutches and a seeing-eye dog, two pints of blood, a pound of rhino horn . . . and another fella?" '

Tony came in with the drinks. 'Well, cock, here's to it. I envy you. A small seventeen-day cruise would suit me fine right now. November is for the birds.'

'So, I hear, are small seventeen-day cruises.'

'Aye, one hears. I wonder if it's true. Drop me a line or two and in return I promise to try to remember to write back.'

I left Tony at eight, another 'last' accomplished. Time was now slipping fast and when I got to Tania's flat at nine o'clock I had exactly thirteen hours left until I boarded the train at Waterloo for Southampton.

We had a late dinner at a little Spanish restaurant near by. The atmosphere seemed right, cheerful yet quiet, neither of us wanting to kick our heels up. Tiger remained gay for most of the evening, telling me about the rehearsal and about the girl who split her tights in close up, but I knew she was tired and I knew she was very aware it was my last night, our last night. It was as we entered the flat that she showed how she felt. She suddenly came close and put her arms around me.

'I'm so glad I'm going away this week-end. I couldn't stand being here by myself. It's been awfully good, Russ.'

'It's been beautiful, love. I . . . I have a little present for you.'

She raised her face. 'Have you?'

'Mm.' I took the case from my pocket and handed it to her. She opened it slowly, then, smiling with delight, she took out the fine gold bracelet I'd had engraved for her. On one side it said 'Tania', and on the other 'My Tiger'.

She looked at me and her eyes flooded with tears. 'Thank you very much. Put it on for me. It's very lovely.'

'You are very lovely, Tiger. And I thank you—for your soul.'

She smiled and came into my arms. And stayed there until morning.

We left together at eight o'clock, Tiger off to her day-long dress-rehearsal and a glittering future, me to Waterloo. I chased her down the highway to a roundabout where we finally had to part and with a prolonged blast on the horn and a wave she zoomed around the corner and was gone.

It wasn't until much later that day, on the boat, that I opened my case and found the little painting. It was the colonel, of course, resplendent in uniform, seated on a white charger. And on the back:

A day, a week, a month, a year;
It's not how long, but how precious, how dear.

Tiger.

THIRTEEN

At ten o'clock I was on my way, in a corner seat of a First Class compartment of the Southampton train, tingling with anticipation. I felt like a kid on his first holiday. You'd have thought I'd never been on a train before, never been abroad.

The compartment was full, presumably with fellow boat travellers. Sitting opposite me was an elderly couple, South African from their accent, returning home after a holiday in England, I gathered. Next to them was a wispish woman in her fifties, dressed in tweeds and sensible shoes. She read Dostoyevsky all the way.

Sitting next to me was another elderly couple, Jewish in appearance and loaded in appearance—if the diamond rings on the old girl's fingers were anything to go by. A bunch of real swingers. I knew, of course, I was associating with this type because I was travelling First and the fear I had in Frank Chappell's office returned. If this lot was representative of the people I'd be eating with on board, I'd be asking for a transfer down to Tourist before we cleared the Channel.

'Ach, 'ow beutiful England is, Friedrik,' the South African woman was saying, looking out of the window. 'So grreen and verrdant. Y'know, I'd just love to be able to tek some of this wonderful grarse back 'ome and lay darn a lawn.'

Within half an hour there wasn't a green and verdant blade to be seen. It was snowing like it meant it and the nearer we got to Southampton the harder it came, whipping past the windows in a blizzard. And was I laughing? I was doubled up. Goodbye, England! Goodbye, snow! Do your damnedest, you icy winds. Freeze the knockers off somebody else for the next five months, Tobin's off. What a wonderful day to quit the sinking ship.

What more appropriate farewell than a howling blizzard and ten feet of snow.

'Ach, it's so prretty,' sighed the daft old bird. 'Just like a Christmas card.'

You wait till May, mother, and it's still doing it. Wait till it ruins your fourth consecutive holiday-at-home and see what you think of it.

But mother learned soon enough. When the train finally pulled into the open sheds at Southampton, the hurricane blew her open umbrella inside out and took her hat four hundred yards down the quay.

I trundled my two cases into the reception hall and was amazed at the number of people already in there. There were hundreds of 'em, young and old, some in uniform, and a lot of howling babies, everyone with cases and carrier bags and overcoats and all the paraphernalia of travel.

With usual British efficiency there was a bar big enough to cater for ten people and some three hundred had already formed the traditional queue for a cup of tea or a beer. I plonked down on a seat, lit a cigarette and watched the passing tableau. Actually I was sizing up the talent. I was not unduly depressed at my findings. There were at least thirty or forty quite passable birds going aboard. Granted there were about two hundred men, too, but then what is life without a little competition.

The crowd began to move, snail-paced, through Customs and Passport Control. It took me fifteen minutes to reach the desk, a quick nod from the gestapo and on, with the icy tang of the sea now in my face, through the sheds ... there was the quay, just ahead ... and a gangway rising steeply to a doorway in a towering lavender-coloured wall of rivetted metal plates. Could this be the ship! The roof of the shed prevented me seeing too much, just row after row of portholes, portholes, portholes.

I reached the foot of the gangway and looked up. The *Windsor Castle* loomed above me like a lavender cliff face, powerful, splendid, elegant and immense, throbbing with excitement, impatient to go.

I climbed the steeply raked gangway, up and up ... and up, watching the quay below diminish to pavement proportions. At the top I was greeted by a reception committee of smiling officers and stewards.

One suave spark with umpteen rings on his sleeve flashed me a Pepsodent smile, and a small emaciated steward came forward to relieve me of the cases.

'Welcome aboard the *Windsor Castle,*' said old smoothy. 'We hope you will have a very comfortable and pleasant journey, sir. Would you like your photograph taken?'

Well, why not . . .

A bloke with a flash camera popped one off and told me the proofs would be pinned up for my inspection in a couple of days and I told him that would be just lovely.

'If you would kindly follow your steward, sir,' said the Teeth, 'he will see to anything you require.'

You see, it does pay to travel First.

I went through the lobby, disbelieving I was on a boat. It was exactly like the foyer of a hotel. The steward jigged around some passageways and stopped at a cabin on the port (left-hand) side, the side facing the quay.

'Here you are, sir. Mr Tobin, isn't it? My Name's Mac. Anything you want, just give us a ding.'

Right, I'll start with a crate of champers, a lark's tongue sandwich, six large Havana's and Bardot.

'Thanks, Mac,' I said.

'Nice to have you with us, sir,' he said, bowing out of the door.

I looked around the cabin. There was a single bed across the width of the room, under the porthole; a dressing table and a wardrobe. In the separate bathroom there was a bath, a wash basin and a loo. The carpet was mauve and the bedspread and matching curtain over the porthole were in chintz floral. It was uninspiring but comfortable—and it was my home for the next seventeen days.

I knelt on the bed and had a squint through the porthole, seeing nothing but the Customs shed roof and forty-seven freezing seagulls perched on the top, squinting at the snow.

I decided to leave the cabin and get back on deck, have a look around. I *had* to be on deck when we pulled away from the quay. I stepped out of the cabin, closed the door and for a moment had the entire ship to myself. Well, Tobin, I thought, you're aboard. The die is cast. Come what may. And with the rolling gait of a seasoned sailor I made my way back to the foyer and up to the open deck.

It was freezing up there and snowing in earnest. I hugged my collar round me ears and hung over the rail. Eight thousand feet below people were pouring up the two gangways, in obvious high spirits despite the cold. Finally it got too cold for me so I moved into the covered way and watched through the windows. Within half an hour the flood of people boarding diminished to a trickle, then to an odd one or two, then finally we were all aboard. It was almost one o'clock and time to go.

The lively music that had been playing all over the ship through the tannoy system was suddenly interrupted for an announcement. Would visitors kindly leave the boat. In a few moments traffic on the gangways proceeded in the reverse direction. A hundred people crowded the quay, straining their necks, grimacing against the blowing snow, waving, shouting goodbyes and good lucks and have good trips and come back soons. Derricks swung out and lowered the gangways to the quay. The massive retaining ropes were loosed from their bollards. The ship was free. Our umbilical ties with Britain had been severed. The music from the tannoy gave way to a rollicking sea-shanty —A life on the ocean wave. Bells clanged. The great ship trembled and began inching away from the quay, gently pulled by a couple of straining tugs.

The quay receded ... fifty yards ... a hundred. Still the visitors waved and shouted and wept. All along the deck, passengers hugged the rail and pressed against the windows, waving ... waving ... waving ... and then the quay was gone, swallowed by the squalling snow. An announcement came immediately—would passengers kindly take their seats for lunch. Good. Very well organized. Get them busy immediately. Give the stewards time to unpack the bags; give the ship time to settle down.

I stood for another moment or two looking at England, at the shadow of docks and quays and cranes, thinking of what I was leaving. Goodbye Patrick, Tony, Tiger. So long Albert. Tarra you green and verdant sometimes land. How long, I wondered, would it be before I set foot on your soil again. Would I ever set foot on your soil again? Where will it end, Tobin, where will it end?

Gripped by a mixture of emotions, excitement, nostalgia, expectation and awe, I turned from the window and entered the warm, bustling interior of the ship, sure of one thing at least—that I was hungry.

FOURTEEN

Extract from the Ship's Official Log of R.M.S. Windsor Castle.

November 11th. 1300 hours: departed Southampton. Cloudy, snow. N wind, force 6. Passengers on board: 187 First Class. 422 Tourist Class. Cocktail music daily by Leslie Ashdown. Recorded music. Cinema—The Pit.

Extract from Russ Tobin's Official Log.

November 11th. 1320 hours: deposited overcoat in cabin, spruced up a touch, entered dining room First Class.

The uniformed bloke on the door greeted me effusively. 'Mr. Tobin ... let's see, yes, you're at table 75, sir, this way.'

I followed him across the plush dining room to a round table set with six places in the left corner of the room. The atmosphere was brisk, excited and talkative. My impression of the room was of snow-white tablecloths, heavy silver cutlery and very good food. It had the smell and aura of a first-class restaurant.

I attracted quite a lot of attention as I passed between the tables because everyone was having a good decko at who was on board. For my part I didn't see a single individual face, merely a sea of faces and a pretty ancient sea at that. From my fleeting impression I'd have said the average age was sixty and before I'd taken my seat I was wondering how long a walk it was to Tourist.

There were three people already seated at table 75—two women and a man. The much older woman glanced up, beamed a smile and dug her husband in the elbow. It was the Jewish-looking couple I'd travelled down with on the train, the momma with the entire 1972 output of De Beers diamonds on her plump fingers.

'Hello,' I said. 'We meet again.'

The man was short, very round and very bald with a dark complexion and a huge bulbous nose the size of a 100-watt light bulb. He had a nice, kind avuncular face, fleshy and gentle. His wife was grey-rinsed, treble-chinned and enormously double-breasted. She was embalmed in a blue floral dress and was keeping her wrestler's shoulders warm in a silver mink wrap.

The old man made a gesture at rising, then flopped back and held out a veined, speckled hand. 'Rubinstein,' he announced.

I almost said, 'No kidding' and did say, 'Tobin. Russ Tobin.'

'This is my wife, Mr. Tobin. And this is Mrs. Felton.'

Mrs. Felton was a knockout—a beautiful, very elegant woman in her early forties, I mean a real beauty. Wonderful hazel green eyes, gently waved ash-blonde hair to her shoulders, lovely mouth. She sat tall and slender, dressed in a green jersey dress, high at the neck, decorated with a gold medallion on a fine gold chain. Her hands were long and slender and the rings she was wearing said that in addition to everything else, she was wealthy. She gave me a charming smile and shook hands and resumed her inspection of the menu.

I sat down. The chief steward handed me a menu and departed. I pretended to read it, using it as cover to settle in.

'How strange we should travel down on the train together,' said Mrs. Rubinstein. 'Are you going all the way to Cape Town, Mr. Tobin?'

'Further still—to Durban. And from there to Nairobi by air.'

Mrs. Felton looked up and smiled questioningly. 'Hardly the most direct route but infinitely more leisurely.'

'I'm killing time the pleasant way, Mrs. Felton. I've got three weeks to spare and I've always wanted to do a long sea trip.'

'Very adventurous,' she remarked, and somehow I was delighted she thought so.

I lost myself in the menu again, wondering about the two empty chairs on my left and who would occupy them. So far so good, the company seemed highly compatible. And it would need to be. If the others were all travelling to the Cape we'd sit here together for three meals a day for fourteen days. Forty-two meals that could either make or mar the cruise. I hoped nobody else would come.

But they did come. Mrs. Dorothea Klein swept in breathlessly, gushing like a Texas oil-well, swamping us with a personality as out-going as a tidal wave, colourful as a circus tent in an orange trouser suit fringed with white bobbles, her baubles, bangles and beads jingling like a toppled grandfather clock, her reddish-blonde hair an untidy cluster of ringlets.

'Hi, there, everybody, I'm Dorothea Klein, glad to know you this is my daughter Ellaleen my God what *wea*ther I sure am glad to be leaving old England now the snow's come I just couldn't *stand* a winter in England and I am just *starved* y'know we've travelled all the way from Scotland since yesterday afternoon and I feel I've been on that train for a *month* thank you steward say could we have some drinks here before lunch I just couldn't *face* anything solid without a drop of something nice an' cool to pave the way say would you folks join me in a small aperitif . . .?'

I stood and turned to greet Ellaleen and felt the heart skip a beat. She was standing there, loose-limbed, bored, insolent, listening to her mother rabbiting on and hating her. She was a fairly tall girl, mid-twenties, with long dark-brown hair and a very slender figure, a boyish figure, though quite well endowed bosom-wise. She was wearing jeans and a midnight-blue silk blouse, open one button too many for the First Class dining room, though not for me. She was good-looking but strange, sloe-eyed, moody, perhaps truculent, obviously spoilt. A weirdie.

I put out my hand. 'Hello, I'm Russ Tobin.'

She took the hand and sloe-eyed me with startling directness. 'Hi,' she said, unsmiling, just looking.

She sat down, giving me an overhead shot of her bra-less breasts and knowing it, then picked up the menu and ignored everybody for the next five minutes.

I sat down and glanced around the others to see what effect the arrival of the Americans had had on them. The Rubinsteins were smiling attentively at Dorothea who was still rattling on like a Gatling about the wonders of London and Edinburgh and the shops and the parks. But Mrs. Felton, serene and half-smiling, was taking them apart. Her eyes moved languidly between Dorothea and Ellaleen, then stayed on Ellaleen, narrowing with thought, obviously intrigued. Suddenly they switched to me and the corners of her mouth twitched and she had to lower her eyes quickly to avoid laughing. Mrs. Felton and I had established raport. I had found an ally.

We all accepted Dorothea's pressing invitation to join her in aperitif, though the Rubinstein's ordered only tomato juice. Mrs. Felton asked for a small sherry. I ordered lager.

'Ellaleen?' asked Dorothea.

'Gin,' she answered tonelessly, without looking up from the menu.

'Two gins and tonics,' Dorothea told the steward. 'And make mine a large one, I feel the need.'

Dorothea turned immediately to Mrs. Felton, remarking on her gold medallion, and it gave me a chance to nip in quickly with a question to Ellaleen. With Dorothea at the table it was always going to be necessary to nip in quickly to get a word to anybody.

'Are you going to Cape Town, Ellaleen?'

She raised her head and, before she answered, covered my entire face in a slow, unsettling, feature-by-feature examination and was so long in answering I thought she wasn't going to.

'No,' she said finally, caressing the word, playing with it, dramatically, leaving it teasingly on an upward inflection as though she was going to add more. But she didn't. She left me in the air and just looked at me with those sultry eyes and a suggestion of a smile, toying with me. She was mad . . . crackers . . . like one of those crazy method actresses, all twitch and effectedness.

'Oh, then, you're getting off at Las Palmas?'

'Yes,' she replied, in the same way.

And stuff you, too, love, I thought. Body or no body, you're not putting me on for three days. You can fasten your blouse and get knotted, I'll talk to old man Rubinstein instead. Ha! Just my luck—the only decent looking and young bird in First and she has to be a nut.

I turned towards Rubinstein and was about to ask him if he'd been on holiday in England when Ellaleen asked in a husky, sexy, caressing voice. 'And how far do *you* go, Mr. Tobin?'

I abandoned Rubinstein and swung round, finding myself pinned to the floor by her sloe eyes. 'I . . . er . . . I'm going all the way . . . to Durban.'

Rivetting me with her gaze she said slowly, 'Mm . . . it must be nice—going all the way. I think I'd like that.'

'You would?' I croaked.

'Mmm. I think a *long* trip is so much more satisfying, don't you?'

'Y . . .' I cleared my throat. 'Yes, I suppose so.'

'Still . . . I'll just have to make the most of the three days I've got, won't I.'

'Is . . . that all you've got . . . three days?'

'Do you . . . know anybody else on board?'

'No . . . no, I don't.'

Her eyes left mine and did a lazy sweep around the room. 'Where's the action—Tourist?'

'Yes, Tourist.'

'I need some action. I've been dragging around Scotland and England for two months.'

'Just you and mother?'

Her lip curled as she nodded. 'Just me and mother.' She looked at me, curling my toes. 'You swing, huh?'

'Swing? You mean dance?'

She gave a curious smile, strangling me. 'I mean swing.'

'Oh, yes . . . yes, I swing.'

'O.K.' she said, making it sound as though I'd just been hired for something. 'After lunch we hit Tourist—all right?'

I grinned. 'Fine.'

Lunch was a ball. Dorothea got very tight on three more gins and kept up a non-stop commentary about their travels. I gathered she was a widow (gee, poor Milt woulda just *loved* the changing of the guard . . .) and that Milt had been some big wheel in the film industry, which explained Ellaleen's histrionics more than somewhat.

Nobody else got a word in. The Rubinsteins tried to contribute the odd experience but made no progress at all in the face of Dorothea's onslaught, but from the little he said, I gathered he was connected with the diamond business.

Mrs. Felton said a great deal with her eyes, the gist of it being that if the Kleins hadn't been getting off at Las Palmas she would have been sitting at a different table by that evening.

Ellaleen said nothing. She ate in a desultory way with her

mind on other matters, all of which had to do with our conversation, I was sure; the realization of which took the edge clean off my own appetite. I had the immovable impression that something had caught fire inside her, a switch had been triggered, and it wouldn't be long before she exploded.

The party broke up around three. As we wandered out I said to Ellaleen, 'What time do you want to recce Tourist?'

'Give me an hour, huh? I wanna bath, I've been on that stinkin' train all night.'

'Sure. Where will I meet you?'

'Where do you live?'

'B60.'

'We got A15. Give me a knock about four thirty.'

'Yes, all right.'

Momma and daughter wandered off, Dorothea laughing at something Rubinstein had said, quite smashed. Ellaleen was good to watch. She moved like a lynx, long-legged and sexy, as though she'd studied hard to learn how.

As I turned from watching her, I caught the eyes of Mrs. Felton who I'm sure had been watching me. 'Enjoyable lunch, Mr. Tobin?' she enquired with a naughty smile.

'Very enjoyable, Mrs. Felton. Very ... entertaining, I thought.'

'Eminently. I'll see you at dinner, then.'

'I look forward to it.'

Still smiling, she walked away. It was the first time I'd seen her from head to toe. So help me, she moved better than Ellaleen. Mrs. Felton was a very intriguing woman.

I went back to the cabin, lay on the bed and tried to read, but Ellaleen kept filling my mind. I wondered if all this sexy inuendo was genuine nymphomania or just teasing. You could never tell with a bird like her. They could jump this way or that in an instant, totally unpredictable. She could either be the wildest thing on board or the type that got you all worked up and then wanted to discuss disarmament. But try as I might to push fantastic expectancy from my mind, the prospect of what might happen if she did cut loose was too exciting. Somehow I *knew* she wasn't just a tease; this crazy bird was genuine.

At four thirty, tingling with anticipation, I crossed over to the starboard side and went up one deck. A15 was one of the De luxe twin-bed cabins. I knocked ... and waited. I knocked again. Ellaleen opened the door, eyes puffed with recent sleep and her hair dishevelled. She was wearing a loosely-tied turquoise silk kimono. I was a bit narked; she'd said four thirty.

'Oh, hi. I fell asleep.'

'So I see. Look, you take your time, I'll meet you in the lounge at six, O.K.?'

'No, come in, I won't be long.'

I followed her into the narrow corridor. On my right was the bathroom and next to it the loo. Wondering where Dorothea was, I walked into the main cabin ... and found where Dorothea was. She was in one of the single beds, fast asleep on her back, mouth open, quietly snoring, her hair a forest of pink and blue curlers.

'Sit down,' said Ellaleen. 'I won't be long.'

'Hey, I'd better wait outside.'

'Why?'

'Well, your mother ...'

'She won't wake. Gin always blasts her.'

I lowered myself nervously into a chair, keeping an eye on Mom. Ellaleen went to the dressing table, inspected her appearance in the mirror, took up a brush and swiped at her hair a couple of times, inspected herself again, head on one side, then hooked a thumb into the kimono sash and dropped the garment to the chair. I gaped, heart thundering. All she had on was the minutest pair of completely transparent knicks.

I couldn't believe it was happening. She stood there, looking at herself in the mirror, then turned sideways, her front towards me, and looked at herself in profile.

'What d'you think?' she said, flatly.

'Mm?'

'Am I too thin?'

'Mm ...? Er, no ... I ... I think you're perfect ... beautiful.'

'She says I'm getting too thin.' She raised her hands to her breasts and pushed them together, studying them in the mirror, then released them. 'To hell with her, I think they're good.'

Without looking at me she crossed to her bedside table, lit a cigarette and waltzed off towards the bathroom. 'Won't be long.'

I watched her gorgeous bottom disappear from sight and sat there in shock. It hadn't happened. I had to get out of there. They were all mad! What if momma suddenly woke up and started screaming—with Ellaleen poncing about in the noddy? I'd be clapped in irons or something—a round trip back to England in the brig. I could see the headlines: White Marvel man attempts rape of mother and daughter aboard *Windsor Castle.*

I jumped as momma choked on a big snore and with the disturbance changed her position in bed. She drew her knees right up and seemed to settle, still on her back. Then I watched horrified, as her feet began to slide down the bed and her legs straightened. Down ... down ... down they went, taking the covering sheet with them, exposing, inch by inch, her shoulders ... then her chest ... I stared, pop-eyed. Momma was starkers! The edge of the sheet began to rise, to climb the hillock of her breasts. It reached the summit, paused for a breathtaking moment, then slid down the other side, leaving momma naked to the waist.

What could I do! Just sit there and not look? Go and cover her up? What if she woke while I was bending over her? She'd scream bloody blue murder—either that or whip me into bed, if she was anything like her daft daughter. Should I go and tell Ellaleen? Maybe she'd scream bloody blue murder, thinking I was trying to break into the bathroom. In any case, what could I say? Er, 'scuse me, Ellaleen, but your ma's bristols are showing ...?

Dorothea suddenly let out one almighty snore and in a flurry of movement shot her legs up and out and booted the sheets clean over the bottom of the bed, finishing in a sprawled position, legs wide akimbo, totally starkers!

I had to get out. I couldn't sit there until Ellaleen came out. Perhaps I could read a paper ... turn my chair round with my back to momma ... I looked around the cabin. There was a magazine on the far side of momma's bed. I stood up. I sat down again. I would ... I wouldn't. Yes, I would. I got up and crept around momma's bed and had just got my hand on the magazine when the bathroom door flew open and out marched Ellaleen, transparent knicks on, hair piled high with one hand holding it. She glanced at me, at the magazine in my hand, at her mother, muttered, 'Slob', picked up the sheet from the floor and flung it carelessly over her naked mater, walked round the bed, stuck three hairpins in her hair and went back into the bathroom.

I stood as though pole-axed for a full minute, then I moved. I dropped the magazine and knocked on the bathroom door.

'Er, Ellaleen, I need some cigarettes. I'll be back in a few minutes ...'

'There are some in my bedside table.'

'I, er, well ... I only smoke English.'

'They're English.'

'Er ... ah! Peter Stuyvesant, are they?' Fingers crossed.

'No, Benson and Hedges.'

'Ah, I only smoke Peter Stuyvesant ... I won't be long.'

I was out of there in a flash, almost running along the corridor. My God, what a family. But that Ellaleen ... wow! Oh, something was going to happen there, all right.

I messed about for twenty minutes and in trepidation knocked again on their cabin door. Ellaleen opened it, dressed like a red Indian—beaded suede skirt and jacket and a coloured headband round her forehead.

'How,' I grinned. 'I mean hi! Sorry for the delay but the shop sort of ...'

'I'm ready, let's go.'

She swept away down the corridor and, so help me, she would have left the cabin door open if I hadn't closed it.

Well, I chased after that bird for half an hour or more and I was getting so fed up with her flashing here, dashing there, covering the entire Tourist section like she was looking for the rest of her tribe or something and hardly saying a word to me that I made up my mind to ditch her and pretend I'd got lost. Then we hit the Tourist Lounge and she saved me the trouble.

The lounge was crowded; I reckoned the entire 422 were in there, all having a riotous knees-up to a piano-accordion. It looked as though they couldn't wait for the official amusements to start so they'd rolled up the carpet and taken things into their own hands.

We'd hardly crossed the threshold when a mad-looking Scotsman with flaming red hair and a kilt swooped down on Ellaleen, crying, 'C'mon my bonny Minnie Ha Ha, let's gi' it a whirrrrl!' and whisked her away in a flying reel. That was the last I saw of her all night.

After ten minutes or so I got fed up waiting and somehow knew she wouldn't be back, so I perched on the arm of a chair and watched the fun. Aha!, yes, this was the place to be, down in Tourist. Apart from meals, First wouldn't be seeing much of Tobin for the next seventeen days. Here was the life, the fun—and the girls. Dozens of 'em. I did a slow recce around the room. Yes, scores of them that would make ideal playmates for a fun fortnight. *But* ... the competition was strong. I'd have to do something about it fast, like right now, or by midnight all the good-looking birds would be snapped up for the voyage.

Aha! There ... on the edge of the crowd ... a nice looking blonde. Quiet looking, just standing there, tapping her pretty foot to the beat of the music. I slid off the chair and with casual haste made my way towards her.

'Excuse me, would you like to dance?'

Her expression of cool sophistication disintegrated in a stupid, eye-fluttering grin. 'Ooh, yers, ta ever so, love to!'

Oh, my God, the voice! A top-C squeak from London's east end. How dare they shatter a man's illusions by opening their bloody mouths.

As we took the floor she launched herself at me, wrapping her arms around my neck in a step-over back strangle.

'First time on a big boat, then is it?' she squeaked, breathing onions at me.

'Er ...' Cor, bloody 'ell.

'First time for me, too, i'n it excitin'?'

'Fabulous.'

'How far you goin', then?'

To the nearest exit, luv, soon as you let go of me.

'Durban.'

'Oh, that's nice, I'm goin' there, too. 'Ere, I didn't see you at lunch, did I? I'm sure I'd 'ave noticed.'

'No, I'm travelling First, actually,' I said, feeling mighty glad of it for the first time.

'Oo, I say, posh, ain't we. Wot's it like up there, then?'

'Incredible. Gold bath taps and dinner plates. Every cabin has it's own personal maid.'

'No! Really? Ooh, I say. 'Ere, wot's yours like, then?'

'Unbelievable. She's a Swedish sexpot. I had to come down here for a rest. Won't leave me alone. Keeps nipping in pretending to make the bed. She's made it three times since lunch.'

' 'Ere, you 'aving me on?'

Love, with respect, I wouldn't have you on, off or any other way if you were the only bird on board.

'Well, a little,' I admitted.

'Oo, you're naughty, you are,' she giggled and snuggled a bit closer. 'I bet you're the sort that would take advantage of a girl on board ship. I've been told to watch out for men like you.'

I'll bet. Would the bloody music never end! I was suffocating.

'Will you, er, be coming down later on, then—after dinner?' she asked with unabashed directness. 'I expect I'll be 'ere ... you know, what with travelling alone I like to be where the fun is.'

'Er, no, I don't think so. There's a chess tournament in First Class, I'll probably enter that. Ah, what a pity the music's finished. Well, thanks very much ...'

'Don't you want another one. I'd love another one.'

'Well, not just now, it's me bad leg. Have to give it a rest.'

'Oo, how did you do that, then?'

Running away from birds like you, luv.

'Skiing accident. Olympics last time. Well, have a good time ...'

'Ta ever so—and you. See you later, maybe?'

You'll have to look behind the potted palms, angel.

Off she went, straight into the corded arms of a one-man demolition gang. Good luck to both of them.

Well, I was doing quite nicely. Tally to date: one cuckoo Yank and one squeaky Cockney. Would this good fortune hold forever?

Now let's see ... ho ho! over in the corner—a big handsome bird with excellent legs and a bosom you could smother in. Let's give it a whirl, big as she is.

She was chatting to a petite brunette who looked the giggly sort though she wasn't doing it at the moment. I sidled up and waited for a lull in their conversation.

'Excuse me ... would you like to dance?'

The blonde surveyed me, smiled and said in a voice like Lee

Marvin, 'Oh, ja, ja I vill dance. Kom!'

She grabbed my hand in a mitt like a docker's, hauled me on to the floor and launched into a wild polka like it was a field excercise for the Hitler Youth. My feet didn't touch the ground —literally! She lifted me clean off the deck and whirled me round and round, laughing uproariously in a husky bellow, shouting, 'Ach, he is a bee-yootiful danzer, zis man, no!' and the crowd were all gathered round, laughing and applauding and I was getting so fucking mad . . .

'Oh, he's so goot! Just look at his footverk!' she roared, pissed as a barrel bung.

You'll get my footverk where it hurst, Gretchen, if you don't put me down. Jeez, if there's one thing I can't stand it's big butch birds who pick up twelve stone fellas and throw them around like they were two stone six.

Round and round she went, shouting and laughing . . . and I knew something disasterous *had* to happen. It did. She was coming round for the tenth circuit and the music was getting faster and faster, inspired by her hilarity, when she tripped, staggered backwards under my toppling weight, crashed through a small table filled with drinks and landed in a bloody great heap, legs flung asunder and me in between them. A roar of laughter from the crowd. Gretchen was killing herself under me, tears rolling down her cheeks, helpless with laughter. Me, I wanted to die. I mean the position! It looked exactly as though I was screwing her. I tried to get up and, stap me, her great thighs swung up and clamped me in a grip that squeezed the breath out of me. Down I went. The crowd were falling about.

'Hey, come *on*,' I said in her ear, but this only brought on more laughter. Then I felt her legs relax. I tried again—and chunk! back came her legs, trapping me again.

'Get a photo! Get a photo!' someone was shouting. 'She's got no knicks on!'

'Oh, my God . . .'

At last she'd had enough. She parted her great limbs and I climbed out, pleased to see she had got knicks on, though only just. I staggered to my feet, in two minds whether to help the silly cow up or not. Anyway, I did—and lived to regret it. She took my outstretched hand and as she came to her feet she grabbed me round the waist, lifted me three feet off the ground and proclaimed, 'The vinner!' then dropped me with a thump.

I'd had enough. I pushed through the encircling crowd, smiling stiffly, and left the lounge. By the heck, a *highly* successful afternoon. Total now to date: One yucky Yank, one cock-struck Cockney and one krazy Kraut. Tobin, it's great to know you haven't lost your touch. You could always pick 'em.

Was there, I wondered, as I headed back to First, or was there not a nice, quiet, unextraordinary, good-looking bird on board with whom I could spend the carefree hours in gentle shipboard play. By midnight I was beginning to believe, to fear—nay, to despair, that there was not.

FIFTEEN

Ellaleen didn't come down to dinner. Dorothea seemed quite unperturbed and I put it down to one of three reasons: (a) that she was so used to Ellaleen's unpredictability that she considered this sort of thing normal; (b) she was thankful for a rest from Ellaleen; (c) she was still half-shickered from lunch and didn't notice Ellaleen wasn't there.

Mrs. Felton took her seat looking so stunning in a green velvet dress with gold accessories that she literally took my breath away. As she sat down she gave me a knowing smile and said, 'Good evening, Mr. Tobin—interesting afternoon?'

So she'd heard—or perhaps seen—what had happened in the Tourist lounge.

'Oh, sort of up and down, Mrs. Felton,' I said and she laughed beautifully.

The dinner passed pleasantly. Old man Rubinstein kept us very entertained talking about the history of diamond mining in South Africa, and I don't know whether it was the subject—so dear to a woman's heart—or that she'd talked herself to a standstill over lunch, but Dorothea listened very attentively and hardly interupted once.

'It all started,' said Rubinstein, 'in the Hopetown district in 1866, when a farmer named Schalk van Niekerk admired a pretty stone some children were playing with. Their mother, a

Mrs. Jacobs, gave it to him. It turned out to be a $21\frac{1}{4}$ carat diamond which he sold for £500.'

Dorothea's eyes popped. 'Well, for goshsakes ... poor Mrs. Jacobs.'

Rubinstein smiled. 'Well, by all accounts van Niekerk was an honest man and shared the money with her. He must also have been a very lucky man because two years later he bought a "charm stone" from a witchdoctor for £250 worth of cattle. The "charm" turned out to be a diamond of $83\frac{1}{2}$ carats and van Niekerk sold it to Lilienfeld Brothers for £11,000. The stone is now known as the Star of South Africa. It was ultimately sold to the Countess of Dudley for £50,000 ...'

The ladies gasped. Dorothea, shaking her head, muttered again, 'Well, for goshsakes ...'

'Which was the largest diamond ever mined, Mr. Rubinstein?' I asked.

'Well, there were several much, much bigger than the Star of South Africa. There was the "Jonker" diamond. That was 726 carats ...'

'What!'

'Oh, yes,' he smiled. '726 carats and so perfect it changed hands in 1934 for £200,000 in rough state—1934, mind you. Worth a lot more today. Then there was the "Excelsior" diamond ... 995 carats ...'

There was a flurry of 'Good Lords' and 'Good Gods' around the table. 'Nine ... hun'red and ninety-five!' exclaimed Dorothea.

'Yes,' said Rubinstein, really warming to his subject now he'd got us. 'That one was mined in Jagersfontein and eventually cut into 21 brilliants. And *then* ...' he smiled, looking at me, '... to answer your question, Mr. Tobin—then came the daddy and grand-daddy of them all—the "Cullinan" diamond.'

'Oh, I've *heard* of that!' said Dorothea.

'The "Cullinan" was discovered near Pretoria in 1905,' Rubinstein began, waxing lyrical over this one, 'and was named after the chairman of the Premier Mine, on whose land it was found. It was actually discovered by the mine's superintendent who was walking one evening along the face of the workings and was attracted to a shiny object glinting in the sunlight. He prised it out of the earth and at first thought it was a huge piece of glass, disbelieving that so large a diamond could exist.'

Dorothea and Mrs. Felton were sitting forward in their chairs, agog. 'How big was it, Mr. Rubinstein?' asked Mrs. Felton.

'Sure you can stand it?' he grinned. 'It was three thousand ... one hundred ... and six carats. Almost 2 lbs in weight.'

'Oh, my ... Gard,' sighed Dorothea, holding her face. 'Can you believe that. A diamond the weight of a bag of sugar!'

Mrs. Felton was shaking her head and smiling.

'Yet ...' Rubinstein went on, 'despite its enormous size—and it's by far the biggest diamond ever found—many experts considered that one of its faces was a cleavage and the original stone may well have been *twice* the size.'

'Twice that size,' Dorothea almost cried. 'Mr. Rubinstein, what would a diamond like that be *worth*?'

'Well, it was bought by the Transvaal Government for £150,000 and presented to Edward VII as a birthday gift. That was in 1907. Then it was sent to Amsterdam for cutting. You know, it took literally *months* of study before it was decided to cut it into nine large diamonds and ninety-six smaller brilliants.'

'Boy, what a decision,' I laughed.

He turned to me. 'Well, if you think the decision was difficult —how about the cutting? Would you have liked the job.'

'No thanks. I'm sweating just thinking about it.'

'Well,' he smiled, 'pity the poor old master-cutter whose sole responsibility it was. Imagine the scene ... February 10th 1908 —D Day. He approaches this enormous stone lying there on his bench. You know, he must have stared at it and studied it until his eyes ached, then, finally, there was no more staring and studying to be done. The moment for action had come. He placed his cleaving blade on the stone ... took a deep breath ... probably said the most ardent prayer of his life ... and gave the blade one tap with a heavy rod ...'

He paused dramatically and sipped his coffee, taking his time. Dorothea's eyes were wide. A thin wail of anguish came from her. 'Aw, c'm*on*, Mr. Rubinstein, don't leave us in sus*pense*! What *hap*pened?'

Smiling teasingly, he put down his cup and wiped his mouth. 'The blade broke. The diamond remained intact.'

'Ohhh, that poor *man*!' groaned Dorothea. 'Then what happened?'

'A second blade was applied and struck. The diamond parted perfectly. The cutter was so relieved he fainted.'

Three pent-up breaths were released around the table. Dorothea clutched her bosom and sank back in her chair, laughing at Mrs. Felton.

'The cutter then began his job of fashioning the gems,' Rubinstein went on. 'And as you probably know, all nine large ones are either in the British Crown Jewels or in the possession of the Royal Family.'

'Which was the biggest of the nine?' Dorothea asked.

'Oh, that's the Star of Africa. It weighs 530 carats. It's mounted in the British Sceptre.'

'Well, how very interesting,' exclaimed Dorothea. 'Gee, I dunno, we just don't seem to have anything that exciting back home . . . not unless you count the odd prison massacre.'

When dinner was over I found myself walking out with Mrs. Felton.

'I suppose you're heading for Tourist?' she smiled.

'Yes, I suppose. There's not much doing up here.'

'There never is—not for young people. I hear there's a discotheque on board.'

'Yes, there is. It's in the Tourist lounge. Are you interested?'

She laughed. 'No, I don't think it's quite my scene, somehow.'

I didn't agree. I think anything would have been Mrs. Felton's scene if she put her mind to it. She had that flare for adaptability, I thought—gracious, erudite hostess at a formal dinner party or swinging in a disco, whatever was called for.

'What will you do?' I asked her.

'Oh, read . . . maybe I'll go to the cinema.'

'Would you like some coffee in the lounge?'

She looked at me, obviously trying to analyse my motive and also probably pondering the wisdom of such a move. Then she smiled and nodded. 'Yes, I'd love a coffee in the lounge.'

We sat in deep armchairs and I gave her a cigarette. She looked gorgeous, sitting there; very feminine, really very sexy.

'Do you live in Cape Town?' I asked her.

'Just outside. Do you know Cape Town?'

'No, this is my first visit to Africa.'

'You'll love it, I'm sure. It's a very beautiful, very fascinating place.'

'So I'm repeatedly told. I'm sure I will.'

'Will you be working out there, Mr. Tobin? May I ask what you do?'

As the coffee was served I told her briefly about the T.V. in London and about Majorca and Centaf, and at the mention of East Africa she said, 'Oh, that's a wonderful place. I've been on many safaris, shooting *and* photographing ... though I personally haven't shot anything. It's very exciting.'

'Are you South African?' I asked.

She shook her head. 'No, I'm English—from Berkshire. I've just been there to visit my parents.'

'And glad to be back in the Cape?'

She smiled. 'Oh, yes. I love London now and again but I'd never go back. About your T.V. work ... I've done a little commercial work myself, you know ...' she tilted her head in a humorous 'so there!' attitude.

'Have you? Were you an actress ... I mean, *are* you still ...?'

'No, I was a model. But I made one or two commercials in the earlier days.'

That explained a lot of things—her walk, her figure, her style ... and probably our instant raport.

'Do you still model in South Africa?'

She shook her head and smiled, as though the idea was a bit preposterous. 'No, not any more. Now I'm just a full-time housewife ...'

I could tell from the way she said it that she regarded herself as anything but 'just' a full-time housewife.

She looked at her watch. 'It's almost nine. I think I will see that film. Thank you very much for the coffee ...' She stood up, '... I hope you have a very ... enjoyable evening in Tourist.'

Damn it, she was so nice to be with I was in two minds whether or not to go to the pictures with her. But something told me not, so I said goodnight to her and wandered down to A Deck and to the bar in the Tourist lounge.

After the funereal respectability of the First Class lounge, the racket in Tourist hit me like the Alamein bombardment. Four hundred souls were crowded in there, determined to have a whale of a time all the way to Cape Town. I bought myself a drink and began wandering around.

She was gorgeous. Long brown shiny hair and a strong, intelligent face. She looked pensive, even sad, sitting there on the sofa all by herself.

'Hi.'

She looked up, smiling pleasantly. 'Hi.' Nice voice, very gentle.

'You going to Cape Town?'

'No, East London.'

'I'm going further still—to Durban.'

'Lovely place Durban—wonderful beaches.'

'My name's Tobin—Russ Tobin.'

'Anita Sherman.'

'Would you like a drink, Anita?'

'Well, that's very kind of you, Russ—but my fiancé is just getting one. Here he is now.'

'Splendid. Well, have a good trip.'

'You, too, Russ.'

Ho-de-ho-de-hum ... the next was a soft, voluptuous redhead with enormous blue eyes and a wondrous mouth.

'Hallo.'

'Hallo.'

'Going to Cape Town?'

'No, Durban as a matter of fact.'

Aye aye!

'Holiday?'

'No, we're emigrating actually. There's much more opportunity there for the children, we think. My husband says ...'

She must have taken her ring off to wash out a nappy or two and forgotten to put the rotten thing back on.

'Best of luck in your new home,' I said cheerily.

'Thanks—and the same to you.'

Da de da de diddledum day ...

I wondered where Ellaleen was. Probably in someone's cabin being rodgered mercilessly, God help him. By God, things were getting rough when I was forced to think of her. Come on, Tobin, get weaving. If you don't land something tonight there'll be nothing left tomorrow—and how does the prospect of seventeen birdless days grab you? Even the thought was painful.

I did a slow circuit, conscious of time pressing in fast on all sides. There wasn't a decent looking buttercup there without a fella. Maybe they'd brought them on board with them. I suddenly felt a bit out of it. Well, served me right for travelling First. I should have gone Pleb.

After an hour the discotheque started. A young with-it officer got the thing organized very efficiently in a matter of minutes, transforming the lounge into a flickering, flashing disco, dim as a crypt and noise by the hundredweight.

I approached a blonde female shape and asked it to dance. It came willingly, even eagerly, and began wriggling very fair hips to the reggae beat, her full breasts jumping in her sweater like a couple of sandbags. We looked at each other a few times during the first minute and grinned inanely, sizing each other up, then I said, 'By golly, this beats dancing any time, what?'

'Pliss . . . you speak Dutch?'

Oh, fuck . . .

'No, love, not a blind word.'

'Sorry, I speak no Eenglish.'

Where have all the flowers gooooone . . .

By midnight I'd danced four hundred times and every one of 'em was either married, engaged, dim, foreign or pregnant. I was fed up. I bought one more drink I didn't really want and decided to call it a night.

In the cabin I undressed desultorily, cleaned my teeth, hopped between the sheets and put out the light. Then I lay there in the darkness, becoming aware for the first time of the sounds and movement of the ship, of its gentle plunging roll through the waves and the rhythmic creaking of its hull.

Outside the tightly clamped porthole and far below I could hear the hiss of the sea. I threw back the bedclothes and knelt up, drawing the porthole curtain. There was very little to see, just rushing flecks of white water lit by the lights from hundreds of portholes below and on either side of mine. No matter what went on inside her, the boat kept ploughing on, day and night, night and day, out of sight of land for two whole weeks. For the first time I began to realize how vast the ocean was.

I closed the curtains and got back into bed. South . . . south . . . south . . . mile after mile after mile, taking me to . . . what?

... and where? The thought brought a stir of renewed excitement. Ah, to hell with the birds. They weren't what I was on board for. If I didn't get one, I didn't get one. I'd use the seventeen days for a good rest, good food and a lot of fresh air and sun, be really fit by the time I landed. And there was always Mrs. Felton to talk to, maybe even dance with; perhaps we'd go to the pictures and sun-bathe on the deck together. Yes, the prospect pleased me. Birds invariably meant trouble and who wanted trouble on a cruise? Relax ... relax ... take it easy ...

The steady rhythmic roll of the ship and the soporific hiss of the sea had me away in no time, sleeping like a babe.

It seemed like ten hours later that the thumping on the cabin door brought me fast awake, heart thundering, wondering, in the dark, why my hotel room was pitching and rolling.

'Wh ... who is it?' I shouted.

'You in bed? Open the goddam door!'

Oh, Christ—Ellaleen!

I fumbled for the light and slipped out of bed. 'Just a minute!' I grabbed my robe, put it on and opened the door. She was leaning against the bulkhead opposite, still in her Indian outfit, headband nicely askew. She was sloshed.

'Ha ... some goddam swinger!' she laughed cruelly.

'Ssssh! What time is it, for God's sake?'

'Who the hell cares.' She pushed herself off the bulkhead and came into the cabin. 'You got anythin' to drink, Mr. Swingy Tobin?'

'Er ... yes, there's some vodka.'

'Christ, there's hope for you yet. Where did ya get to?'

'When?'

'Aw, skip it. Where's the vodka?'

I got the bottle from the wardrobe and poured a couple of slugs.

'Where did *you* get to?' I asked her. 'You took off with that Scotsman and I didn't see you again.'

She flung a careless arm. 'Oh, around. Some guys and cats ... real groovy. Been playin' poker. I won a bundle—about four pounds.'

'Did you have any dinner?'

I added some tonic and she threw back a big gulp before answering. 'Dinner ...! You mean sit there with those old ruins ... listen to my mother going on about sweet fuck all ... you crazy?'

She flopped down on the bed, swung her moccasined feet up and collapsed against the pillow, arms outstretched, spilling the drink. 'Jeez, I'm bushed. Say, this is a nice soft bed. I like it better than mine.'

'Ellaleen ...'

'I'm gonna stay right here for three days, d'you mind?' She looked sideways at me, grinning lop-sidedly. 'No, you don't mind. You want me to stay here ... and you know why? Because you want to sleep with me. You wanna lie next to a nice warm body. And you want to lay me. And you know why *I* want to stay? Because *I* want to lie next to a nice warm body. And because I wanna lay you.'

She sat up suddenly and bashed the drink down on the bedside table. 'O.K. ... if that's what you want—that's what you get.' She reached behind her back and in a quick flurry of practiced movements was standing naked in a puddle of clothes. 'There—what d'you think of that? Do I look good or don't I?'

'I ...' I couldn't speak for the lump the size of an ostrich egg stuck in my gullet.

'Don't you think I've got beautiful boobs? That hag said I was too thin. What do *you* think, Tobin?'

'I ...'

'O.K., let's see what you got, baby ...'

'Now, Ellaleen ...'

She pounced. I had the tonic bottle in one hand and my full glass in the other. I tried to fight her off with my elbows but to no avail. She got a finger in the sash and jerked. The robe flew open. 'Hey ...!' she laughed, 'now look what we got here!'

'Ellaleen, for Chrissake, I'm spilling the drink ...'

'Screw the drink. ...' She jerked the collar of the robe down over my shoulders, pinning my arms, then pushed me backwards on to the bed and leapt on me. I abandoned the glass and the bottle on to the floor.

'Jeezus, you're built,' she mouthed in my ear, following it with her hot, wet tongue.

'Ellaleen ... you're ... hey ... wow! ... you're drunk. You'll regret this tomorrow . . . won't you?'

'Stuff,' she said in my other ear. 'I never regretted a thing in my goddam life . . . and to prove it I'll stay here all night and screw you sober in the morning.'

'Ellaleen, you can't . . . what about your mother?'

'Let her find her own.'

'No, I didn't mean that . . . hey, where are you going?'

'Where the heck d'you think I'm going—to say my prayers?'

'Ohh . . . ooohhh! . . . aaahhh!'

'Good . . . good,' she said from somewhere down there. 'I've waited two months to hear that . . . two goddam months. Now, how does *this* grab you . . .?'

Dawn was breaking through the porthole before she finally collapsed upon the bed and gasped, 'You alive?'

I shook my head; it was all I could manage.

'By the cripes . . . and a goddam Limey,' she breathed, flopping a broken arm on the bed. 'I thought you Limeys were supposed to be cold and impotent.'

'We are . . . I am . . . look at me. Hey, you know it's dawn?'

'Dawn what?'

'Dawn dawn. Won't your mother . . .'

'Hell, why are you always worried about her?'

'I'm the worrying type. I just don't like the idea of her waking the entire boat bashing on my door yelling rape.'

'Relax, my mother never saw a dawn in her life.'

'Hey, you're sober!'

'Sure, I'm sober. No one could sweat like that and stay blipped.' She took a deep breath and sat up. 'O.K. I'm goin'. You're right, if she knows I've been balling she'll cut my allowance.' She skipped out of bed, slipped on her mini-knicks and her Minnie Ha Ha outfit, finger-combed her hair and said, 'You rest up, y'hear. I want you in form tonight. I've only got three days of you and I aim to make the most of them.'

I grinned at her. 'Do, er, I have any say in the matter?'

'None whatsoever. See yuh.'

And she was gone.

It was the last I saw of her. She didn't come down for meals and when I asked Dorothea where she was she gave me a martyr-mother, eyes-to-the-ceiling expression and said, 'Who knows *where* that girl gets to, I'm sure I don't.'

I reckoned our Ellaleen had found a real bull somewhere—or maybe was trying to get as many different ones in as possible before Las Palmas. Anyway Las Palmas came and the Kleins went, with nary a further sign of Ellaleen.

So, there I was—back to square one, with even less chance of finding something now we were three days out from England. Or so I thought.

Her name was Lisa. She got on at Las Palmas.

SIXTEEN

Las Palmas—tiny volcanic dot in the immensity of the Atlantic Ocean, a relative step from the African coast at a point where Morocco meets the Spanish Sahara.

We docked at 1642 hours, teatime, on a warm, sunny afternoon. What with passengers disembarking and new ones embarking there was a lot of activity in the foyer and quite a few passengers, myself included, were idly watching, attracted by the bustle.

I saw the old dear arrive in the wheelchair, brought up the gangway by a couple of stalwart sailors and also by the chick in the very familiar-looking uniform. It was some moments before I realised it was an Ardmont uniform—my old firm in Majorca.

The girl, presumably a courier, was very attractive, as most of them are. She had a good slim figure, short dark hair and was very tanned. She smiled reassuringly at the old girl in the wheelchair and told her she'd stay with her until the ship's nurse arrived.

I just had to have a word with her—talk about Ardmont, you know, so I waited until the nurse came and wheeled the chair away, then I went up to her.

'Excuse me . . .'

She turned and gave me an enquiring smile.

'My name is Russ Tobin. I see you're with Ardmont. I've just finished a season with them as courier in Majorca. I wondered if you knew any of the gang out there.'

Her mouth popped open. 'Really! Oh, yes, I did a season

there myself last year. This is my first in Las Palmas. Who do *you* know?'

'Patrick Holmes?' I suggested and she laughed aloud.

'The lovely Patrick,' she said. 'Yes, I know him very well. He's a dear, how is he?'

'Still breathing—at least he was the last time I heard. At the moment he's confusing Paris. He's on holiday for a few days. We finished together in Majorca on the fourth. How are things out here?'

She shrugged. 'No difference. We still work eighty-seven hours a day—not counting lunch break.'

'You get a break for lunch!' I cracked. 'Sounds idyllic.'

'Are you on holiday?' she asked.

'Yes and no. I'm going the long way round to Nairobi to do a season with Çentaf Tours.'

'Centaf. Can't say I've heard of them.'

'No, they only operate safari tours in Central and East Africa. Might I know your name?'

'Barbara Fells.'

'Are you all through here? I saw you bring the old lady aboard.'

'Yes, I've got nobody disembarking this trip. So I'm through for the day—apart from a week's paperwork that has to be done by tomorrow morning.'

I smiled. 'Like you said—no difference. Barbara, would you like a drink? Have you got time?'

She sagged a little. 'Oh, I'd love a drink, I've been on my feet since eight this morning. But to tell you the truth I'm waiting for a friend of mine. She's a courier with Ransome's. She's embarking two passengers ...' she looked at her watch, 'she should be here any minute. Look, would you like to go on and we'll catch up when she gets her clients settled. Where are you—First?'

'Yes.'

'Shall we see you in the Smoke Room, then—say fifteen minutes?'

'Fine.'

It was nearer half an hour before they came in and just in time to save my flagging ego. I was beginning to have doubts about my personal freshness or something.

Sitting at the bar I glanced towards the door, hearing female voices—and my eyes went funny. The girl with Barbara was gorgeous—a blonde, sun-tanned goddess in a white mini-skirted uniform trimmed with gold. As she walked in she gave the bar a cool, confident search and when Barbara pointed to me she looked at me and kept on looking as they approached.

Barbara said, 'Sorry we took so long, Russ, we had a spot of trouble with a passport. This is Lisa Ord. Lisa—Russ Tobin, ex-Ardmont slave in Majorca.'

Lisa shook hands and smiled. She had very fine eyes, almond shaped, Wedgewood green and long dark lashes. 'My commiserations, I hope you're recovering.'

'How do Ransome's compare?'

'Very favourably. They're happy with a ninety-six-hour day.'

'It obviously agrees with you, though—with both of you. I feel positively pallid. I'd forgotten tans like yours were possible. Now, how about some drinks, I'm sure you both need one. Me—I haven't done a stroke all day. You ought to try shipboard life sometime, it's wonderful.'

Lisa gave Barbara a certain knowing smile and said, 'Yes, we must,' but through ignorance I missed its significance.

They stayed for a good hour, talking shop, telling me some of the terrible and funny things that had happened to them during the year and I in turn told them about one or two of my Majorca fiascos. It was a very nice hour. Barbara finally looked at her watch and said, 'I must go, it's nearly seven. I've got to change, I'm dining out tonight . . . thrill, thrill.'

'So am I,' said Lisa, again smiling at Barbara which I supposed was a shared confidence.

They shook hands, wished me a good trip and success in Kenya and left. I watched Lisa go, captivated by her movement, her long tanned legs. If there's one thing destined to knock me sideways it's a cool, green-eyed blonde in a white mini-skirt. I wasn't at all sure it had been a good thing to meet her. The remainder of the cruise was going to be difficult enough without memories of what might have been.

I finished my drink and went down to the cabin to change, wondering what excitements the next fourteen days would bring, and seriously considering the possibility that I might end up in the chess tournament yet.

No, at least I was saved from that. I didn't even play chess. Oh, death . . .

When I entered the dining room just after eight, Mr. and Mrs. Rubinstein were already seated. I bid them good evening, said howdy to the steward and read the menu. It sounded terrific: Smoked Turkey with spiced peaches to start; followed by Poached Salmon (Scotch) Hollandaise; then Roast Gosling, Sage Stuffing and Apple Sauce; and Souffle Royale for dessert. Ridiculous—but what else was there to do.

I glanced up as Mrs. Felton arrived and caught my breath. Oh, boy, *quelle elegance.* She looked radiant in a beautiful floral gown in silk, mostly dark reds and blues. Well, it was no wonder she dressed so exquisitely—apart from the fact that she'd been a model. I'd had a quiet word with Mac, my cabin steward, and he'd told me she was married to one of the wealthiest businessmen in South Africa. He owned hotels, farms, cinemas . . . you name it, Felton had it. I was very glad for her sake. I only hoped he treated her right.

I stood up as she sat down and received a devastating smile for my trouble.

'Good evening, Mr. Tobin.'

'Mrs. Felton . . . may I say you look . . . you look . . . well, you just do.'

She laughed and said, 'Thank you, that's one of the nicest compliments I've ever had. And may I say you look pretty dishy, too.'

Right then I got the feeling that this was going to be some sort of extra special evening. I was right. It began a few minutes later.

The chief steward arrived at my left hand and eased away a chair. Mrs. Felton looked up and behind me, her eyes expressing surprise and great interest. The Rubinsteins looked up, the old boy taking particular interest. I turned. Lisa was standing behind me, breath-taking in a long orange evening gown. My expression must have been quite comical because she laughed at it.

The chief steward introduced her to the others and when he got to me she cut in, 'Yes, Mr. Tobin and I have already met.'

As we sat down I glanced at Mrs. Felton, knowing darned

well she'd be looking at me. In her eyes was a glimmer of a smile that said '*Now* are you satisfied, Mr. Tobin.'

I gave her a grin in return that said 'Immensely—thank you for asking'.

My holiday began from that moment.

SEVENTEEN

Lisa, we learned at dinner, was South African born of English parents. They owned a ten thousand acre farm fifty miles from Durban and that's where she was heading, for a two-week holiday.

'Oh, I get up late ... play tennis ... ride a lot,' she said, in answer to my question what does one do on a ten thousand acre farm on a two-week holiday.

I could see her in riding gear, in shapely jodhpurs and sweater, a scarf at her throat, striding from the house towards the stables, smacking the leather crop against her leg as she walked. Quite a sight on a bright, sunny summer morning. Lisa would be quite a sight *anywhere* on a bright, sunny summer morning. Lisa would be quite a sight anywhere on a bloody awful winter's morning ...

'... Russ ...?'

'Mm? Oh, I'm sorry ...'

She and the others laughed. She said, 'Where were you just then, you must have been miles away.'

'I was—I was in Durban ... sorry.'

'Oh, you know Durban?'

'No, never been there.'

She shook her head. 'No, that's too profound for me. I was asking whether you'd been down to the discotheque in Tourist.'

'Oh ... yes, yes, I have. It's not bad. Would you like to go?'

'Love to. I haven't danced in a month.'

'How about you, Mrs. Felton?' I asked. 'Will you change your mind?'

She demured with a smile and said to Lisa, 'I refused Russ's kind invitation on our first evening because I didn't think it was my scene. However, with you along for support, I might try it for half an hour. You know, I'm afraid I've never been to a discotheque. What exactly is it?'

'It's dancing to records—plus a lot of frills.'

'Frills or thrills?'

Lisa smiled. 'Both if you're lucky. No, frills—coloured lighting that swirls and blinks and throbs in time with the beat of the music.'

'Sounds ghastly,' said Mrs. Felton. 'It also sounds very loud and very young. Now I'm *sure* it's not my scene. However, I must try it. If I got home and told my husband I hadn't "dug the disco" on board, he'd be terribly disappointed.'

While we were laughing at the unlikelihood of it, Rubinstein surprised us. 'Yes, very interesting this matter of stroboscopic lighting in discotheques. It can, I believe, have a profoundly disturbing effect on the mind. I was reading ...' he then launched into an erudite appraisal of the matter which shattered me because I'd have laid money he'd never even heard of a discotheque never mind strobe lighting. And he surprised me even more by finishing, 'Well, as you're all going down there, may we join you? I'd like very much to see this lighting for myself ...'

'Of course!' I said. 'Provided Mrs. Rubinstein promises to do a Watutsi with me.'

Mrs. R. laughed wih surprise. 'Oh, my word ...'

So at ten thirty, there we were, the others sitting in the shadows, lights flickering and flashing and pulsing all over the place, Mrs. Rubinstein and I on the floor jigging around to Slade, Mrs. R. going at it like she'd been doing it all her life.

'How is it, Mrs. Rubinstein?' I bellowed.

She threw back her head and laughed. 'Ach, *lov*ely, Mister Tobin. I think the lights are *beau*tiful. We never had anything like this in my day ...'

A real swinger, this chick.

When the track finished we breathlessly made our way back to the table to find Lisa missing. I died there and then.

'Well, *Professor* Rubinstein,' chaffed his wife. 'Have you seen enough.?'

'More than enough,' he laughed, rubbing his eyes. 'I think we'll leave it to the youngsters, hey?'

'It was nice of you to come down,' I said. 'And thank you for the Watutsi, Mrs. Rubinstein.'

'Is that what it was? Hear that, Friederik, I did the Watutsi!'

'Well, don't let the tribe know, for heaven's sake, it'll completely shatter their cultural stability. Goodnight, Mr. Tobin.'

Off they went, leaving me with Mrs. Felton.

'She's dancing,' she said immediately.

'Mm? Oh, Lisa.'

'I thought I'd better put you out of your misery quickly,' she smiled. She could conjure up the most most devilishly knowing smiles at times.

'Thanks. Well, shall I put you into your misery in return? Would you like to dance?'

'Just one, then I'll be off. One game I've never been very good at is "gooseberry".'

Ae we took the floor, I said, 'Thank you again, but I'd be very upset if you left here before you wanted to because of me. There's plenty of time yet—another two weeks. Please don't leave on my account.'

'That's sweet of you,' she smiled, 'but it really isn't my scene. Besides, I've got a wonderful thriller in my room I'm dying to get back to.'

'All right, I'll let you go provided you promise to join us for coffee on deck tomorrow morning—provided, of course, that Lisa will join *me* for coffee on deck tomorrow morning. She just may take a permanent fancy to that big gorilla she's dancing with.'

'Ah, you noticed,' she teased.

'Well . . . no disrespect to you of course . . .'

'Of *course* not.'

'. . . I just happened to glance over there . . . and . . .'

'Come on,' she laughed, 'she's heading for the table now. You must get there before the gorilla tries again.'

'Thank you for the dance. You promise about that coffee, now? You won't be playing gooseberry.'

'We'll see. Goodnight, Russ, have fun.'

I left her and went to Lisa. 'Hi, like to dance?'

'Well, it would make a nice change from all-in wrestling. If you're at a loose end tomorrow maybe you'd come back here and help me look for my toes.'

'Ah, what a shame, I'm already booked for tomorrow morning.'

'Oh.'

'So are you.'

'I am?'

'Mm, you're having coffee with Mrs. Felton.'

'I am? Who arranged that?'

'Well . . . let's say . . .'

'You did.'

'Well . . .'

'In other words I'm having coffee with you tomorrow.'

'Oh, you don't have to.'

'I know I don't.'

'But then, if you don't . . . we don't come back here and look for your toes, simple as that.'

'That's filthy blackmail, you know that?'

'I know that.'

We took the floor. She was soft and warm and smelled of the sun and sea and shampoo and the touch of her cheek and her breath in my ear sent shivers through me. We danced until midnight and didn't sit down once.

After that evening the days flew, melting and melding into one another until it was impossible to remember, without conscious calculation, what day of the week it was and how long I'd been at sea.

The daily routine was always similar yet somehow always different. I would wake early to the sound of the swishing sea and the sight of bright sunlight fighting through the curtain to warm the cabin walls. Often I was up before Mac brought my cup of tea, and long before breakfast I'd be up on deck, breathing the unbelievably fresh air, strolling the newly washed decks, nodding good mornings to people as familiar to me as family.

Then down to breakfast and first sight of Lisa, the real start to the day. What with having her *and* Mrs. Felton on the table, I must have been the envy of all the other men in First.

'Good morning, Mrs. Felton.'

'Good morning, Russ, what a wonderfully gay shirt.'

'Thank you—and may I return the compliment. 'Morning, Lisa.'

'You won't get round me that way.'

I pulled a face at Mrs. Felton who raised an enquiring brow.

'Pontoon,' I explained. 'Lisa learned to play pontoon in the Tourist lounge last night.'

'Correction,' said Lisa. 'Lisa learned to *lose* at pontoon last night. And, Mrs. Felton, guess who won Lisa's money.'

'Could it be . . . could it *possibly* have been—Mr. Tobin?'

'It could and was. Mrs. Felton, what sort of man would teach a girl a game and steal her money during tuition?'

'A heel?' suggested Mrs. Felton.

'A heel.'

'That's me, folks,' I said to Mr. and Mrs. Rubinstein who had just sat down.

'How much did he take you for?' asked Rubinstein.

'Thirty . . . seven . . . new . . . pence!'

'Oh, Russ, how *could* you?' gasped Mrs. Felton.

'Easy. Lisa will insist an twisting on nineteens and twenties.'

Mr. Rubinstein tutted and shook his head at Lisa.

Mrs. Rubinstein said, 'Will somebody *please* tell me what day it is today. I'm completely lost.'

'Wednesday,' I said.

They all looked at me. 'Thursday,' said Mrs. Felton.

'It's not. It can't be. Whatever happened to Wednesday?'

'It slipped by yesterday,' said Lisa.

'Well, what's on the agenda for today?' asked Mrs. R.

'I *do* know that,' I said. 'Aquatic sports in the Tourist swimming pool . . . a cricket match, passengers *v* officers, this afternoon . . . dancing this evening . . .' I turned to Lisa. 'Maybe a little pontoon afterwards, hm?'

She shook her head. 'Definitely mm mm.'

'Aquatic sports?'

'Mm mm.'

'Cricket?'

'More mm mm.'

'Table tennis,' I sighed.

Her eyes lit up. 'Yeeesss, table tennis. We'll play for . . . let's see thirty-seven new pence a game.'

'Oh oh.' I looked at Mrs. Felton dejectedly. 'Do you think

she's good? Do you get the feeling the lady's good?'

'I get the feeling you'll be cashing a traveller's cheque before nightfall,' said Mrs. Felton.

And so that day went.

In the evening Lisa and I danced until midnight, then left the smokey lounge and walked along A Deck to the stern, finding it deserted. Here, especially on a beautiful moonlit night such as it was, is the most exciting and dramatic part of the ship. Looking astern, with nothing of the boat to be seen, the boiling white waters of the wake stretch away endlessly into the sparkling moon-splashed vastness of the ocean, lonely, empty and mysterious.

We hung on the rail and watched the tumbling wake for some time before Lisa said, 'No wonder the doctors recommend a sea voyage. It's *so* relaxing. So beautiful.'

She stood and turned towards me, looking over my head at the sky. 'And just look at that incredible moon . . .'

My heart stirred at the loveliness of her face, her eyes, the closeness of her mouth.

'The moon is that way, Tobin,' she murmured.

'Mm?'

'The moon . . . that way . . . up there . . . it's in the sky, you know.'

'Not mine. I've got two moons—right there your eyes.'

'Tobin . . .'

I kissed her and she must have liked it because she forgot all about the moon and about everything else for a very long time. Finally she broke away, gasping, 'That was sneaky.'

'No it wasn't, it was blatant.'

'Well, I'll say one thing for you, you certainly take your time.'

'Kissing you?'

'No, getting around to it. Three days! I was beginning to get worried.'

'About me?'

'No, about me! You're a rare bird. When you've been a courier as long as I have, you count the count-down before attack in minutes not in hours—and *never* in days. You kinda threw me.'

'I apologise.'

'Don't. I liked it. It was refreshing.'

'Have you any idea how much I wanted to—ever since I saw you with Barbara?'

She grinned. 'Of course I have. You fellas are so darned obvious.'

I reached for her again and her grin faded, and this time when she broke away she whispered, 'It's been so very nice—these three days.'

'Yes, it has.'

'And it could be even better, couldn't it?'

I nodded. 'Yes, it could.'

'Do . . . you want it to be better?'

'Very much.'

She moved away from me and looked at me, 'So do I.' She held out her hand and I took it, then with my arm around her we left the moonlight to the sea.

'I like you,' she said.

'And I like you.'

'I hoped there would be somebody on board. I'm an incurable romantic.'

'You're a woman,' I laughed. Then I looked at her, bathed in moonlight. 'Yes . . . without fear of contradiction I can say assuredly you are a woman.'

'I only hope the remaining days . . . and nights . . . are as lovely as this one.'

'I can think of no reason why they shouldn't be. I could say I'll try very hard to make them so, but effort doesn't come into it. You're very easy to enjoy.'

'Then it should be a wonderful holiday.'

'It will be,' I said, kissing her. 'I know.'

EIGHTEEN

'Russ . . .! Russ . . .!'

The whispered alarm and the nudge in the backside brought me awake to find the naked loveliness of Lisa kneeling over me, peering out of the porthole. 'Mm?' I murmured.

'Quick . . . look!'

'What is it? What time is it?'

'Half past six . . .'

'Half past *six*! In the *morning*!?'

'Well, hardly in the evening. Come on, get up . . . look!'

'What is it?'

I scrambled up, full of sleep, and joined her at the narrow porthole, cheek to cheek.

'Africa!' she whispered, excitedly.

My heart leapt at the sight of the still, flat, dawn-lit waters of Table Bay and, beyond it, to the towering, rugged, purple mass of Table Mountain.

'Wow!' I whispered. 'It really *is* that flat.'

'Cape Town! Come on, let's get dressed. I'm going to show you around!'

The boat docked at seven thirty and we were ashore by nine. We entered the city by taxi and Lisa had him drop us in the market place in the Grand Parade. There, on the pavement, I stood rooted, gazing around me.

'Hey, guess what!?'

'What?' she laughed.

'I'm standing on Africa! I'm here! I'm really here!'

'You sound like Cecil Rhodes. Come on, I'll show you the city.'

It is said that Cape Town ranks with Naples, Rio and San Francisco as one of the great scenic cities of the world. Well, I haven't actually *seen* those other places but I'd say whoever said it was dead right. The colour, the palm trees, the buildings, the botanical gardens and the shops, all nestling at the foot of the great Table Mountain which rises behind the city in a sheer precipice 3,500 feet high, slashing the skyline with a dark horizontal mass many miles long.

We stood looking up at it and along its length.

'Right, race you to the top,' I joked.

'You want to go up?'

'Can we!?'

'Sure. There's a cable car from Adderley street. Come on.'

If I boast that I saw all of Cape Town in two hours it's an accurate boast. From the cable car and from the top of the mountain you can see the entire city and a whole lot more including, from one point, a simultaneous view of both the Atlantic and the Indian oceans.

But what can one really say about a view of any city from a height of 3,500 feet except—it was stupendous. Lisa and I stood on the flat plateau of the mountain top with the exhilerating wind blowing through our hair and the view battering our senses. It's a picture you want to capture and hold on to all your life, resurrecting it when life gets a little spiky as a reminder that there is still an awful lot of beauty in the world.

We got back to the boat in the late afternoon, tired, wind-beaten, sunburnt and hungry, and later that evening, standing by the ship's rail, looking out at the night sight of the blazing city, Lisa said, 'Do you smell it?'

I inhaled deeply. 'Yes, I smell it.'

'Africa ... the most wonderful smell in the world. Arid ... wild ... ancient ... and exciting. On the farm it's twice as strong, twice as compelling. I love it. I could never leave it, not for long. It would always bring me back. And I believe that when you get to Kenya it will have the same effect on you. You're a born Afrophile, Russ, I could tell from the way you reacted today. You may as well give up now. Africa has already got you.'

I didn't argue because there was no argument. In my heart I knew she was right.

I left her at the Louis Botha airport in Durban five days later with a weight in my breast where my heart should have been. As the jet took off into the piercing blue of the afternoon sky I gazed down at the receding city and wondered why all good things seemingly had to come to an end, knowing, of course, that their going made way for other good things and life went on. The plane banked steeply, and the city was lost to view, but the vastness of Africa stretched away beneath me to the unreachable horizon.

I lit a cigarette and lay my head back on the seat. Well, I was here. A tingle of excitement returned. What now? What would be the next fateful step in the continuing saga of Tobin's travels.

'You going to Johannesburg or beyond?'

I turned my head, hardly aware that anyone had sat next to me. The face was young and very tanned, the eyes startlingly blue; his hair, bleached by the sun, was unruly, as though he'd made some effort at it but not too earnestly. There was a heap of living in that face, and a heap of mischief. I liked him immediately.

'Beyond,' I said. 'To Nairobi.'

'Really? I'm heading there, mind if I join you?'

I grinned. 'Be my guest. Pull up a seat.'

He held out a corded, sun-burnt hand. 'Bob Eastman.'

'Russ Tobin. You work up there?'

'Yes, there—all over, really.'

'I'm flying up to work with Centaf Tours. D'you know them?'

He smiled, showing good teeth. 'Yes, I know them. Good outfit. I work for them occasionally.'

'Really! What do you do for them?'

'I take their clients on safari. I'm a hunter.'

'Well, by God . . .'

'What's the matter?'

'It's the coincidence. I'm going to work for them as a courier. I'm replacing Jim Fuller.'

'Would you believe it? Yes, I know Jim well . . . well, hell, what a small world. Russ, would you like a drink?'

'I'd like twenty-seven. I've just left my heart on the ground.'

'Yeh,' he grinned, 'I know the feeling.'

I'll bet.

'Let's get a stewardess and pour a little Scottish balm upon the sorrow,' he said.

He got a stewardess, just like that. She came down the aisle as though beckoned by silent dog whistle—or as though she'd been watching him.

'Yes, Mr. Eastman, what can I get you?'

'A couple of big scotches, Kay, lots of ice, hm?'

She flashed him a dazzling smile and went away, her trim

bottom wiggling flamboyantly. Eastman turned to me and grinned. 'You, er, been to Nairobi before, Russ?'

'No, I haven't. I haven't been to Africa before.'

'Hm,' he went on, scratching his chin. 'Y'know, you sound to me like a chap who needs cheering up a bit—and showing around a bit. What are you doing tonight?'

'Er, tonight I'll be trying to find Johannesburg.'

'Ah, bit of luck there, I happen to know where it is. Right, we start tonight in Johannesburg. A couple of pals of mine own a club. If you know the right spots you can really swing in Jo'burg. This is one of the right spots.'

You know I believed him.

Well, all that happened two days ago ... or is it four. And I'm now in Nairobi ... I think. Oh, man, that Eastman! If I were to tell you the things we've done and the places we've been! But I can't—at least not right now. He's due downstairs in the hotel foyer any minute and we're off to a party—I think, out at a farm—I think, all part of my African initiation—I think. I just don't know anything for sure any more. Boy, they really *live* out here—at least Bob Eastman really lives out here. He's chatted more birds in the past forty-eight hours than Patrick and I did all last season ... hang on, the phone's ringing. It'll be him.

'Hello ...? Yes, Bob, be right down. Mm ...? No, I haven't ... what to*night*! Well, O.K., if you say so. Sure, love to. If I've got to learn sometime, may as well be tonight. Right ... two minutes.'

There, see what I mean? This, er, party we're going to ... well, it isn't. We're going crocodile hunting. *Croc*odile hunting!

Well, I've got to fly. Fly! Ha! My feet haven't touched the ground since I boarded the plane at Durban. Well, provided I come out of this alive I'll drop you a line and let you know how I got on. All right? Tarra ...

Crocodile hunting!

Exit Tobin, singing nervously.

Oh, once there was a travellin' man
Who got a terrible shock.
He went out one night for a bit of fun
And the damn fool not knowing what he was doing stagger-

ing half-smashed in the dark put his big foot on the wrong part of the boat and tipped the whole flaming issue into the black waters of the Upyagoogoo river—and got eaten by a croc . . . !

Yerk!

Where *will* it end?
Tarra.